MARRYING THE MISTRESS

Juliet Landon

MILLS & BOON®

Pure reading pleasure™

First published in Great Britain 2008
Paperback edition 2009
Harlequin Mills & Boon Limited,
Eton House, 18-24 Paradise Road, Richmond, Surrey TW9 1SR

© Juliet Landon 2008

ISBN: 978 0 263 86762 6

Set in Times Roman 10½ on 12¼ pt.
04-0209-79528

Printed and bound in Spain
by Litografia Rosés S.A., Barcelona

MARRYING
THE MISTRESS

Juliet Landon's keen interest in art and history, both of which she used to teach, combined with a fertile imagination, make writing historical novels a favourite occupation. She is particularly interested in researching the early medieval and Regency periods and the problems encountered by women in a man's world. Her heart's home is in her native North Yorkshire, but now she lives happily in a Hampshire village close to her family. Her first books, which were on embroidery and design, were published under her own name of Jan Messent.

Recent novels by the same author:

ONE NIGHT IN PARADISE
THE WIDOW'S BARGAIN
THE BOUGHT BRIDE
HIS DUTY, HER DESTINY
THE WARLORD'S MISTRESS
A SCANDALOUS MISTRESS*
DISHONOUR AND DESIRE*
THE RAKE'S UNCONVENTIONAL MISTRESS*

*Ladies of Paradise Road

Prologue

❦

It was hardly more than two miles from the centre of York to the racecourse at Knavesmire, a distance that only a few months ago, the Honourable Linas Monkton would have been happy to ride on horseback without the least discomfort. On this occasion, however, his young mistress, Miss Helene Follet, had put her foot down and ordered the barouche to be made available, for nowadays Linas's cough left him weak, sweating with pain and gasping for breath. She dared not allow it, although she would have liked to ride her own black mare that weekend.

'I feel sure we're in for some showers,' she said, noting the bending tree-tops as they passed out of Micklegate, 'and I don't fancy getting soaked as we watch your brother's horses go through their paces. If it turns out fine, I'm sure he'll lend us two of his hacks to ride. Did you remember to pack the new linctus?'

'I expect Nairn did. You look very nice, my dear.'

Linas's compliments rarely went beyond 'nice' or 'smart', which Helene thought more appropriate for soldiers. 'Thank you.' She smiled. She had made the outfit herself, including the beaded panel down the front and the frilled chemisette that showed inside the neckline. The matching bonnet of ruched blue-grey silk had been made by her, too, after the latest French styles.

Linas himself ought to have been tucked up warmly in his Stonegate home on such a raw April day, but it was the start of the York racing season and nothing would have persuaded him to refuse his twin brother's invitation to stay the weekend at Abbots Mere, so close to the racecourse. The invitation had been to stay for a week, but Helene had balked at that and Linas, aware of a certain tension between his mistress and his brother, had not insisted on more than two nights.

Helene would rather not have gone at all. Although she enjoyed the races and the sight of horses in a herd at full gallop, bright with silks and shine, she could not look forward with anything like the same enthusiasm to meeting the Abbots Mere set, which, as like as not, would include a similar herd of Lord Winterson's mistresses, past, present and hopeful.

The twins were unlike each other in most respects, Linas being far from robust but still trying to emulate his brother in so many ways, by taking a mistress, for instance, and by trying to prove his fitness when it was plain to see, to Helene at least, that he grew weaker with each passing season. Lord Winterson's rude health needed no proof, for one look at his powerful physique was enough to convince any critic that his parents' recipe had favoured the first of the two to emerge with good looks, intelligence, and enough charm to ladle out whenever he felt he could spare the effort. At other times he could be insufferably proud and offhand, and it was said that one of Winterson's set-downs could cause a recipient's disappearance for as long as a six-month.

Linas had never indulged in that kind of high-handedness except occasionally to the servants, and it was this brand of gentle courtesy that had won Helene over. After insisting that she would never again become intimate with a man for money, however high-born, she had relented and become Linas Monkton's mistress, companion and nurse. That had been two years ago when she was still seventeen, two years in which there had been no sign of pregnancy, in spite of her desire to bear his child before it was too late.

Perhaps it was already too late, for Linas had not visited her bed once in the last two months on the pretext that any physical exercise brought on his coughing spasms. Tomorrow would be her nineteenth birthday. She hoped he might visit her, if only to be held in her arms.

It was unproductive to speculate on the welcome they would receive, Helene having no reason to suppose that they would be treated with anything but courtesy and, in her lover's case, with affection too. The brothers were very fond of each other, and although no obvious favour was offered to Linas when taking part in the usual manly activities, Helene nevertheless suspected that Lord Winterson kept a very careful eye on his brother, stopping within his limits or suggesting an easier route, ostensibly for his own benefit. Visiting Linas's home on Stonegate, Winterson never stayed long enough to tire him, nor was anything ever said in her presence about the array of medicines at Linas's elbow.

Helene hoped it was obvious to Winterson that she was taking every conceivable care of his brother without molly-coddling him, but the feeling persisted that he thought her a young social-climbing nobody on the look-out for a wealthy patron who would feather her nest for as long as possible. If he had taken the trouble to find out, she thought, he might have discovered the truth of the matter, that Miss Helene Follet was in fact a certain Miss Helen Follethorpe of Bridlington, only thirty miles or so away on the Yorkshire coast, where her father had once been mayor. Had it not been for Leonard Follethorpe's unfortunate experience, she would still be living with her family in comfort instead of selling herself to support those of her family who remained. Five years ago, taking a lover had been the very last thing on her mind, but she could be of little help to her family on the pittance she had earned as a York mantua-maker's assistant, and one could not be too finicky when near-starvation was a real alternative.

To say she resented Winterson's thinly veiled contempt would not have been an exaggeration. His manner was correct and as icy as if she'd been a crusty old dowager of fifty instead of a sleek raven-haired beauty of nineteen, giving her no opportunity to be as sisterly as she was with her own two young brothers. Not even for Linas's sake did Lord Winterson do anything to endear himself to her, and now as he strode

out of the great Tudor porchway of Abbots Mere with
three gigantic wolfhounds at his heels, his smile
skimmed over her as if she were merely the housekeeper or Linas's nurse. The hand he extended came
just a little too late to help her out of the barouche.

'Miss Follet,' he said, keeping the hand out so that
she was obliged to accept it. 'Welcome to Abbots Mere.'
The greeting was formal, and not particularly convincing.

She had tried to ignore the ambiguous emotions that
bedevilled her, but the contrast between Linas and his
twin was so transparent, and she herself so receptive to
all the differences between one man in the prime of his
life and one whose prime had never quite materialised,
that she now found it easier to accept it than question
it. Winterson did not have his brother's lanky loping
frame of a tired racehorse, but the deep-chested, well-
toned solidness of a hunter.

Helene watched him move gracefully aside, her eyes
taking their own wayward course over the broad
smooth line of his riding coat, the bulge in his tight
breeches, the tan-cuffed riding boots with spurs, and the
muscled calves. Reprimanding herself, she refused to
acknowledge the stark truth that she might have wished
this man's physical endowments upon his sibling,
forcing herself instead to smile at the brotherly embrace
and the genuine laughter accompanying it. The stifling,
insistent beat of her heart, so long starved of its own
special excitement, was quelled with some effort as
she diverted her thoughts towards Linas's pleasure and
what she could do to maintain it.

Noting how Linas caressed the ears of the nearest

wolfhound, she could see how happy he was to be here and to spend time in the stone-built rambling place where he'd been born. As a concession to his asthma, he kept no animals except horses, but any excuse to visit his brother's racing stable was worth the sneezing fits and the itchy rash on his wrists that Helene cooled with witch-hazel and chamomile. The prospect of sleeping in his old room at Abbots Mere brought back the laugh lines to his pale winter face and lit up the sombre darkness of his eyes, as did the appearance of Somerton, the elderly butler.

Linas took Helene by the hand. 'Good to see you again, Somerton,' he said, creasing his papery skin with deep folds.

'And you also, Mr Linas, sir. M'lord Burl here has had us all up since dawn to get everything ship-shape. We've even polished the hounds' collars. Welcome, Miss Follet,' he said to Helene, courteously.

'Thank you, Mr Somerton.'

Perhaps being made aware by his butler that something more was being required of him, Winterson turned back to her to offer his arm, taking both her and Linas through a panelled passageway into the Great Hall. Again, the differences returned with the memory of that first meeting at the York Assembly Rooms when they had danced together just before she and Linas had first met, when she had seen the fear in Linas's eyes that she would surely prefer his brother Burl, as any woman would. But she had never been seriously attracted to men like Winterson with reputations for breaking hearts, nor could she afford the indulgence of falling in love. If Winterson had ever suspected that she was more interested in a long-term relationship, then he would have been correct. She was. But her affection for the Honourable Linas Monkton was none the less genuine, for all that, and her good care of him had grown into a kind of love far beyond convenience.

The company that weekend was exactly as Helene had expected it to be, noisy, good-natured and gossipy, flirtatious and with an air of competition she felt no need to be a part of, since she was unavailable. Not that she was entirely safe from the attentions of the men, but her status and devotion were sufficient to keep all dalliance at a very superficial level. And because she posed no threat to the women, they sought her friendship and asked her advice about even the most personal matters, especially about fashion. Yet they were not the kind of people she would have chosen to spend a weekend with, and she wondered why Lord Winterson enjoyed their company so much, unless it was to watch them compete for his attention.

Although Winterson must have known about Helene's previous employment as a seamstress, she had told neither of the brothers the full story of her transformation from well-brought-up mayor's daughter to mantua-maker's assistant. If either of them ever wondered how she had acquired such singular style and elegance, how she came to be fluent in French, or why she spoke English with only the odd vowel sound to betray her northern roots, they were either too uninterested to ask, or too well bred.

But the mantua-maker herself, once she saw what a gem she had taken on, had put those accomplishments to good use, transferring her from the workroom to front of shop, using her as a mannequin to model her creations and to suggest other ways of using accessories and fabrics with the kind of flair the older woman could only dream of. When Helene borrowed an evening dress now and again to attend the nearby Assembly Rooms with a beau, this was seen as a cheaper way of rewarding her than with money, for she was sure to tell admirers where such a beautiful gown could be made. Those years had been for Helene a time of intense learning in which she had absorbed every skill of the dressmaking trade, since then she had designed and made all her own garments, including her bonnets.

Despite her undeniable fashion ability, her popularity with Winterson's guests could not be called complete as long as Lady Veronique Slatterly was on hand to shoot down any woman perceived to be receiving more than her fair share of attention from the men, particularly from Winterson himself. Her envy of Miss Helene Follet was out of all proportion to her influence with anyone except Linas. But according to Lady Slatterly, Helene was almost one of the family whereas she herself had not yet achieved that status, nor had she any guarantee of success. Helene's superior position was too close for comfort, and the consequent trivial and ungenerous remarks that Lady Slatterly rained upon her, almost unceasingly, eventually drew even mild Linas's displeasure at dinner.

Handing Lady Slatterly a silver dish of sugary things, he told her, 'Take a few, Veronique dear. Chew them slowly to grind your teeth down.'

Frowning, she took the dish from him. 'What are they?' she said.

'Little sweet things, dear. Keep them by you. You need them.'

Damned if she did, and equally damned if she declined, she glared at Linas as everyone around them laughed, but the caustic remarks stopped for the rest of the evening.

This personal sniping would not in itself have caused Helene too much concern had she not already been feeling vulnerable, vaguely insecure and unsettled by not knowing how to relate to a host who treated her with such polite indifference as if it was no possible concern of his that she was caring so well for his ailing brother. As if she was doing it more for her own benefit, rather than his. Not that she expected their undying gratitude at every end and turn, nor even their thanks. Men only rarely went in for that kind of appreciation. But nor did she appreciate being taken for granted in the offhand way these brothers had. Linas was a very dear man, but he appeared to suppose that what Helene was doing for him was no more than he deserved after what he was doing for her. And since the question of the future was a subject he particularly wished to avoid discussing, it seemed not to occur to him that Helene would have benefited from some clarity on the issue. She had a house, servants, a horse and enough money to pay her bills, but presumably those would all disappear one day, unless she could make some other arrangement.

Had relations between Helene and Lord Winterson been more cordial, she might have broached the subject to him. But not the way things stood. There was a younger brother who also lived on the outskirts of York, a new country parson named Medworth whose profes-

sion and family kept him totally occupied. No doubt he
was relieved to know that his brother was being cared
for, but his absence showed that he had his hands full
enough without involving himself in Miss Follet's
problems.

Mindful of Linas's enjoyment, Helene made every
effort to enter into the excitement of the first day, during
which two of Winterson's racing thoroughbreds were
competing. The day had begun with an earlier-than-
usual breakfast and, since the weather was blustery but
dry, Helene and Linas borrowed two of his brother's
hacks to ride with the others, she in her habit of nut-
brown velvet and matching plumed hat that drew many
a compliment. Linas had retired early the previous
night, well before the others, and had fallen asleep even
before Helene could go in to wish him goodnight. His
valet had told her that his master had been too tired even
to take his usual night-cap of port, sharing with her a
look of concern that did not bode well for the busy day
ahead.

So it did not surprise her that no reference had been
made to her birthday on the morrow, and it seemed to
her inappropriate to mention it when all the attention
was focused on the races, the guests, the winners and
owners, the sumptuous feast, the meeting of old friends
and the excitement of Winterson's successes. Linas had
completely forgotten, and Helene had already decided
that his guilt would serve no good purpose. Even so,
there were moments during the day when her lovely ex-
pressive eyes must have revealed something of her hurt
and disappointment, the ache to be at home with her

family on this special day, enjoying their warmth and love instead of maintaining a position for which she had no real appetite, which she would once have reviled before she lost her innocence.

Turning to look at Linas, she checked that he was comfortable on the well-mannered hack, heaved a sigh, and looked away into the distance to where the newly white-painted grandstand swarmed with racegoers. A large horse and rider moved up beside her, blocking her view of Linas. It was his brother. At first his eyes followed where hers had been and then, returning to find that she was looking down at her hands as if deliberating whether to go or stay, said, 'No, don't go. We have not spoken all day.'

'To each other, you mean? What is there to be said, except congratulations?'

'Oh, dear. You're angry.' His voice was deep and apologetic.

'Not at all. But you must not be seen talking to me, my lord. That would look *very* odd, wouldn't it? See, we're being remarked already.'

'What is it, Miss Follet? You *are* angry. With me? Linas? Has he been flirting with someone?'

'I don't know *what* he's doing. Does it matter?'

His horse stretched its neck, pulling his hand forwards as it shook its head and jangled its bit, keeping its rider occupied with its sidling before he brought it back, almost touching her leg with his. She watched as he humoured the great beast with patience, as if he enjoyed controlling its movements, his face strong, impassive, astonishingly regular, for a man. His dark hair was too long, she thought, noting how it curled over his cravat at the back.

He had obviously been thinking of what she said. 'Or what he's *not* doing? Is that it? He's forgotten your birthday?' he ventured.

She knew it to be a stab in the dark. It must be. Yet the sudden surprise in her velvet-brown eyes escaped before she could hide it, and the denial that followed was worse than useless. 'Of course he hasn't. He…'

'He has, hasn't he? He was never any good at birthdays, Miss Follet. He rarely remembers ours, either. Shall I remind him for you?'

'No!' The word shot out, compounding the earlier denial. 'No, please don't.'

'Ah! You mean you'd rather remind him yourself in a week's time? Or you'd rather he didn't know at all?'

'I mean, my lord, that it's of no possible concern to anyone but me. Please say no more about it.'

'If that's your wish, then I must obey. But you're wrong to think it concerns only you. You are my guest and you're not entirely enjoying the experience. That concerns me. What can I do to put it right?'

'Nothing at all. Your hospitality is the finest, and if Linas is content then that is all I ask for.' She heard the emptiness of her reply and was not proud of its insincerity. She could hardly expect him to believe her.

'Fine unselfish sentiments, ma'am. But I fear I'm too cynical to be taken in by them. To say that my brother's contentment is all you desire, a woman of your age, is moonshine. Have you not thought ahead a little, to the time when you might wish for more?'

Like a ball of slow fire, a sob of pain rose into her throat to sear her with a longing so intense that she had once cried out in the night with it, soaking her pillow with tears, for it seemed at times that her thoughts were of little else. Before she could take herself in hand, her eyes had begun to flood with scalding tears, showing him what was in her heart as clearly as if she held its doors wide open. This man, of all men, to see her weakness, a man who had rarely condescended to speak to her until now.

She would have wheeled her horse away, blindly, but he caught at her bridle before she could do so, leading it away from the Abbots Mere crowd towards a deserted area of long grass where both mounts dropped their heads to snatch at a juicy mouthful. He held her reins and waited, keeping their backs to everyone but making no comment.

'I'm all right,' she whispered. 'Do forgive me. I had no wish to embarrass you, my lord.'

'I am not in the least embarrassed, Miss Follet. I tend to be outspoken, and I have touched a raw spot. I am concerned, but not embarrassed.'

'Yes, my lord, you have. Shall we say no more about it, if you please?'

'Of course. Are you quite recovered?'

'Yes. Quite.'

'Then we shall return.' Handing her the reins, he took stock of her smooth curvaceous lines under the habit, the neat waist and long back, the white lace at her throat. Black glossy hair was bundled into a gold net under her saucily feathered hat, and the deep reproachful eyes spiked with long black lashes were like pools to drown a man. Her full lips were mobile upon a skin of peach that he knew his brother had begun to abandon as his illness progressed and that this, as much as anything else, was a prime source of her distress.

Their return to the others, side by side, did not escape
the notice of Lady Veronique Slatterly, whose displeasure bordered on extreme folly. 'Where have you two
been?' she demanded, wheeling her grey mare round in
circles ahead of them. Her blue eyes were cold and
hard upon Helene.

Winterson's reply did nothing to thaw them, though
her skin turned a healthy pink. 'I have not had to account
for my whereabouts since I was fourteen, Lady Slatterly, and I don't intend to start again now. Nor, I
imagine, does Miss Follet owe you an explanation.'

Snubbed in no uncertain terms, the astonished
woman hauled her mare savagely away and, though
Helene caught sight of her several times during the afternoon, she did not approach.

It was Linas himself who answered Helene's query
about the exact nature of Lady Slatterly's relationship
with his brother. Was she his mistress, or merely one
of the hopefuls?

'He has no official mistress,' Linas told her on the
way back to Abbots Mere. 'Veronique believes she
stands a good chance, but she'll have to toe the line and
curb her sharp tongue if she wants to get anywhere
with Burl. He doesn't like the controlling kind of
woman. Not even our mother had much success there.'

The parents, Lord and Lady Stillingfleete, had never
exercised much control over any of their three sons, and
had left the family home at Abbots Mere to live in a
smaller Georgian house in Harrogate, within reach of
the healing baths. Their large estate was now in Winterson's capable hands, visited only once or twice a year
by the owners when they wanted a change of scenery.

* * *

As a result of Winterson's reprimand, Lady Slatterly's rudeness seemed to abate on the second evening, giving Helene some respite from the woman's jealousy. It also seemed to Helene that Winterson's manner had changed too, even if she was the only one to notice that, this time, he took part in her conversations instead of distancing himself, showing more of an interest in her well-being.

Linas was exhausted after missing his afternoon rest, and at dinner Helene could see how he fought against his fatigue. Not wishing to prevent him from drinking more wine than usual while so many were there to see, she was obliged to watch in dismay as his glass was refilled time and again. His speech began to slur, and his pale skin became unhealthily mottled.

Unable to hide the concern in her eyes, she found her looks intercepted by Winterson's equally worried frown. It was getting late, yet no one had deserted the gaming tables or the chatting groups arranged on couches and floor cushions. She shook her head at the young footman holding a tray of filled glasses in front of Linas, but too late to prevent one being removed, clumsily, sloshing the contents over white knee breeches and carpet.

She went to him, hoping to offer some unobtrusive help, but Winterson was there before her, lifting his brother under each armpit and good-naturedly ignoring his protests. 'Come on up, old chap. Enough for one day.'

'Stay with your guests, my lord,' Helene said. 'I'll go up with him.'

'No, you stay here. I'll see to him myself. Nairn is on his way.'

'He'll be at his supper.'

'I sent for him. Leave him to us.'

His commands offered her a certain comfort for, although she had not wanted to stay amongst the guests for much longer, the alternative was even less appealing. To hand control over to his authoritative twin would be no great sacrifice.

She stayed in the drawing room for another hour, managing to convince all except one that she was as light-hearted as the rest of them. Winterson reappeared to lead a silly game of charades, but the pace slackened and, two by two, the ladies withdrew to their rooms to prepare for the night, still giggling and flirting. Helene was relieved that she and Linas would be returning to York in the morning. She would leave him at his spacious Stonegate home to rest and recover, and she would go to her well-ordered house on Blake Street, which was not really hers but Linas's. She would pretend to be its mistress when the reality was that she could stay only as long as Linas was alive.

If she could have given him an heir, her future would be more assured, but that was unlikely to happen, for both of them had realised some time ago that one of them must be infertile. Having as much pride as he, Helene preferred to believe that the fault must lay with him, but Winterson's wounding enquiry about her future had inflamed a painful truth that was never far from her darkest thoughts that, no matter which of them was responsible for their childlessness, the outlook remained bleak.

Deep in thought, she allowed her maid to undress her and to lock away the few jewels Linas had given her since their first Christmas together. He had never thought it necessary to shower her with gifts, but now her birthday had come and gone without a word, and the thought re-occurred yet again that their relationship must be on the wane. Ought she to leave him now, before he did? Should she find another lover, and be passed from one to the next until…until what? Had his brother anticipated the end of the partnership? Was that another reason for his coolness?

With a pang of guilt, she decided not to go to Linas's room, knowing how the scene would do nothing to lighten her spirits. His brother and valet had tended him, and now he would be snoring heavily under a mountain of extra blankets with all the windows tightly shuttered and a lamp left burning next to the mahogany commode. The air would be heavy with the odour of medications and sweat. It was no place for lovers.

For a few moments longer she watched the rain beat upon the night-blackened window and run down the glass, parting and joining, lashed sideways by fitful gusts of wind. Then, drawing the curtains to shut out the sight of her distorted naked reflection, she parted the cool sheets and slipped between them, gasping at the sting of freshness upon her skin, her feet seeking the places where the warming-pan had recently been. The maid tiptoed across to the candlestick and blew out the flame, leaving her mistress to her rest.

Not for many weeks had Linas stayed overnight at her Blake Street house, nor had he invited her to stay

at his, and so it was with an immediate sense of consolation that, in unthinking half-sleep, she accepted the
gentle movement of the sheets behind her and the slight
dip of the feather mattress as his weight tipped her
against him. She had been asleep, that much she knew,
for the wind had whipped itself into a howling spring
gale that rattled the old casement windows, and
drowsily she wondered whether it was that which had
disturbed him or the sudden remembrance of her
birthday. With a grunt of contentment she snuggled
deeper into his warm body and took the weight of his
arm upon her hip, expecting that he would straight
away resume his sleep.

But the weeks of abstinence were testimony to the
way her senses remembered him, for instead of the
tang of friars' balsam, laudanum or linctus, there was
a fresh moorland smell of heather and larch trees after
rain, and instead of the heavy limpness of his arm, this
one was thick and prickly with fuzz, moving over her
skin with a purpose, his fingers spread wide to cover
hers.

Her breathing behaved strangely as she struggled to
bring back to her sluggish mind some memory of what
she'd been used to, yet even with her back to him she could
not reconcile those vague familiarities with the pulsing
firmness that now pressed against her. Could she be
dreaming? Had her tiredness, resentment and yearnings
taken her too far? Reaching backwards, she took hold of
the hand to feel for the signet ring he never removed.

But the hand slipped away quickly to grasp her wrist
and hold it immobile, and as she turned to him in sudden
alarm, he moved faster than she could ever remember

him doing without stopping to cough and regain his breath. She found herself under him, pressed softly by wide shoulders that covered her, arms that enclosed her, and a large head of thick hair that touched her face with its softness, imparting a scent of new-washed linen. His lips found hers with none of the usual tentative pecking by way of introduction that was Linas's way, but with the assured and competant kisses of one who knew how to suspend a woman's protests in a limbo of delight, and it was not until he had taken his fill of her lips that her terrible doubts were able to surface and demand verification.

Pushing at his shoulders, she struggled against him as her body tried to recognise the deception, her mind still trying to persuade her not to delve too closely for fear of discovering the truth. Wordlessly, so as not to shatter the dream entirely with accusations and denials, she put up a fight that was disadvantaged in every way, which he countered in silence and with ease, and ultimately with the potency of his kisses that she allowed with nothing like the opposition she ought to have offered. Once, holding his head between her hands, she traced his features with sensitive fingertips over broad forehead and brows, over closed eyelids, cheeks and nose, firm mouth and chin, wider than the one she was used to. He kissed her fingers as they passed across, and she melted at that small tenderness before exploring the depth of his hair and the deeply muscled neck that led her on over the contours of his shoulders, down and down.

It occurred to her that he might have mistaken her room for that of another, but he would surely know where his guests were being accommodated. If any other thoughts of reason or common sense sneaked into her mind that night, they stood no chance of being heard against the deeply urgent need that sedated her fears like a potent drug, a need borne of starvation and a sense of waste that had dogged the last year with her lover. Gradually closing the doors of her mind, she began again to lose herself in the lure of his closeness, in the touch of his hand exploring the full roundness of her breasts. Perversely, she joined him in the treachery, forbidding herself to think about the consequences or to seek answers to a host of questions that were sure to follow. She would take what he was offering her, on her birthday, the only gift of comfort she was likely to receive.

Whatever reasons he had for doing this, he was not inclined to share them with her, nor did she ask him to, for she knew this would never happen again. Ever. He was making use of her and she would do the same with him, just this once. She might have pretended it was against her will, but she knew it was not, her token struggles having lacked any conviction against his gentle but determined restraint.

Savouring every moment as never to be repeated, excited by his mastery, she refused to allow the lack of endearment or word of comfort such as lovers use to detract anything from the fleeting glimpses of heaven she saw that night for the first time. Her unlikely lover-of-one-night was not a man she could ever want except for this, for he had never done anything to court her favour, and an exchange of tender words between them would have been meaningless as well as hypocritical.

It was her experience alone that told her of his pleasure in her body, his delight and satisfaction with her loving. At the same time, he was a careful lover, taking time with her as had never happened for her before, bringing her to a state of ecstasy again and again, taking pleasure from her wonderment and indicating by his lips and hands the journey they would take. Yet each time was different, his energy and eagerness phenomenal.

He stayed with her until dawn to take full advantage of her newly awakened passion, feeding from her willingness and giving generously to satisfy her hunger. And as the light crept between the curtains, he disappeared as silently as he'd come, thinking that she was asleep, and she had let him go because the time for words was past. She knew it to be one of those rare events that happened without rhyme or reason to change one's life for ever, and that the experience was worth the heavy guilt she would have to bear as long as her relationship with Linas lasted. Although Linas was not faultless, he had never been disloyal to her in the way she had been to him. She could only hope he would never discover it. The worst part would be having to pretend that nothing *had* happened.

In the months that followed, that pretence was shattered when she found herself to be with child. Then, because she could not keep the information from Linas, she broke the news to him, expecting that he would put an end to their association and reclaim everything that was his, including her home. To her utter astonishment, he did not, preferring to accept the unborn child as his own along with the congratulations of his friends and family, even though he must have known it could not be. Helene had assumed that pride in his manhood was more important to him than the truth, for he asked no questions, nor would he allow her to offer any explanation and, when the child was born, Linas's joy was as great as hers. At last, he had the heir he wanted.

The boy seemed to provide Linas with a renewed lease of life and, for the next three years he hung on as if to escort the lad through his first formative contacts with the world. But the effort could not be maintained, his hold began to slacken and, just after his son's third birthday, Linas was taken to Abbots Mere to end his days where they had begun, with his twin.

By that time, Helene had begun to suspect how adroitly she had been used by the two brothers. Now, she was sure of it.

Chapter One

York—January 1806

It would usually have taken me only a few minutes to walk from the workrooms of Follet and Sanders on Blake Street to Linas's house, but that day was an exception. That day, I was wearing my pretty fur-lined bootees, not designed for three inches of snow that had fallen in flakes the size of halfpennies since mid-morning, and by the time I reached the corner of Blake Street and Stonegate, where Linas's house was, the freezing wet had reached my toes and I was dizzy with slithering over a bed of snow-covered ice. I'm a tough northern lass, I reminded myself, clutching my thick woollen shawl tighter round my shoulders. I've been in many a snow storm before. The scolding did little to ease the situation.

The steps up to Linas's front door were thickly packed with the stuff, the shoe-scraper at the side piled with it, which should have warned me that someone had entered quite recently. But my hood was falling wetly over my face as I went inside, sending a shower of snow on to the already puddled black-and-white chequered tiles, and it was only when I threw my furry hood back that I saw more of Mr Brierley than his serviceable boots. Mr Brierley was Linas's lawyer who had, I suppose, as much right as me to be standing in the hall of his late client.

His greying forelock was plastered across his head, his spectacles speckled with snow, catching the light of the single lamp, and his attempted smile was cooled by the unusually low temperature. Linas had always maintained an uncomfortable warmth in all his rooms. Now, they were uncomfortably cold. But then, nothing was going to be usual for Linas any more after yesterday's funeral and today's thick white blanket being gently laid over him.

'Mr Brierley,' I said, returning his half-smile, 'I didn't expect to see you here so soon. Not for weeks. Well, days, anyway.' Shaking the hem of my pelisse, I showered his toes with snowflakes and saw him step back. My glance at the hall table verified what I feared: two grey beaver hats, two pairs of gloves, one antler-topped cane and a riding whip that I recognised. Silver-mounted. It was not what I had expected, or wanted, so soon after yesterday. I ought to go, I thought, before he appears. We shall only bicker.

The lawyer must have recognised the hint of unwelcome in my greeting, which, I admit, was not as fawning as it might have been from a client's mistress. Client's mistresses usually have expectations. 'No, indeed, ma'am,' he said. 'We lawyers are not known for speeding things up, I agree, but Lord Winterson asked me to meet him here, to—'

'To take a look round? Yes, I quite understand, Mr Brierley. Shall I leave you to it? Is that your inventory?' There was a black leather notebook tucked under his arm, and my accusatory tone drew it from its pigeonhole to prove itself.

'Er…no. Not to take an inventory. It was Lord Winterson's wish to attend to other pressing matters before the snow delays things. Perhaps that is also why you are here, Miss Follet?'

Yes, I suppose he was entitled to ask my business now. 'The snow will make no difference to me. I come here every day, sir. The servants need direction at a time like this.'

'Which is exactly why we're here. To help re-settle them. I have here some contacts…' he tapped the notebook with white fingertips '…and they'll need the references Mr Monkton prepared for them.'

Ah, yes. References. Linas would have discussed the futures of all his employees with his lawyer and brother. Mine too, I hoped. What a pity he had found it so difficult to take me into his confidence at the same time, to spare me the worry of how I would manage on my own. I had made plans, as far as I was able, but it would have lightened my heart if he had shown as much concern for my future as he had for the rest of his household. My repeated promptings, gentle or insistent, had brought no response except irritability and fits of coughing, and finally I had stopped probing for any kind of assurances concerning me and Jamie.

'Of course,' I said. 'Then I shall bid you a good afternoon.'

My feet were wet, my fingers inside my woolly gloves frozen, the hall was bare and gloomy, and I did not want to see Linas's brother that day. Or any day. I reached back to pull up my hood, numb fingers fumbling with an edge of wet fur, icy water running up to my elbows.

'I believe,' said Mr Brierley, 'Lord Winterson would like you to be present at the reading of his brother's last will and testament tomorrow, Miss Follet.'

The shake of my head was hidden from him. 'No, I think not,' I mumbled. 'That will be no place for a man's mistress, sir. Please excuse me.' But my fumbling had obscured the quiet entrance of the one I hoped to avoid, and suddenly he appeared in the corner of my eye through the wet points of fur.

In almost six years there had never been a time when I'd been able to control my heartbeats at the sight of him. In the last four years—almost—there had hardly been a day when some detail of that night had failed to appear, or the wounding deceit of it fail to hurt. Between them, they had used me and I intended to make *him* aware of my anger as I had not been able to do with Linas. I could hardly bite the hand that fed me and my child, but I could and would refuse Winterson's attempts, such as they were, to make me see him in a better light. And who could blame me?

The day before, with so many people there, I had done my best not to look at him. Or not to be *seen* looking at him. Now I did, and was astonished to see the shadows of deep sadness around his eyes, the unease of his mouth and the sagging tiredness of his shoulders that leaned against the doorframe into the study. Like me, he had kept his coat on, a long buff-coloured caped affair that barely cleared the floor, hanging loose over charcoal-grey riding coat and breeches, black waistcoat with a row of gold-figured buttons and watch-chain. His neckcloth, as always, was immaculate. His hair, as always, needed cutting.

I am ashamed to say that, in my own grief at the loss of my lover, I had spared too little thought for how he must be feeling at the loss of his twin, having to watch him fade away like a candle flame, burn low and finally extinguish. I had no cause to grumble that I was excluded, for Winterson sent a carriage for me at the end so that I too could be there for Linas's last moments when it seemed, perhaps for the first and last time, that the three of us had shared a special tenderness and compassion, putting aside the complexities of our relationship. He had even allowed me some time alone with Linas at the end, which was remarkable when his parents were waiting to do the same. I was grateful to him for that. Returning home afterwards, my life seemed to be suspended and without cause, except for little Jamie. The funeral had upset me and I had slept badly, and I suppose it must have showed in my manner.

'Miss Follet?' he said. 'Could you spare me a moment of your time?'

'I told Jamie I would not be long.'

'Please? Just a moment?' He moved to one side, holding his hand out as if he was sure I would comply.

I left my hood up. And I left Mr Brierley in no doubt

about my reticence as I swept past them both into the green book-lined study that had been Linas's retreat during his last, most painful year. The once cosy room, always littered with books and papers, was now unnaturally tidy and distressingly naked. Incomplete. I turned the wick up in the oil lamp on his desk before going to stand by the white marble fireplace, putting some distance between us, hitching up my woolly scarf against a sudden chill. 'My lord?' I said, to convince him of my impatience.

'Miss Follet…Helene…' he said, wearily. 'Brierley and I had…' he sighed and looked away as if the room was affecting him too '…had hoped to have the will read here at Stonegate tomorrow. But, as you see, that may be prevented by the weather. If it carries on like this, those who ought to be here will be unable to manage it, or even get home again. I think we shall have to postpone it till it clears. I don't know how you're fixed for funds, to put it bluntly, but since Linas's accounts are frozen for the time being, I wondered if you might need some help until we discover what arrangements have been made for you.'

'How kind,' I said. 'If I had not chanced to see you here today, you might still be wondering.'

'It was not chance. I know you still visit daily. Such habits are hard to break. I called at your home, but you were not there, so I came here to meet Brierley and to wait for you.'

'You called…home? You saw Jamie?'

'Yes,' he said, raising an eyebrow at my tone. 'Is there some reason why I should not? He's grown in the last few weeks.'

'I should have been there. He's already missing his father.'

Unthinking, I stepped straight into the bag of worms. There was a crackling silence broken by the loud ticking of the bracket clock.

'Then this may be the best time to remind you, Miss Follet, that his *father* has just made contact with him, which you have so far been at pains to prevent by every means known to you. I could hardly have said so while Linas was with us, but now we must both try to accept the truth of the matter and do whatever is best for the child. You surely cannot be too surprised that Linas wished me to be Jamie's legal guardian?'

'That is probably the one thing that will *not* surprise me, my lord. It's well known that a child's guardian must always be male, you being the obvious choice, but that does not alter the fact that I am Jamie's mother and, as such, it is I who will decide where he will go and what he will do. And who he'll do it with.'

'Which is why I want you to hear Linas's will at first hand.'

'So you know the details of it, do you?'

'Yes, I know more details than you. That's only natural. We discussed it as brothers do.'

All too eager to display my wounds while I had the chance, I could not resist putting another slant on it. 'Oh you *did*, didn't you? Four years ago you discussed it. In some detail. Linas wanted an heir. You obliged. And I fell for it like an idiot. Like a resentful birthday-gift-starved fool. I paid for it, too.'

'You got Jamie. He was what you wanted. Don't deny it.'

'But one does like to have a say, nowadays, in who the father is to be. Even mistresses appreciate some warning of *that* event.'

'Think about it,' he snapped. 'Had you been *warned*, as you put it, there'd have been no Jamie, would there?'

'No, my lord. There most certainly would not.' I had to admit defeat on that brief skirmish, and I had no stomach for a prolonged argument on the topic. I closed my eyes with a sigh, holding a gloved hand to my forehead. 'This will not do,' I whispered. 'It's too soon for recriminations. Or too late. I'm tired. It's time I went home.'

He watched me, saying nothing as I recovered.

'I know there will be changes,' I said. 'I've had time to prepare for them, whatever they are. And thank you for your offer of a loan, but I think we shall manage for the time being. I also owe you thanks for allowing me access to Linas at the end. That was generous too, and…and appreciated…' My voice wavered and caught at the back of my throat, dissolving the last word. I took some deep breaths to steady it.

'It was no more than you deserve. It was your careful nursing that kept him alive longer than his doctors had predicted.'

'I think it's more likely to be Jamie who did that.'

'Yes, that too. Jamie was your other gift to him. Linas was a very fortunate man. He told me so more than once.'

'Did he?' I remarked, tonelessly, wistfully.

'Did he never tell you so?'

'No. Not even at the end. I think the pain made him forgetful. Or perhaps he thought I was the fortunate one. I don't know. It doesn't really matter now, does it? But I mean what I say about not hearing the will read, my lord. I would be out of place. I am not family and I have few expectations, except for Jamie, having fulfilled the role I was employed to do, to everyone's satisfaction.'

'You were not *employed* in any capacity, Miss Follet. You were my brother's partner. It was his decision not to marry when he discovered he had so few years to live, and our family agreed that for him to do so would serve no useful purpose.'

'Rather like good farm management, I suppose. You see, I am well able to think it out for myself, Lord Winterson. Having a mistress to support for just a few years was safer than taking on a wife. Linas preferred an illegitimate heir able to legally inherit and keep his estate intact, to a widow who would remarry and siphon it off into another man's pockets. But don't tell me that I was not employed, for that is certainly what I was, and I shall not sit with you round a table to be told that my golden goose has gone and left me nothing except my bastard child to care for. You may be very sure I shall guard my only treasure against any attempt to siphon *him* off into another man's pocket. He may be the Monkton heir, but he is also my only legacy. *Mine*, my lord.'

I should not have said it, not then when emotions were so raw, Linas barely out of earshot, and both of us so tired. But my resentments were begging for release, freeing up words that I should have kept tightly controlled, as I had always done. I could have blamed my outspokenness on my northern roots, but that was too easy an excuse. So I held my breath and waited for him to retaliate in the usual Winterson fashion, with a set-down meant to silence me for months. Which he had every right to do.

His reply, when it emerged, was a calm reiteration of his claim. 'And he is mine too, Helene. Linas has made me his legal guardian and you will have to get used to the idea, like it or not.'

'I *don't* like it.'

'But I think Jamie will. He needs an active father, now he's growing up. He needs more to do than walks with his nurse.'

'He's still only a babe. He needs only me.'

'So let's wait till we've heard what provisions Linas has made for you, then we shall know better what his needs are, shan't we? You are exhausted, and so am I. It's time you were home. Come. I have to get back to Abbots Mere before the snow gets deeper.'

'What about the servants?' I said, relieved to have been let off so lightly. 'You came here to—'

'Brierley can stay to deal with that. He lives on Petergate. You should trust him. He's an honest man.'

'I'm sure he is. He'll have your interests at heart.'

'And Jamie's. Is that such a bad thing?'

Still, I could not help myself. Perhaps I wanted to provoke him, to make him react, in spite of his courtesy to me. Perhaps I was a little mad that day. 'If I was retaining him,' I said, 'it would not be such a bad thing. But I'm not, am I?'

We had reached the door where his hand rested upon the large brass knob but, as my stupidly caustic remark stung him into action, he turned to me with characteristic speed, taking me by the shoulders with hands that bit through all my woollen layers. Holding me back against the deeply carved doorcase, he bent his head to look inside my hood and, whatever anger he saw on my face, it could have been nothing to the fury on his.

'Stop it, woman!' he snarled. 'You think you're the only loser in this damned business? You think you've had the thin end of the wedge, do you? Well, *do* you? Forget it. He was my brother. You had him for the best part of six years. I had him for thirty. We both…you and me…did what *he* wanted us to do, and if you had less choice in the matter than you'd have liked, well, I had just as little. I did it for him, and you believed I did it for you, didn't you? That's why you're so angry. D'ye think I make a habit of creeping into my lady guests' beds while they're asleep?'

Since he was being kind enough to ask my opinion on that, I'd like to have said that he must have had a fair bit of practice at it. But, no, I said nothing of the kind. Nothing at all, in fact. I simply shook my head, which made my hood fall off. I noticed two new hairline creases from his nose to his mouth. I noticed that his eyelids were puffy, as if he'd been weeping. I noticed a sprinkling of silver hairs in that luxurious dark mop, just above his ears.

'I'm sorry,' I whispered. 'I'm overwrought. We both need to rest.'

He sighed through his nose with lips compressed, and I thought he was going to say more because his eyes held mine, letting me read the sadness written there more eloquently than words. Then he released me, and I felt the tingling where his hands had been, and I stood still while he pulled up my hood and settled it round my face. I was under no illusions; he would do the same for any of his closer woman friends, I was sure. Perhaps their minds would empty too, just for those few seconds.

'Calm down,' he said, gruffly. 'Go home and get warm. Come on.'

Outside on the pavement, the lamplighter clambered down his ladder into the horizontal white blizzard, having cast a halo of light dancing across the ghostly snow-covered figures below. Lord Winterson's groom emerged from the narrow alley that led to Linas's court-yard and stables, riding one horse and leading the mighty grey hunter that blew clouds of white into the freezing air. 'Follow on,' Winterson called to him, taking my arm and linking it through his.

'I can manage,' I said, ready to pull away. 'Really I can.'

But he clamped my hand with his elbow and, bending his head into the snowstorm, began to escort me home, not far, but far enough for us both to struggle against the conditions. His only conversation was, 'Mind…take care…hold on…you all right?'

Standing under the porch before the door, I thanked him.

'Stay at home till it clears,' he said. 'I'll contact you as soon as I can get through. See Brierley if you need anything. He'll help.'

I nodded and watched his effortless leap into the saddle, wheeling away as if the snow was no more than a mild shower. Across on the other side of Blake Street, the lights in the workroom, more properly known as Follet and Sanders, Mantua-maker, Milliner and Fabric

Emporium, had been extinguished earlier than usual to allow the girls to get home, though I knew that Prue Sanders would still be working at the back of the shop on the new year's orders, the alterations on ballgowns, fur trims and muffs. The cold weather had swept in from the north-east with a vengeance that year, and I had ordered that the fire in the sewing room should be kept burning constantly to keep the place warm. It was an expensive luxury I had not budgeted for, and my recent assurances that I could manage were not nearly as certain as I'd made them sound. But not for any reason would I have accepted a penny from him. Prue and I would have to manage on what the business earned.

That evening, however, my thoughts were in turmoil, for although my contacts with Lord Winterson had always been as brief as I could make them, this was the first time he and I had spoken about what had gone before, about his claim to Jamie, or about my feelings on the matter. As long as Linas lived, the subject had been studiously avoided, and now the impromptu un-veiling had shaken me, if only because I had believed until then that he and Linas were alike in refusing to discuss things they found too uncomfortable. I had been proved wrong.

Only a day after his brother's funeral, Winterson had brought out our shameful secret for its first airing, along with the reason for it and the well-planned result of it. My Jamie. He was right: I *was* angry, not because I was mistaken about his motives—for those I knew by then—but because *he* had known how easily I would give myself to him that night, repeatedly, willingly, and with little conscience. He had known, and my pride was wounded to the quick that all our mutual antagonism had been so easily suspended in the face of a temptation like that. How shallow he must think me. How disloyal. How easy.

What he would never know, though, was that I had fed off that experience since it happened, savouring it every night through each amazing phase, knowing that it would never be mine again. And since he had been unconvinced of my dislike of him *before* the event, I must of necessity try harder to convince him of it afterwards. His accusation about keeping Jamie at a distance from him was a part of my strategy but, with him now as Jamie's guardian, I would find that more difficult, thanks to Linas.

Chapter Two

Thanks also to the weather, that part of my plan held up well when all the traffic in and out of the city was stopped for more than a week until men could shovel paths through the deep drifts, allowing access to the suburbs. We heard reports of farmers losing sheep, of snow burying hedges and cottages, trapping the mail-coach miles away with all its passengers, and the drowning of some young lads who had played upon frozen ponds. Fresh falls of snow added more depth to the fields each morning and broke branches off trees, the dropping temperatures killing everything that was too old, frail or poor to keep warm. The thermometer in Linas's hall registered thirty degrees Fahrenheit, and a few days later we had twenty degrees of frost. I had never experienced such cold.

All through the freeze, my daily visits to Stonegate continued, partly to check on the remaining servants and partly to mentally mop up what was left of the essence pervading each room. In one way I had to be

thankful that his suffering had ended at last, for I had
not found it easy to watch him die and know that there
was no way of stopping it happening. Jamie's birth had
done more than anything to extend the reprieve, but
Winterson had been right to suggest that, when his
brother's illness began to distress the little fellow, a
move to Abbots Mere would be best.

So I'd had a chance, at the end, to spend more time
with Jamie, to begin some small rearrangements of our
life in preparation for the future, to involve myself more
with the thriving dressmaking business, to make another
buying trip to Manchester and to pay an extended visit
to my family without having to account for our absence.

Even so, I felt the gaping hole in my life where my
Linas had been for, although we had not been lovers in
the true sense for years, we had shared a real need for
each other that was not wholly material, but emotional
and spiritual as well. We never actually spoke of it: he
was not good at speaking of love, and any attempt on
my part only embarrassed him. But we were aware of
our need for each other, especially so since Jamie's appearance, and I was not foolish enough to end that prematurely when I knew the end would come soon
enough. Had I remained childless, I might have thought
differently, but I could not take a gamble when there
was the son of a noble house to care for.

The River Ouse that brings boats up to the York
warehouses froze all river traffic to a standstill, offering
a quicker way to cross without using the bridge or the
ferry. Those who could skate had a merry time of it, and
Jamie's nurse and I took him there, astonished by his
pluck and persistence.

While Linas was alive, the natural tendency had been for everyone to compare him to the one he called papa, but by three years old his sturdy little frame and bold wilful nature, dark eyes and thick curly hair indicated characteristics that I was able to identify only too easily. Fortunately, my own dark colouring disguised the truth, but then, that must also have been taken into account at the outset, I supposed. It was so clever of them.

The nine seamstresses in the sewing room were loath to return home each evening during the freeze when the conditions at work were so much more comfortable than their own. Remembering how I too had been one of them, fourteen years old with only my clothes to my name, how Prue had sheltered and fed me, I tried to do the same for them, many of whom had worked there longer than me. Oh, she had worked me harder than hard to make it worth her while, being a canny Yorkshire woman, but I had not resented it, nor did the girls appear to resent me moving up the ladder rather faster, so to speak. Now, Prue Sanders and I were partners in the business, having expanded sideways into the house next door to the Assembly Rooms. A perfect situation, if ever there was one.

My own house was placed diagonally across the road, so convenient for us both especially during those exceptionally cold weeks when the ice seemed to creep into our veins. All our stores of potatoes froze solid. Few people could reach the mill for flour, nor could the miller use his wheel, sending up the price of bread accordingly. Fish was locked under the ice and people had to delve earlier than usual into their reserves of dried and pickled foods, feeding cattle with precious hay.

I did better than most in that respect, for as soon as a narrow passage was cut through the drifts, two pack-ponies and men arrived at my kitchen door having trekked from Abbots Mere at their master's command. Into the kitchen were carried sacks of flour, oats and barley, chickens and geese, a brace each of pheasant and grouse, rabbits and a hare, baskets of apples, pears and plums, butter and cheeses, eggs and half-frozen milk, a half-carcass of lamb, hams, and trout packed in ice, all piled on to the table while cook stood with jaw dropping. I saw this gift as an answer to my refusal to accept a loan. For all our sakes, I was bound to accept this.

Gulping down beakers of mulled ale and wedges of fruit cake, the men would give no more information than, 'Compliments of Lord Winterson, ma'am. And ye're to let him know when you want some more. He hunts most days.'

'What, on horseback? In this snow?'

'Usually on foot, ma'am.'

Jamie jumped up and down at the end of my hand. 'Oh, can I go too? I go on foot with Uncaburl?'

'Nay, little 'un,' said one of the men, replacing his woollen hood, 'tha'd be mistekken fer a rabbit.'

'Would I, Mama?' said Jamie, looking worried.

I lifted him into my arms. 'No, sweetheart. Your ears are much too short to be mistaken for a rabbit. But the snow is too deep. Now we must say thank you to the men and let them go. It's starting to snow again.'

I sent my thanks to 'Uncaburl', thinking how ironic it was that food was more available to him out in the country than it was to me here in the town. Winterson's revolutionary farming methods would see him through any crisis. According to Linas, Abbots Mere had never produced so much since his brother took it over. In truth, I had started to worry about what my own family would suffer if the freeze continued much longer, living several miles from York and completely cut off from supplies.

Perhaps I exaggerate. No, they were not *completely* cut off, only in the sense that they were invisible to all intents and purposes, living in hiding in a deserted village between York and our old home town of Bridlington on the east coast. There, the North Sea hurls itself at the cliffs in easily provoked anger.

For several years, my perceptive partner, Prue Sanders, withheld all questions about my family and why I was cut adrift from them. When the time was ripe, she knew I would take her into my confidence. So it was after I had borne Jamie and gone into partnership with her, extending the shop to twice its size, that I felt she was owed some kind of explanation as to why a woman like me had had to look for work as a lowly seamstress in York.

She was not the kind of woman to express astonishment; it was as if she had already guessed parts of the story, reversals of fortune being no new thing in those uncertain war years. When I told her my father had been mayor of Bridlington, she simply nodded and carried on pinning a gathered skirt on to a bodice. 'Mm…m. Wealthy?' she mumbled, without looking up.

'He was a merchant. A ship owner, and Customs Collector.'

'Oh, yes,' she said in the kind of voice that expects

the Customs Collector to be up to some shady business, as a matter of course. 'Smuggling, was he?'

Her assumption was correct, of course, for every villager along the North Sea coastline had a hand in the 'Free Trade', and few could afford not to be involved in the carrying, the hiding, the converting of boats, the warning systems, not to mention the putting-up of money to buy the goods from northern France and Flanders. The new French aristocracy led European fashions, and all things French were much in demand, imports that were taxed so highly by the English government that smuggling became a kind of protest against the unaffordable import duties.

'Yes,' I said. 'He got caught. Informed on by a so-called friend.'

'Nothing new there, then,' she said, pinning. 'Good rewards.'

'Yes, it was the Customs Controller who shopped him for half the value of the contraband and five hundred pounds extra. Father wouldn't accept the man's offer to marry me, so that was how he took his revenge.'

'And did you want him?'

'Lord, no, Prue. I was fourteen and he was thirty-something.'

'So your father was arrested. He'd not be found guilty by a local jury. They never are.' She was so matter of fact. So dispassionate.

'No, but he used a firearm, Prue.'

The pinning stopped as she straightened up to look at me. 'Oh,' she said. 'That's serious. That's a hanging offence. Confiscation of property. The works. Is that how you came to be…?'

I remembered those weeks when the world turned upside down for our family, how my father was dragged off by the local militia to the gaol at York. 'Yes,' I said. 'More or less. But his friends from Brid rescued him and hustled him away to Foss Beck Common. My mother and the rest of us joined him there, but he died soon after.'

'Foss Beck?' Prue said, taking the last pin from between her lips. 'Is that where they are? I always thought…'

'Yes, I know you did. I'm sorry I deceived you, but it's not a story to boast of, is it? It's easier to call Brid home than a deserted village. Linas doesn't know about what happened. No one does.'

'Aye…lass!' she said, sitting down at last. It was unusual for her hands to be idle. 'Dear, oh dear! You lost your father too? And your home?'

'He was wounded, but he kept it quiet. It seems so absurd that, only weeks earlier, he could have afforded the best attention in England. My mother has never quite recovered from the shock of it all, so it fell to me and my two brothers to survive on what we could find. We have a French relative who lives with us too, and he's been very good. We have a few servants to help out, and friends from Brid brought us food and bedding and tools. Even hens and goats. We managed.'

'I didn't think any of the houses at Foss Beck were still habitable.'

'The manor house has been half-ruined for centuries since the plague killed everyone off, but we manage to live in half of it.'

'And there's no chance of returning to Brid?'

'My brothers were nine and eleven, and I was

fourteen when we went into hiding, old enough to be arrested as substitutes for my father's crimes. It's a risk we daren't take, Prue. Not even after all these years.'

'So that's when you came looking for work in York. I see.'

'While I still looked half-respectable. Sewing was one of the things I could do to earn money. You must have seen in me something you could use.'

'Yes. Your skills, and the fabrics you brought in each month.' Picking up a bobbin of tacking-cotton, she pulled off a length and snipped it with her teeth. 'I've never asked where it came from, Helene, and I don't intend to ask now. If I don't know, I can't tell any lies, can I? Where did I put my needle?'

'On your wrist.' She wore a piece of padded velvet like a pincushion around her wrist. With Pierre, our French *émigré* relative acting as a go-between, and me not asking any questions about the source of his merchandise, everything he obtained for us was passed straight into the dressmaking business, the only one in York at that time to sell fabrics and designs too. The money from the bales of muslins and lace made it a lucrative trade that allowed me to supplement the poor wage I had earned and to take money and goods back to my family. Had it not been for Pierre and his French connections, we would certainly have starved. Prue must have known how the precious goods were obtained, and our customers must have guessed. My only thought was how to keep myself and my family alive.

'Yes…well,' she went on, threading her needle in one quick move and rolling a knot between finger and thumb, 'you've been a godsend to me, Helene love. Not

just the fabrics, though I'll not deny they've done a lot
to help things along. Your business ability, for one thing.
Your looks, for another. Your style. Your knowledge of
French too. And I know how hard it's been for you,
though I don't know what your ma would say about
how hard you've had to work. Does she know?'

'That I've had to sell myself?'

'Mmm,' she said, rippling the needle through the
gathers.

'No, Prue. She doesn't. The boys do, and Pierre. But
beggars cannot be choosers, can they?'

'No, love. You've had to grow up rather fast, haven't
you? But it's not made you bitter, has it?' The needle
delved and pulled up, finding its own rhythm.

'Yes, it has,' I said.

The needle stopped in mid-air as she looked up at
me. 'Then don't let it,' she said. 'Regretting is a waste
of time. What's done is done. You have a man, and a
child, and a partnership in this, and youth, beauty, and
more common sense than most women of your age. So,
you've got responsibilities.' The needle began again.
'Well, most of us have, one way or another. Nothing
stays the same, Helene. Believe me.'

'I do believe you,' I whispered.

Things would *not* stay the same. For one thing, I was
determined that my infant would not suffer the same
deprivations I'd suffered. Little did I know then how his
future would pass out of my hands with such finality,
nor did I fully appreciate the wisdom of Prue's advice
about my bitterness.

Lowering Jamie to the ground, I took him by the
hand and led him back to the warm kitchen where the

piles of food were being sorted by cook's eager hands. He stroked the hare's soft fur and spoke into its huge reproachful eyes. 'Sorry, hare,' he whispered. I showed him the intricate pattern of the pheasant's feathers and the long banded tail that I would save for the millinery girls. 'I want to see Uncaburl,' said Jamie, sadly.

'Yes, love. But you saw Uncle Burl only last week, and the snow is very deep. I don't think our horses would like it.'

He barely understood. 'We could go to see Nana Damzell, then?'

Damzell Follethorpe was my mother, who had not seen him for over a month and Jamie now able to talk so well, I dared not take the risk, with Winterson being a Justice of the Peace and Jamie so willing to chatter about all he knew. 'Soon, darling,' I said.

'She'd like some of this, wouldn't she, Mama?'

'Yes, love, she certainly would.' The same thought had passed through my mind too, but I could not see how to get it there.

Mrs Neape, my cook, understandably not wishing to see the supplies dwindle so soon, had the answer. 'Don't you worry, young man,' she said. 'This lot will stay frozen solid down in the cellar for weeks. Then you can take some of it to Bridlington to your Nana Damzell.'

It was where all my household believed my family to be living, about forty miles away on the coast. Foss Beck was less than half that distance, and the only person ever to accompany us there was Jamie's formidable nurse, Mrs Goode, who would not have disclosed the smallest detail of my secret. She had once been a man's mistress, too. 'As soon as the snow begins to melt,' I promised, 'we shall go. What shall we take her?'

'Eggs. She likes duck eggs, Mama.'

That would be like taking coals to Newcastle. They had hens, ducks and geese roaming freely, and no shortage of eggs. But bread would be a problem.

'Tell me when you're going and I'll make you some of my meat pies,' said Mrs Neape, hoisting the side of lamb on to her padded shoulder. She would not, however, see any need to send loaves of bread.

With little improvement in the weather, the reading of Linas's will was delayed for almost three weeks and, even then, several of the family were missing, so Mr Brierley told me, owing to the impassable roads. It was he who called to say that he hoped I would not mind hearing at second hand what concerned me, since that was how several of the others would receive news of their endowments too.

What they were endowed with I have no idea, never having shown much interest in what Linas owned, or whether he relied on his wealthy father for an allowance, as many sons did. Even when they were twins, second sons rarely prospered as well as their elder siblings in the property stakes, although I had no doubt that Linas would never have been left wanting. As his mistress, I was probably the most expensive of his few extravagances, albeit not as costly as some I've heard of. I had, after all, reorganised my own business after Jamie's birth, and thank heaven for my foresight, Mr Brierley having no outstandingly good news to offer me that day.

At first, I could hardly believe what I was hearing.

That Linas wanted me to continue living on Blake Street came as a great relief, though no real surprise. Mr Brierley's assurance was quite clear that the house would be made available to me for as long as I wanted it. But when he kept his balding head bent while unnecessarily sorting papers out across the polished table, I guessed that he was seeking not figures, but a kind way to break the news. It came very quietly and deliberately.

'As for pecuniary endowments, Miss Follet,' he said, glancing up at last, 'that's *money*, you understand…'

'Yes?'

'Mr Monkton has left you the sum of three hundred and fifty pounds per annum for the rest of your life.'

'Yes?'

'Er…yes. That's all.'

I stared at him, frowning, puzzled. 'All? Three *hundred* and fifty?'

His finger pointed at the yellow page. 'Yes. That was his wish.'

'But how am I supposed to manage on that? Has he left no provision for our son?'

'Certainly. Master James Frederick Linas Monkton has been left, you will be pleased to hear, a substantial trust fund, to remain in the hands and to be administered by his sole guardian, Lord Burl Winterson of Abbots—'

'Yes, I know where Winterson lives, but what else is there? Surely Linas left me something for Jamie's needs until he comes of age? I cannot raise him on three hundred and fifty pounds a year, Mr Brierley.'

'You are not supposed to, Miss Follet, if I may say so. The trust fund to be held by Lord Winterson is designed to cater for all your son's needs, as and when he needs them. This will include all his living expenses, his clothes and education and so on. All you will have to do is to apply to James's guardian for—'

'But that's ridiculous!' I yelped, jumping to my feet. 'Are you saying I shall have to request money for Jamie's food, but not for mine, candles and coal for Jamie, but not for me, his nurse's wages, a groom…'

'No…no, Miss Follet.' Mr Brierley smiled, waving a hand in my direction. 'I don't suppose it will come to that, will it? I'm sure Lord Winterson will see that you have what you need for young James. A kind of allowance? Monthly? Weekly? But Mr Monkton's wishes are quite clear that his brother shall have every say in his ward's upbringing, and I have Lord Winterson's assurance that he intends to exercise his guardianship with the authority of a father. It must surely be comforting for you to know that your son will have a guardian who is so committed to his immediate welfare.'

I stood by the window, stunned by the chilling austerity of Linas's tight-fistedness. I felt I deserved better than that, after almost six years of devotion. I wished then that my life had taken a different turning. Gripping the rose-velvet curtain, I spoke my thoughts out loud. 'The house will have to be sold,' I said. 'And I shall have to find a husband. Yes, that would be best for both Jamie and me. Even with a house to live in, it's going to take every last penny I can earn to keep it going.'

'Ahem!' Mr Brierley coughed, shuffling the papers again. 'I believe Mr Monkton did add a clause concerning that eventuality, Miss Follet, if I can find it somewhere. Ah…yes, here we are.' He adjusted his spectacles. 'Should Miss Helene Follet decide in the future to take a husband, then my son James Frederick Linas Monkton shall live permanently and exclusively in the home of his guardian at Abbots Mere in the county of York. There. He's saying that—'

'Yes, thank you. I believe I know what he's saying, Mr Brierley. In short, I shall lose Jamie if I marry.'

'Correct. You will also lose the use of the house too, I'm afraid.'

'What?'

He nodded, pursing his lips. 'Mmm. Well, you can see his point.'

My head reeled as I sat down with a thump upon the couch. Oh yes, I could see his point quite clearly. No wonder he'd been loath to discuss it with me. Not only had he decided by whom and when I should bear a child for him, but now he was asserting that he could take it away again if I did not conform to his wishes. How dictatorial was that? As for Winterson exercising his guardianship like a father, well, yes, he would. *Exactly* like a father.

'That is most unfair, Mr Brierley, and *highly* unethical. That is interfering with my right to take a husband and to keep my child.'

'Surely, Miss Follet, it is better for your son to have a guardian he knows and likes than to have a stepfather he doesn't know? I do believe Mr Monkton had this in mind when he made this wish.'

Did he? I struggled to think *what* Linas had in mind when he saw fit to interfere in my life even after he'd gone. Jamie was precious to him too, I understood that, but he could not realistically expect me to see eye to eye

with his brother on any matter relating to Jamie's upbringing, when Winterson had no experience whatever
of children. I felt insulted that he could not have left
matters in my hands and made funds available to me
for Jamie's use. Did he think that, although I could
manage a business, nurse him day and night, run my
own household and care for a three-year-old, I could not
be relied on to handle a trust fund? No, probably not.
There had been times when I wondered whether Linas
spared much thought for me at all. Now I knew the
answer.

'This will have to be contested,' I muttered. 'It
won't work.'

'Miss Follet,' said Mr Brierley, removing his spectacles and sitting back in his chair, 'one cannot contest
a will simply on the basis that one thinks it might be difficult to put it into practice. There is nothing here that
is unworkable. You may have found it disappointing,
but the terms are not so very unusual. Mr Monkton's
reasoning was sound at the time, and he does not state
that you should not marry, only that his son shall live
with his guardian if you do.'

'And you see nothing sinister in that, sir? Is it
remotely likely that I would allow that to happen, do you
think?'

'Ahem! I really cannot comment on that, Miss Follet,
except to say that Mr Monkton's prime concern was for
his son's well-being.'

'Which I find difficult to understand, sir. One would
have thought that his son's well-being would be all the
better for knowing that his mama was happy too. Oh,
yes,' I said as he opened his mouth to speak, 'I know

that wealth is not happiness, but how am I supposed to pay the servants' wages, keep the place warm and in good repair, and maintain the standard of living that Jamie is used to, I wonder, on three hundred and fifty pounds a year? Not to mention my own requirements. I shall be obliged to look for a little cottage to rent. That seems to be the only solution. Thank you for coming, Mr Brierley,' I said, holding out my hand. 'I think the best I can do now is to speak to Lord Winterson personally and see if we can come to a more sensible arrangement. Even he must realise what an impossible position this puts me in. Good day to you, sir.'

He shook my hand and gathered his papers together. 'Mr Monkton's servants will be gone from Stonegate by Friday,' he said. 'All of them except the top four have been paid and found new positions. The house will then be locked, prior to the new administration of the estate. If there is anything in the house that belongs to you, Miss Follet, I wonder if you would mind letting me have a list of the items so that I can isolate them. Oh… er…one more thing. If I may have your key to the Stonegate property?'

I took it from the drawer of my writing table and gave it to him. There were several things at Stonegate that belonged to me: a pair of miniature cameo portraits, my silver pill box that Linas used once, the embroidery workbox I kept there and a set of ivory combs, brushes and manicure tools. They were private, and I'd be damned if I'd make a list for him to hum and haw over.

It occurred to me much later that night as I lay sleepless, that Mr Brierley had not brought with him the title

deeds to my house, or things to sign that would estab-
lish me as the new owner. Well, I must remember to
mention it next time we met.

Chapter Three

$\mathcal{C}\!\!\!\sim\!\!\!\mathcal{D}$

Had I misunderstood? Had I not listened to him with
enough attention? Had he *really* said the house would
be mine? Mr Brierley had made no response to my
angry comment that I would have to sell it and find a
small cottage with fewer servants. Reduced circumstances I was familiar with, the fortunes of women in
my position being notoriously unstable, but was that
really what Linas had wanted for me and Jamie? I found
it hard to believe.

My house on Blake Street was newer and more fashionable than our old family home had been, furnished
with woods that shone like satin, hung with soft tones
in velvet and silk, carpeted with Axminsters and
matching Persian rugs, my bedroom patterned with
birds and trees. My canopied bed was carved by George
Reynoldson of York, no less. I had a family of loyal
servants who gave me no trouble at all, and Linas had
paid their wages without me ever having to worry about
the cost. I kept a phaeton and two horses in his stable

at Stonegate with no clear idea of whether they would still be mine to use. I ought to have asked Brierley at the interview, but perhaps he had given me enough bad news for one day.

My first call on the following day was to Follet and Sanders. Leaving Jamie at home with Goody, his nurse, I trudged over new layers of frozen snow. Every rooftop and ledge was capped with rounded pillows of white, blown like lace into every crevice and beyond where the great white minster reared its spiked towers, draped like a bride, silent and virginal.

The workroom door let in a fall of snow as I entered. Shivering in the chilled hallway, I met Prue with chattering teeth. 'It's as cold in here as it is outside,' I complained. 'We'll never attract any customers at this rate.'

Unmoved, she kissed me daintily on both cheeks, casting her eye over my black outfit with the grey squirrel fur up to my ears. For all her fair, petite, middle-aged looks and elfin ways, she was as tough and sensible a businesswoman as any in York, with the typically dour sense of humour that can poke fun at what is difficult to accept. 'No, dear,' she said, without a hint of levity, 'but we're selling fur muffs and knitted gloves like hot cakes, so we can't have our customers getting overheated, can we?'

'And fur-lined capes? Those fur hats, too?'

'Fur-edged handkerchiefs,' she replied, dead-pan.

'No!'

'No,' she agreed. 'Come and see.'

'It's not warm enough in here either,' I said, entering the large workroom where women sat at the oak table, each with a mound of fabric before her, reels of cotton on revolving stands, pincushions and tapes, scissors, lamps and lace edgings. They looked up and smiled, all of them swaddled in woollen shawls and fingerless mittens. The windows were white, patterned with ferns.

'No coal delivery this week,' Prue said. 'We're having to eke it out. I can't keep the fire going all night any more, and now the pump is frozen.'

'I'll send some coal across. Get cook to make some soup.'

'That all adds to the costs, you know.'

Faces looked up, grinning slyly. Prue never starved them.

She followed me into the fitting room, draped with discreet pale curtains and peopled by miniature figures on shelves wearing the latest Paris modes. In here, I paraded gowns before our best customers, where they called me 'Madame Helene', impressed by my French pronunciation and having no qualms about our poor relationship with France. War or no war, French modes were all the thing, and our supplies of silks and lace was wondered at, bought, but never queried.

'Brierley came about the will,' I told Prue, quietly.

I told her what had been said. She listened, unruffled.

'Then go to Stonegate and collect them,' she said. 'Go now. You don't need a key. Go in by the kitchen door. If you delay till Friday, it'll be too late.'

'Do I care enough to go and help myself?' I asked.

'Of course you do. Go! Mr Monkton's servants will let you in.'

She steered me through into the shop festooned with fabrics where customers were being attended at the long counter. 'Good morning, Mrs Barraclough. Miss Fairweather. Lady Bess, good morning to you.' She flicked a fair eyebrow at me and ushered me out into the snow, closing the door, setting the bell tinkling again.

At Stonegate, it was easy enough to pass through the ginnel into the courtyard and from there to the kitchen door. The cook, butler and coachman were there, huddled round the fire, surprised but not unwelcoming. I explained my mission and was led courteously up the back stairs into the echoing hall. 'Would you like some assistance, Miss Follet?' said the butler. 'Or would you prefer to be alone?'

'To be honest, Mr Treddle,' I said, 'I'm not even sure I ought to be doing this. Mr Brierley said to make a list, but I really don't… well, you know.'

'I understand perfectly, ma'am, and I feel sure Mr Monkton would too. May I suggest that you place your possessions on your bed, and I will personally wrap them and have them conveyed to Blake Street later on today. Would that do, do you think? That way, you'll not have removed them, will you?'

'Thank you, Mr Treddle. That will do perfectly.'

'Very good, ma'am.' He bowed, leaving me alone and feeling as strange as I had at my first entry, seventeen years old and on the cusp of something new. Yet again.

Upstairs, the sour smell of medication had gone and the tables had been cleared of the usual healing clutter. My silver pill box, brought from my old home, was still in his bedside drawer, yet even now I hesitated to take it. Smoothing the grey fur coverlet, I sat down on his bed as I had so often done to comfort him, to talk, to watch him sleep. Dear Linas.

The door, left open, gave on to a wide landing and the curve of polished elm, and if my eyes had not been closed by memories, I would have noticed, long before my return to the present, the tall great coated figure who had come to stand just inside the door frame.

I started with a gasp of shock, only half-believing.

'Miss Follet,' he said, softly.

I took a breath, summoning my matter-of-fact voice. 'Oh…you! You've saved me a journey. I was going to pay you a visit today.' He looked less weary, I thought, wishing my heart would not be so feckless.

'In this weather? I should hope not. Was it urgent?'

'Mr Brierley came. You must know, surely.'

'And?'

'There are things to be discussed.' Glancing at Linas's open drawer, I explained. 'He wanted me to give him a list. I don't do lists of possessions. I've lost too many possessions for that.'

'I don't blame you. Was there something in the drawer? Treddle told me why you're here.'

'Well…yes. That pill box. It was my father's.'

'Then take it.' When I did not, he walked over to the drawer, removed the pill box and gave it to me. 'There. Now, what else is there?'

'You don't mind?'

'Why should I?' he replied, wandering across the room with his hands clasped behind his back beneath the greatcoat. 'My staff are not going to know what belongs and what doesn't when they start next week.'

'What do you mean…*your* staff?'

He stopped his wandering and turned to face me with a searching look as if he was deliberating what to say. Yet again, I felt that this must be the prelude to some unwelcome news. 'Some of my staff from Abbots Mere. The house belongs to me now.' Then, as the shock dawned upon my face, he added, 'Oh, dear. Brierley didn't tell you? It was remiss of him to keep you in the dark. The staff you saw downstairs will remain, and the housekeeper too. I can use a house in the city as well as one outside it.'

What a fool I was. Why could I not have drawn more realistic conclusions about this? Guessing the answer to my next query, I asked it nevertheless. 'So who owns the one I live in on Blake Street? Mr Brierley said I would maintain the right to…'

'To live in it as long as you wish. Yes, that part was not in the will, but Linas and I agreed it between us. It belongs to me, you see. It always did. I lent it to Linas for your use.'

My guess had been correct. My arms prickled, but not with the cold. I stood up and closed the drawer with a snap. 'If I'd known *that*…'

'You'd what? Have refused to live in it?'

'I had thought…*hoped*…that Linas would provide me and his son with a roof over our heads, at the very least. Now, I cannot even sell it to make ends meet.' I could not deny that one of my main reasons for wanting to bear Linas's child was to do with the security it would bring. It had, as it happened, brought much more than that, not least being great happiness to his last few years. I had never regretted that part of the experience.

'You don't *need* to make ends meet, Miss Follet. I intend to continue paying all the running costs, as I have done since I lent it to my brother. You won't have any more expenses than you did before, except personal ones for which Linas has left you a modest sum.'

'You…*you* paid for its upkeep? And servants too?'

'Well, of course I did. Linas didn't have many extravagances, apart from…'

'Apart from *me*!'

'…from yourself, which I was quite content to finance. There was no sense of obligation, I assure you.'

'I've heard enough. No obligation, you say, when I was well and truly shared, wasn't I? You even *paid* for me. How do you expect me to feel about that, my lord? Grateful? Flattered? Slightly bewildered? Who exactly *have* I belonged to all these years, I wonder? All neatly contrived to live as the mistress of one twin whilst bearing the other one's child. Someone should write a play about it, shouldn't they? What a *comedy*!' Clutching the pill box, I strode past him, but was held back and swung round by his hand beneath my arm.

'Come back, Helene. You can't walk off in the middle of a discussion.'

'I'm not in the *middle* of it,' I snarled at him, pulling my arm away. 'And you can keep the other things I came for, since you probably paid for them too.'

'Listen to me, woman,' he growled, preventing my escape with his great bulk, legs apart, a black silhouette against the light. 'You're blinded by your anger because what Brierley told you was not what you expected. But be reasonable, will you? You want to continue living on Blake Street and you want the funds to maintain it properly, to give Jamie the stability he needs. And now when I tell you that's exactly what you *can* do, you fly off the handle and say it's *not* what you want. Well, make your mind up, but try to think what's best for Jamie instead of getting all hoity-toity about it. Does it matter *who* the house belongs to as long as you can both live there? Who else should pay the bills except me, I ask you? His guardian. Come down off your high horse for a moment. You'll have all you need.'

'What I need, my lord, is control of my life, for once. Control of Jamie's life, too. And that is still being denied me.'

'Then try being realistic. Sons remain in the control of their fathers or guardians and there's nothing you can do about that. You must have known as much. So, if you want to stay with him, you will have to accept the same constraints and try to regard them as benefits. Which they are. Linas knew that, and his will reflects it.'

'Is that so? Even to a ban on my marriage.'

'What marriage?'

I shrugged. 'Well, to a future husband, of course. Who else?'

'Do you have a candidate in mind for the position?'

'It would make no difference if I did. I stand to lose my son if I do.'

'Nonsense. You wouldn't lose him. He'd be with me.'

'That's the same thing, isn't it?'

'No. You know full well it isn't.'

There was something in his voice which I could not identify, but which I preferred not to enquire into too closely. Far from simplifying matters, our discussion had taken me further into obligations I would rather not have had, for while the crisis over costs appeared to have a solution, the acceptance of it for little Jamie's sake was not at all to my liking.

'Just the same,' I said, 'it's a risk I'm not prepared to take.'

'A risk? Is that how you see it? As risk? What on earth do you think I might do to the little chap?'

The risk, of course, was not about what he might do but what he might *not* do, namely to protect my son from the kind of racy lifestyle enjoyed by the Abbots Mere set, the foolish irresponsible blades and the Lady Slatterlys of society. She, for one, would enjoy finding my Achilles' heel in Jamie and, having found it, would twist the dart till it hurt. I was certain of it.

'The kind of life you lead is quite different from the one he's been used to with Linas and me,' I said, turning away. 'And you are not used to children.'

'I'm willing to learn. And he has a nurse. Anyway, you take him to see Medworth's family and to play with the animals there. He can do the same at Abbots Mere, and more. He'll have his own room, a pony to ride…'

'He's too young for that,' I objected, weakly.

'Of course he's not!' he scoffed. 'I learned to ride at three.'

'The question doesn't arise. Jamie will stay with me. A child of three needs his mother.' I hoped he would hear the finality in my tone.

'Nevertheless, Miss Follet, I think you will have to accept that Jamie will want to visit me, and that I shall want to see him. Often.'

'I have to, don't I? Perhaps one day a week, or alternate—'

'No. My work doesn't run like clockwork. I have a large estate, and I do things as and when they need doing. When I send for Jamie I shall expect him to come, and that will vary from week to week. I shall also expect him to stay, sometimes. You too, if you wish. I shall have rooms put aside for your personal use.'

Alarm bells rang. 'For my personal use. How thoughtful. So tell me, my lord, what kind of signal that will send to family and friends? Will your current mistress vacate her rooms for my benefit? Shall I be seen as the newest member of the harem? It could get quite cosy.'

He didn't react, this time, as he'd done before, but looked down his straight nose at me with his eyes narrowed, his mouth beginning to lift at the corners. 'So…o, *that's* what's bothering you, is it? Ah, I see.'

Suddenly I was having to defend myself to him in a way I'd never had to do for years. Linas seemed so very far away, which was good, for I did not want him to hear this conversation. 'Yes,' I snapped, heading for the door, 'that *is* what's bothering me. How *could* you be so insensitive as to think I would ever agree to stay there after…' My cheeks flamed. Why had I brought that up now, of all times?

I stalked off into the room next door that I had always used, scarcely more inviting than Linas's, especially in the cold blue light of winter. 'You must know,' I mumbled, 'that for me to be seen as one of the Abbots Mere crowd is the last thing I ever wanted, even when Linas was with me.' I started to rummage. 'I have a few things to look for. Treddle said he'd send them on, but if you'd rather I left them, I shall quite understand.'

He caught up with me and perched on my delicate stool with the petit-point cushion, his greatcoat swamping it, his long booted legs looking very out of place in a lady's bedroom. I glared at him, bristling with hostility.

He held my glare with those supercilious brown eyes. 'I know,' he said. 'You wish me to hell. But some matters have to be tackled head on, and we're going to have this out whether it embarrasses you or not. You must have learned by now that you've met your match, Miss Follet.'

What I *had* learned was that Linas and his brother were even less alike than I thought, one refusing point-blank to discuss the future, even mine or his son's, the other one impatient to settle every detail. One, a prevaricator with no future to see into, the other with bountiful years ahead. Linas must have thought my future would take care of itself. I was not his wife. Why should he bother?

'Shall we postpone the debate about whether or not I have met my match, my lord? If you're asking whether I ever felt a certain imbalance in my relationship with your brother, then, yes, I cannot deny that. It could hardly be otherwise, could it, with Linas unable to see far ahead. Happily, I can see far enough for myself, so I shall not go hungry. You must tell me how to apply for Jamie's allowance each month, and perhaps arrange for Mr Brierley to make it available. I shall keep every receipt, naturally. I pride myself on being able to keep my own accounts.' It was immodest of me, but I thought he may as well know.

'Mother. Mistress. Businesswoman. Is there any-thing at which you are not proficient, Miss Follet?'

'Yes, I am not a good liar, my lord. The other day you were kind enough to remind me that your high-minded act of self-sacrifice was entirely for Linas's benefit, not mine. So I would be lying if I failed to point out, in case you should misunderstand, that I thought only of him too. I wonder you did not hear me call out his name, once or twice.'

'We spoke no words, as you well know.'

'Which only goes to show the limitations of your memory, my lord.'

'I'm flattered to know that yours is still sharp, Miss Follet.' He stood up, damn him, as if to claim the last word on the subject. 'And since you were also kind enough to point out the undesirable nature of what you call the Abbots Mere crowd, perhaps I may be allowed to voice similar concerns about your dubious connec-tions. Not quite the kind of thing Jamie ought to know about. You entertained young Solway for a few months, I believe, as well as Standish's middle son. What's his name? Bertrand, is it?'

'For money, my lord,' I snapped. 'I was obliged to sell myself.'

'Ah, of course. For money. Well then, you need hardly be too concerned about visiting Abbots Mere with my ward, since none of the women who stay there are ever paid a penny. They do it voluntarily.'

'In which case, then, one would expect to see the place swarming with your other little wards. *That* part must cost you a small fortune.'

'No!' he said, picking up a porcelain plate from the

mantelshelf and looking at the back. 'You and Jamie are the only ones to cost me anything.'

'How sad. That's something I can easily fix, my lord.' Boiling, churning, *seething* with anger at being outmanoeuvred, I gulped down the rest of my venom in a pointless threat that meant nothing at all, since there was no way in which I *could* fix it, except permanently.

Looking back on it later, I suppose that's what he thought I meant, for when I moved towards the door again, thinking only to get away from the haunting place, he slammed it shut before I could reach it, catching me like a silly sheep against the wall.

'Admit it or not, lady, as you please,' he said, but no more than that before he pushed my head on to his shoulder and brought his mouth down to cover mine, making me forget what it was I was not admitting, and a lot more besides.

He must have known…oh, yes…he *must* have known how much of that night I remembered. He must have known too how desperately I needed comfort instead of conflict and how much I would have preferred matters to go my way, for a change. He must have known, with Linas no longer to care or be cared for, that I felt both free and guilty, grieved and confused and not as well organised as I pretended to be. So I half-expected his kiss to taste of revenge after our session of deliberate wounding, our first close contact in all those difficult years. I thought he was about to put me, finally, in my place.

But it was not like that, not bitter, but meant, I think, to remind me of the magical beauty of that night without words, passionate but tender too, wanting, taking and giving. Predictable was not the way to describe Burl Winterson, yet I could taste the hunger in his kisses that roamed slowly across my lips, and I felt the desire in his hard arm across my shoulders, the soft hand holding my face. Feel, taste, scent…ah, yes…the scent was there too. Moorland. Fresh linen. Trees after rain. How could I not be reminded?

He must have heard the moan, faintly, in my throat.

'You're right,' he whispered, 'about not being a good liar. I think we'd both better stick to the truth in future. And let us get another thing straight before we leave. You and Jamie will continue to live under my protection on Blake Street without any more argument. You will bring him to visit me and you will both accept my authority as you did with Linas. I do not need to remind you again whose son he is.'

'And I suppose the next thing will be that you'll expect him to call you Papa, will it?' I said, trying to stiffen in his embrace, and failing.

'That'll come too. One thing at a time.'

Squirming out of his arms, I steadied myself against the blue-flocked wallpaper. 'I was being sarcastic,' I said, pettishly. 'I have no intention of giving you that satisfaction. And what is it I'm to admit, or not, as I please?'

'That you've met your match, at last. Now, where are these other things of yours? Come and show me.'

Chapter Four

$\sim\!\!\!\sim\!\!\!\sim$

No expectations, I had said, choosing not to hear the unreality of such a boast. But it was not true. I *had* expected, and yet again had failed to take into account the uncanny affinity between the twin brothers who, although unlike in many ways, had shared the same birth and the same life.

To hear that Linas had never owned my home on Blake Street had shocked me. To discover that he had not personally been responsible for its running costs, and mine too, had left me totally bewildered and very angry, making me revise my assumptions about why he had wanted an heir so much when he had so little to leave. A trust fund, yes, but no property. Linas had owned the Stonegate house, but Winterson had lent *his* property on Blake Street to Linas for my use, and Jamie's. And now, he was adamant that we should stay there while he made use of the larger one, as well as Abbots Mere. It was going to be difficult for me to escape him or to avoid his promised interference in our lives, our freedom being the one thing to which I had most looked forwards.

And the kiss? Well, no more than a reminder, a clever way of exposing my pathetic lie that had been intended to hurt him as he had hurt me. He said we should both start telling the truth, but I had no wish to tell him anything. To do that would be dangerous for a woman in my position. All the same, it was his kiss that kept me sleepless for most of the night.

Long before dawn, I had reached the decision not to delay any longer my visit to Foss Beck Common. My family's food situation must now be getting desperate, I thought, though there were other reasons for me to go too. They would not have heard of Linas's death, and I had to speak to them about the future. Mama would be suffering from the extreme cold, and I also needed to collect whatever Pierre had managed to acquire for my business. There was also money to be taken to him from the sales of my last consignment which, even when shared between us, was almost always a considerable amount. He never told me exactly how much it cost him to pay for these goods in the first place, or even whether he paid in kind and, if so, what kind. But I had recently felt that whatever he paid was nothing like as much as the returns we were getting.

So I had my horse saddled at daybreak, loading the packhorse with gifts and supplies and, wrapping myself thickly with extra shawls, set off along the snow-packed Roman road towards Bridlington. Jamie had not been pleased to be left behind: so unpleased, in fact, that his screaming tantrum was the last sound I heard as Goody hauled him away with both threats and promises. I knew what Jamie needed most, but my firmness was sometimes not enough, and nor was Mrs Goode's. Did he really need to see more of me, or less?

There had been no new falls during the night and, although the wind was still biting hard, the sky was blue and cloudless, the sun's rays bouncing off the dazzling white of moor and valley. I went alone, sure of the way, expecting to meet very few travellers, and certainly no coaches. Only a mile or so out of York, however, I realised what a big risk I was taking, for the road was treacherous with ice, the snow blown into drifts by the north-easterly against which the poor horses had to battle with heads down.

The sky was beginning to darken under a full moon by the time I reached Fridaythorpe and found the turn-off southwards to Foss Beck, another three miles of deep drifts and hidden tracks. Then, the land spread out before me like a laundered sheet stained with the dark shadows of trees, and I cursed myself for my impetuosity and foolhardiness while thinking of how I needed to see my family, and how they needed the food. It was quite dark before I made out the squared shapes of buildings ahead, before I rode, exhausted and chilled to the bone into the rambling desolate place, after a journey of less than twenty miles usually accomplished in three hours. Four, at the most.

The dogs picked up my shouts, baying with excitement when they heard my voice, yelping as the torches waved. My brothers ran out to take my bridle, catching me as I fell into their arms. Finch was nineteen, Greg seventeen, and as strong as young oxen. 'Sister! Are you *mad* to come here in this weather? Here, hold on to me. Can you stand? Shall we carry you?'

'I'll carry her,' called a deeper voice. 'Unload the horses, lads.'

'No one shall carry me,' I protested, hearing the authority in Pierre's command. Five years older than me, he had assumed the position as head of the house since my father's demise, which did not go down well with anyone except my mother. Careful not to add my approval to hers on that vexed question, I greeted Pierre as I had done my brothers, with a hug and a frozen smile that hurt my face. 'Yes, unload the horses and tend them. I'll go on up to Mama.' I staggered like a drunk towards the stone steps.

High waves of snow broke over the outbuildings in the courtyard where deep passages had been cut to the doorways, the paths marked out with straw. Now half-ruined, the large house had been built in the thirteenth century for the lord of the manor, with walls three feet thick and living quarters, as usual, on the floor above the undercroft. The place had been derelict until my family took possession of it, believing like everyone else that the abandoned village belonged to no one and that the land had reverted to common useage.

Carrying what I could manage up the flight of steps, I almost fell into the vast space that had once been the great hall. This had been my home too, though still a far cry from our grand house on the coast, as well as the one I used in York filled with polished wood, glass and fine paintings. Here, the massive beams under the thatch were thick with cobwebs, the bare walls flaking with centuries-old limewash.

'Helen! It cannot be…my lassie…my little Helen.'
My mother's wail, squeaking like an untuned spinet,
sounded to me like an angel choir. It might, I thought,
have been the real reason why I had to make that
dreadful journey, to hear her voice and find the warm,
eager, clinging welcome of her arms, her hands, her
lovely smile, her tear-filled eyes. We sobbed, laughed,
and sobbed again, rocking and cooing in wordless
mothering sounds.

Anxiously looking over my shoulder, she croaked,
'Ye've not brought the little one, have ye? Not in this
weather?'

'No, Mama. But he wanted to come to see Nana
Damzell.'

'Then what's wrong, lassie? Is it your man? He's
worsened?'

'Gone, Mama,' I sobbed. 'He's gone.'

'Aah! *Gone.*' The words were merely breaths of
sound as she studied me. 'Gone. Oh, my poor wee lass.
Tch! Oh, lassie. After all that you did.'

With our typical northern philosophy that sympathy
was best expressed in practicalities, she began to bustle
about, removing my frozen layers, drawing me to the
roaring log fire to seat me with a blanket round my
shoulders and a cushion beneath my numbed feet.
Croaking, she called to the two elderly family servants
to fetch bowls of broth, which they were already doing.
'Gone,' she kept whispering as her fingers wrapped and
tucked. 'Tch! Gone at last. So sad. Here, eat it up,
lassie. You're home now.'

That kind of care, and the exhaustion, was all it took
to release the flood, and for some time I could neither

hide my grief nor tell her about the events that had changed my life once more. Though I tasted nothing much, the warming broth began to send my blood back into my aching limbs, thawing my brain. Then, like a runaway child returned to the fold, I was quizzed about my eating, sleeping, monthly periods, keeping warm, exercise and rest, overwork, moods, mine and Jamie's. None of this did I resent. It was one thing to laugh at the banality of such an inquisition, but quite another to weep at the loving intent behind it. And if it was intrusive, it was the kind of intrusion I had missed and longed for.

Naturally, I had questions of a similar nature to ask Mama, though the state of her health had patently not improved since my last visit just before Christmas. Like her energy, her voice was fading away with each passing season, and I think she knew that the ailment that devoured her lungs would not be held back for her as it had been for Linas. Living in the fresh country air had its advantages, but the raw winds that scoured the Yorkshire Wolds that winter could be mightily unkind to all but the sturdiest beings. Some patients retired to nearby Scarborough to recuperate, but no doctor ever recommended an isolated place like Foss Beck Common. Yet when I suggested that she might consider coming back with me to York, her indignation flared like the protective mother she had always been.

'What? Leave the boys and Pierre?' she said in her hoarse whisper. 'I would not dream of it, love. They're making a grand little farmstead of this place, you know, and as soon as we can afford it, we shall rebuild the other half of the house so we can spread out a bit. We may do the same to one of the cottages too. It'd make more sense if you and young Jamie were to come and live with us now. Wouldn't it? You know how he loves the place.'

It was true that he did. As soon as he was old enough to travel, I had taken him to see them and to ask for their understanding. A bastard in the family was not something they had ever thought likely, but I need not have been concerned, for there was no criticism of the methods I had used to earn money for us all. Only Pierre was less than enthusiastic, never having made any secret of his hope that I would one day agree to be his wife. I suppose it must have irked him that others had been where he'd wanted to be first, but I had given him no promises or even the expectation of any. I looked upon him as one of my brothers, but never as a future husband.

Unpacking the goods I had brought, woollen clothes, medicines, new boots, Mrs Neape's pies, and at least half the food sent from Abbots Mere, I told them about Linas's will, about my plans and disappointments, my fears, and the unlikelihood of Jamie being allowed to live anywhere except York. It looked, they agreed, as if I might have to stay there too, at least for the foreseeable future.

If it was not what any of us wanted to hear, it was even less acceptable to Pierre, who took me to one side before we settled in for the night. Only an inch or so taller than me, he was yet strongly built and pleasant of face, and certainly the man my father had earmarked for me, when the time came. I cannot say that I was glad not to have my father there with us, but he would have put a very strong case for that connection, and I doubt if my unwillingness would have had much to do with it.

As a terrified twelve-year-old, Pierre had been smuggled out of Paris and across the English Channel, having lost both his aristocratic parents to the guillotine during the Revolution that put an end to France's royal family. Though that particular danger had passed, Pierre looked upon our family as his own so much so that, after my father's tragic end, he had taken much of the responsibility upon himself, for by that time he was a comely nineteen-year-old with a noble manner, unafraid of work or danger, assertive and enterprising. It was he who maintained the connection with the Bridlington smugglers, though he never volunteered any information about how exactly he was able to procure such large quantities of costly fabrics for me to sell in York. And I never asked him to. Yet it was due to Pierre's involvement with contraband that I had been able to take a partnership in Prue's thriving business on Blake Street.

Sometimes I would travel to Foss Beck to pick up whatever he had obtained for me; at other times Pierre would bring it to York on pack-ponies and leave it at Follet and Sanders. Occasionally he would call at the house on Blake Street as a distant relative from Bridlington, but never with the goods. The pack-ponies, it was assumed, were to take supplies back home from the shops and warehouses. There was never any question of him meeting Linas, and to Jamie he was 'Uncapare'. I was, of course, very careful not to be seen handing him any money, nor did I have any doubts about Pierre's honesty.

'Helene,' he said, speaking to me in French as he always did when we were together, 'I'm so glad to see you again. But you ought never to have made the journey alone. It's far too dangerous.'

'I had no choice, Pierre, if I'm to keep our family a secret.'

'Well, I shall ride with you tomorrow when you return. I can take the new goods to the shop. As it happens, I have some other business in York, so I can kill two birds with one stone.' His teeth shone even in the gloom, startlingly white against his healthy outdoor skin and black hair, like my own. 'Does one throw stones at birds?'

'Not nowadays. What business?'

'Oh, a message to pass on to friends, a contact to make, some purchases. Who is this brother-twin of Mr Monkton? The guardian. What's he like?'

'He's good to Jamie. He adores him.' I knew it was an ambiguous reply, intentionally so, for indeed it was a mutual adoration that I had done little to foster, to the frustration of them both. Jamie's strong will, having turned more recently to noisy tantrums, was never witnessed by Winterson for whom my beloved infant was a lamb, obedient and obliging, trotting after his idol and beaming with good nature when he was allowed to ride on Uncaburl's shoulders. To see them like that made my heart flip like a seaotter, and to ache for hours afterwards.

'And you?' said Pierre. 'You adore him too?'

'Pierre,' I replied, wearily, 'I have just lost the man I lived with and cared for. The father of my child. Except for Jamie, adoration has no place in my heart at the moment. I love my mother and brothers, and I am very fond of you as a brother, and I am grateful to you for your care of us. But things are not moving on for me in quite the direction I hoped for. Rather, they seem to have come to a standstill. Perhaps it's too soon to expect them to. Let's just see, shall we? I wish Mama would come to York where I can tend her. I'm very concerned about her.'

'She won't, Helene. Your father is still here, remember. She will not leave his grave. She wants to stay beside him.'

I nodded, aware that my tears, so recently shed, were by no means spent. 'Then I had better not mention it again. But try to understand my position, Pierre. Please. I'm being torn two ways at present.'

'My understanding matters to you?'

'Certainly it does. You are family. It will always matter to me.'

'Forgive me,' he whispered, touching my arm with a tentative forefinger before withdrawing it quickly. 'You're right, it's too soon for you to see ahead, and you are weary. It's only that…' he sighed '…that we meet so rarely and, when the chance arises, I must take it before you're gone again.'

'Then we shall talk more on the way home. Goodnight, Pierre.'

'Goodnight, Helene.'

I turned away, but not before I had caught the 'my love' whispered in my wake, which I pretended not to hear, dismissing it from my mind as one more complication I could do without. Even so, I had witnessed yet again the small signs of rebellion from Finch and Greg as they deliberately ignored Pierre's commands that ought to have been requests, and I prayed that, if only for my mother's sake, the boys would not cause any trouble.

* * *

I had slept that night in my underclothes upon a duck-down mattress with a feather pillow and thick furs to keep me warm. Yet I awoke with limbs that hurt as if I'd run all the way from York, and a splitting headache. Whatever my ailment, I dared not delay my return home, for the thought of Jamie missing me, being upset and refusing to eat was more than I could contemplate. Heaven only knows how I clambered up into the saddle, more thankful than I expected to be that Pierre was with me to lead the pack-pony. Tearful farewells were not my style, but knowing what I did of Mama's condition, I could not have said for certain whether she would still be there to welcome me on my next visit. And for some miles I was very poor company, wondering how and when I would be called upon to bear yet another loss.

Even with Pierre for companionship, the return to York was no more comfortable than before, as by that time I was feeling wretchedly unwell and not at all inclined to converse. With the wind at our backs for much of the way, we made marginally better progress, but the sky was again heavy with snow, darkening by the hour, and we reached York speechless with cold and tiredness. For me, it was another nightmare of a journey, but one that could not have been put off, all the signs being that reserve food supplies at Foss Beck had run drastically low.

With the light almost gone, Pierre was anxious to unload the goods and then to conduct at least some of his business before it was too late. So although I was desperate to see my Jamie again, we went first to deliver the much-needed stocks to Prue, and I took the pony and horse back to Linas's stable, grateful that Pierre had agreed without a quibble to leave me to myself. I was sure by then that I was coming down with something more than a cold, for my joints ached unbearably, and I was shaking like an aspen leaf. The walk back to Blake Street took all my last efforts.

Hoping for whoops of joy at my appearance, I encountered only my maid's anxious face as she dealt with my enquiries about Jamie. 'He's gone, ma'am,' she whispered, round-eyed. 'Mrs Goode and him.'

'Gone? What d'ye mean…gone?'

'Let me help you with your coats, ma'am, and I'll tell—'

'No! Tell me *now*, Debbie. Where *are* they?'

'At Abbots Mere, ma'am.'

'*What?*' It was one of those inane responses that only buys time to think up every dreadful reason and result, every terrible revenge and almighty row that will follow if the matter is not righted that same instant. There was to be no hope of that.

'Lord Winterson came yesterday after you'd gone, ma'am, and there was Master Jamie—' she pointed to the hall floor '—kicking his little heels and screaming and crying, and there was nurse trying to reason with him and could hardly make herself heard, ma'am. Rolling about, he was.'

My head swam; I had to sit. 'And Lord Winterson?'

'Strode through the door, ma'am, took one look and said, "Hoy! Enough!" And do you know, ma'am, Master Jamie just stopped and ran to him, just like that. He was sobbing his heart out, mind. Poor little soul.'

I held my head in my hands. I *thought* I had done the right thing, but clearly I had not. I was the worst mother in the world, at that moment. 'Then what?' I whispered.

'Well, Lord Winterson picked him up and talked to him, and told Mrs Goode that she should pack things, that they would go to stay with him at Abbots Mere till you returned from Bridlington.'

Where I had not been.

'Ma'am, you look terrible. Are you all right?'

I swayed unsteadily, holding my head before it fell off. 'Yes,' I said. 'I'm going over to Abbots Mere. I shall have to go back to Stonegate first to get a horse. You stay here, Debbie, and tell Mrs Neape where I've gone.'

'At this time of night, ma'am?'

'*Yes!*' I yelled. 'At *this* time of night, girl. I want my *son!*'

She was a Leeds lass, and not easily browbeaten. 'Then I'm coming too,' she said. 'Just wait till I get my coat and boots on, ma'am.'

'Debbie, I have no time to argue. You can't come.'

'I can, ma'am, and I will. You're not going on your own.'

'There's only one horse.'

'Then I'll walk it.'

I turned and went out. It had started to snow again, but Debbie caught me up before I reached Linas's stables. She was carrying a portmanteau. 'What's that for?' I asked.

'Things, ma'am. We might have to stay.'

What a treasure she was, that girl. I was wrong about there being only one horse; there were several, most of them newly arrived. I chose two of the heaviest, ordered them to be saddled and gave the worried groom a silver shilling when he told me Lord Winterson would probably kill him. 'He won't,' I said. 'Help me up.'

It was dark and snowing fast, laying a clean white cover upon what was already there. The two black, wet, agonising miles took us almost an hour, with me clinging to the saddle to stay upright and often my beast stopping when it felt me slip or slouch. Gritting my teeth against bouts of faintness, I forged ahead with Debbie calling and encouraging me to stay on. Then, at last, we passed through the old Tudor gatehouse and headed for the lights of the house and for the fearsome battle that would be raged within minutes of my arrival.

Being no rider, Debbie fell off her horse into the snow, picked herself up and ran to the door, hammering upon it with the heavy iron ring until it opened. The crashing noise in my head stopped; I heard her yelling at someone, echoing from a long way off, then shouts. My face was in the horse's snow-covered mane and I could not move it from the hot-cold sweat that beckoned me into its arms, to sleep. The horse tipped, throwing me sideways into a black gulf.

A deep voice rumbled against my ear. 'What in heaven's name possessed her to come…?'

'She would do it, my lord. I tried to reason, but she's unwell, and I could not let her come alone.'

'But at *this* time of night, in this weather?'

How many times had I heard 'in this weather' recently? 'In this weather,' I muttered, 'I've come for my son.' The world was still moving, swinging me this way and that. 'Jamie,' I said. 'I want Jamie.'

'You want for some common sense too, woman, coming out here in a blizzard, in the dark too. And how you managed to get to Bridlington and back in two days in this lot is going to take some explaining. Did you fly?'

I was being carried, and not expected to answer. Which was just as well for, at that point, I suppose I must have passed out again.

Chapter Five

Nights and days merged into a timeless blur during which I was fed like a fledgling without knowing whose nest I was in. Shadowy figures lifted and bathed me, tucking me into warm feathery layers, soothing my aching body, cooling my fever. I dreamed, but never managed to trawl them up from the depths. I wept, they said, but could not explain why. And at last the snow-white glare from the casement seeped into my eyelids and brought me back into the room I had sworn never again to occupy, for any reason. I think I felt then that this was one of those bizarre situations that could only have been engineered by Fate itself. It was only with hindsight that I was able to see how I had made Fate a convenient scapegoat.

My infant's delight at finding me silenced all my earlier fears that he would bear me a lifelong grudge for breaking my promise to take him to see Nana Damzell. Without a mention of that particular dilemma at Blake Street he bounced into my room, picking up the thread of his life from where he'd left it the moment before to tell me about the snowman, the ride with Uncaburl that morning, and the promise of a pony of his own. Of screaming tantrums, Mrs Goode assured me, there had been none, not even when he was opposed.

I saw nothing of my long-suffering host, however, until the fifth day of our visit when I was at last able to find the energy to walk a few steps. Winterson himself was allowed into my room to carry me downstairs, swathed in blankets, to the warm parlour where he placed me upon a long cushioned chair with eight legs and a woven rattan back. I had been in no position to appreciate the first carrying. With the second, however much I tried to hide the thrill of being helplessly buoyant, the closeness of his face and the memories it evoked must have shown in my eyes whenever he glanced down at me. Which he did several times.

Abbots Mere had once been the abbot's own guest house for visiting dignitaries to the great minster of York. Since the dissolution of the monasteries, the house had been sold off, enlarged and altered at the convenience of each successive owner, though no Georgian styles had been allowed to interfere with the sixteenth-century interior that still showed in every part of the building. The parlour was a large low-ceilinged room, exquisitely plastered and oak panelled, with brightly painted coats-of-arms around the plasterwork frieze. The walls were hung with lace-collared ancestors, the floor covered with mellowed pink-and-blue Persian carpets, furnished with dark oak tables, chairs with tall

backs and barley-sugar legs. In the massive stone fireplace, a log fire crackled and blazed behind cast-iron
firedogs, and silver oil-lamps were reflected in polished
surfaces. I had been in this room many times before, but
always it had been Linas who lounged on the long chair,
and never had I been here alone with his brother. I had
always seen to that.

He sat opposite me in a red upholstered wing-chair
with his face partly shadowed so that I could not tell
his expression, though he rarely allowed one to know
what he was thinking at the best of times. 'Inscrutable'
sounds like a cliché, but it suited him well. A long-case
clock chimed softly, musically, and his three great
hounds flopped quietly behind his chair.

'I've sent for some tea,' he said. 'Will you join me?'

'Thank you. I hope Jamie and I have not been an
imposition. I really had no intention of…well…' I
thought he might interrupt me with a polite denial, but
he did not, and when I couldn't think of what to say,
he was unhelpful.

'No intention of what…taking a fever? Coming all
this way in a blizzard to rescue your child from my
clutches? Well, you can see he's suffered very little
from the experience.'

Being in no mood for an argument, not then, I sighed
my annoyance and looked pointedly towards the
window. 'Has the snow stopped?' I asked, hoping he
would catch my meaning.

'If you mean, can you escape, then I'm afraid the
answer is no. You've missed three days of snowstorms
and now all the roads are impassable, according to my
information. I hear that the road to Brid has been

blocked beyond Fridaythorpe since the snow started. No one's been either in or out.'

'That's annoying,' I said, ignoring his reference to Bridlington. 'I had hoped to go home tomorrow.'

'You'll do no such thing,' he said, quietly dismissive. 'You've been ill. My bailiff forecasts a thaw before long, so you'll have to be patient until you're stronger and the roads are dug out.'

'I have a business to run. Anyway, I'm not ill. It's only a chill.'

'Yes, and I dare say you've been too busy chasing about the countryside in the snow to give any thought to your own needs. Perhaps it's time you began to think of them, unless you want pneumonia too. If I were you, Miss Follet, I'd take this as an indication that you need some rest, after all that's happened.'

That made me angry. Take a rest? How like a man. Ignore everything that needs attention and everyone who depends on you and take a rest. How *could* I rest?

Winterson's housekeeper, Mrs Murgatroyd, came in with a silver tray of tea things and, while she set it out and poured the steaming amber liquid into fine Queen Anne teacups, I was able surreptitiously to knuckle away a tear of impotent fury and to mop my nose on the back of my hand. Very unladylike. My hand shook as I accepted the teacup, rattling it on the saucer, so she removed it with a smile and set it on the table beside me. Then, bobbing a curtsy, she withdrew.

'How *can* I?' I said. 'Customers still need new clothes, even in midwinter.'

He plopped a lump of sugar into his tea. 'Well, for a start, you can allow Jamie to spend more time here.

Mrs Goode is a very sensible woman and I'm perfectly willing to share the duties of caring for him. Medworth and his wife are too. Their eldest is just about Jamie's age, you know, and there's nothing more respectable than to be related to a country parson's family. He enjoys his visits there, I believe?'

I nodded. 'Yes, very much, but…'

'But what? Too countrified for you?'

'I am a countrywoman too, my lord. Mr and Mrs Medworth Monkton are delightful and charming, and so is little Claude. But Linas was never very happy to see pigs and geese, hens and goats wandering through the house, especially when there are small children and babies about. Last time we were there, the goat chewed the baby's layette; when the donkey wandered into the dining-room, they allowed Claude to feed it with his own bread. I'm used to animals, but I would never go quite that far.'

'No, I wouldn't feed good bread to a donkey, either. It's far too rich. But you know Linas's attitude to animals, Miss Follet. He could never see the need for them except as food or transport, or inside a kennel. It would be a pity, wouldn't it, if our Jamie adopted the same indifference to them. He's quite fearless with them, you know.'

Our Jamie. *Our* Jamie. 'Yes,' I replied, stepping gingerly over the implications. 'I do know. He has a little temper, too.'

His voice dropped, soft and indulgent. 'That's not temper, lass, it's sheer frustration at not being able to express himself, to tell you how he feels. You offered him the alternative of twiddling his thumbs at home with his nurse while I offered him the chance to ride in the snow, without you. There's no magic in that. He's a lively little lad, bright and bursting with energy and curiosity. He doesn't always want velvet suits and silk shirts. He's not a puppet. He needs coveralls and some muck to stamp in, and things to climb.'

'You make it sound as if you know about such things.'

'I do. I've *been* a three-year-old boy. You have not.'

I had brothers. I knew he was right, but how could I offer Jamie those more alluring alternatives while keeping to my intention not to get involved, more than I must, in Winterson's life?

My silence prompted him to ask, 'Does he enjoy seeing your family? He was very disappointed not to go.'

'Yes, he loves it. I promised to take him, then I couldn't.'

'Because of the snow?'

'Yes, it was too dangerous.'

'But you had to go, did you?'

'Yes, I *had* to go. My mother is ailing. The same as Linas. I knew they'd be snowbound and running low on food.'

'But they were not snowbound, if you got through to them.'

'They were, almost. My brothers knew that, if they got away, they'd probably not get back again and, as it was, I only just managed to find them, knowing that I could stay overnight. They told me I was mad, but I'm the eldest and I have a responsibility to them. My mother needs medicines. I cannot let a snowfall stop me, but nor could I have taken Jamie and his nurse. I tried to make him understand—' I stopped and held a hand to my face.

'You're not the monster-mother you thought you were, you know. He was as right as rain, once I picked him up.'

He was trying to reassure me, I knew, telling me that there was no magic in it. But Jamie would run to him without any promise of rewards or alternatives, but simply to be noticed by his hero. It had been the same when Linas was alive. Jamie doted on him.

'Who is Nana Damzell? Your mother?' he said.

I nodded.

'I see. And there are animals there too. They have a farm?'

'Yes. Please don't ask me any more, my lord. I cannot tell you.'

'Why? Are they outlaws, like Robin Hood?'

'Not at all like Robin Hood,' I said, glancing at my cooling cup of tea. My hand still shook, but I managed not to spill while I drank, wondering how much my chatterbox son had divulged about his uncles and their isolated home. I suspected that Winterson would have liked to ask me about the Bridlington connection, but he apparently thought that enough had been said for one day, for he did not pursue the question of why anyone living in a town the size of Brid should run out of food. Or indeed how I had managed to get there. Or not.

'Miss Follet,' he said, after a pause.

'My lord?'

'I wouldn't like you to think that I shall make a point of asking Jamie about his maternal family. I shall not. I can see that you'd rather not talk about them, so I'll wait until you do. But neither do I want *you* to use Jamie's inclination to chatter as an excuse to keep him away from me. You're entitled to your privacy, and I shall respect it. That's what Linas did, I believe.'

The truth was more stark than that. Linas had not the slightest curiosity about my family. Not only did he never ask me about them, but even when I visited them for two days at a time, with Jamie, he didn't ask where, who, or how they were, whether they had what they needed or what had happened to their former lives. I didn't complain, for I was able to share my earnings with them and that was all that mattered. But I often found it strange how Linas's life revolved only around himself, until Jamie came.

'As you know,' I said, very quietly, 'Linas was a very private kind of person, and I sometimes think that he tended to ignore the possibility that I had a family in case I brought them into the life we shared. I would never...ever...have done that, but I think he believed it was a risk. Some mistresses' families can be quite demanding, as I'm sure you've heard.'

He smiled at that. Lady Emma Hamilton had recently lost her beloved Lord Nelson and, anticipating that he would leave her substantial wealth, the poor woman's relatives were already hounding her day and night. That, at least, would not be happening to me. 'Well,' he said, 'now you see how differently Linas and I view matters. I can accept that you have a responsibility to your family whose privacy you wish to protect and who you need to visit from time to time. But to take Jamie all that way without a proper escort is a risk I do not want you to run. In the future, you must take at least two men with you. Either my men, or your own.'

While we were on the subject, I thought I might as well tell him, though I could easily foresee the reaction. 'When I told them about Linas, there was some discussion that I might go and live with them again. With Jamie.'

'Who suggested that?'

'My mother would like it. She wants me to look after my brothers.'

'Yes, I can understand the reasoning, Miss Follet, and you must do whatever you can for them, but I would not allow Jamie to live so far away. He will be either at Blake Street with you, or here with me.'

'I told her that I could not do so. I have my business to attend to, you see, and I need to be on hand. It brings me an income, and, if that were to go, *they* would be much the poorer.'

'Oh, so your business supports them, does it? I thought…'

'You thought it was another way for me to line my pockets? Yes, well, that is what mistresses often do, I believe. They usually move on when the going gets rough, and I didn't do that either, my lord. Nor did I shirk from telling Linas that I was pregnant, even when I feared he would surely turn me out. *That* was a risk, I can tell you. A very uncomfortable one.'

'I can see why you are bitter, Miss Follet.'

'At the way I was used, and still *am* being used? As Jamie's mother, being told what I must and must not do, as if I were married? Which I cannot do either?'

'Have there been no compensations?' he asked from

the depths of his chair. His long legs crossed and re-crossed, and I saw the pinpoints of fire reflected in his eyes as they turned again in my direction.

'Jamie. And a place to live in comfort, and a thriving business and good friends to work with. Yes, and I still have *some* freedom left, which I shall fight tooth and claw to keep.'

His tone sharpened to match mine. 'You have no need to fight tooth and claw, lass. We're on the same side.'

I swung my legs off the long chair, ready to go. 'Correction,' I said. 'We have *never* been on the same side, my lord. Not even before I became your brother's mistress, when you tried to warn him off me. Too unreliable, you told him.'

'Is that what he told you?'

'That's what he told me. We laughed about it. We shall never be on the same side, except where Jamie's welfare is concerned. Now, if you will excuse me, I'm getting rather tired.' I tried to stand, but the room swayed dangerously and I had to sit down again with an ungainly thud, my hands clutching to keep me upright. 'Oh!' I said. 'Oh, dear.'

He was beside me instantly. 'Steady…steady, lass. God's truth, but I've never known a woman fly up into the boughs so fast. Now wait. I'll take you back, but I shall not allow you to walk. It's time you were taken in hand.'

I let the remark go, for he was justified in thinking that I was on edge, snapping and snarling as if I was being threatened. 'I'm all right,' I said. 'It's just dizziness, that's all.'

'No, you're not.' Busily re-wrapping me, his hands came to rest upon my shoulders where the blanket

pinned my arms to my body. Holding it tightly so that
I could not protest, he swung me once more into his
arms where I lay with my head upon his shoulder,
utterly powerless. Wordless, too.

'Now, my beauty,' he said, sternly, 'let's get one
more thing straight, shall we? It will be better for Jamie
if we both try to show him that we're friends, not rivals.
I shall not use him to score points, nor should you do
that. If you want to fight me, we'll do it in private, not
in front of him. Agreed?'

'Yes.'

His eyes narrowed and his lips moved, and I knew
there was more to come. 'Fierce woman,' he whispered.
'My God, but the lad has a warrior-mother to defend
him, doesn't he? You don't have the physique to go with
it, though, so don't even think about going home yet.
You need some care and attention first. I expect
someone can take care of the shop?'

'Yes.'

'And the house? I'll get a message to them as soon
as I can.'

'Yes. Thank you.'

'Saints, lass. Have I silenced you at last? No,
perhaps not. I remember there was another way to do
that, wasn't there?'

'Please!'

'Hah!' Throwing back his head, he bellowed with
laughter as the door opened, letting Jamie and his nurse
into the room to make what they could of me in the arms
of Jamie's guardian.

It could have been worse, as it happened, for Jamie
was too young to think anything of it and Mrs Goode

was one of those rare creatures whose experience of life runs just ahead of one's own. She was approaching middle age and still handsome, and the flash of interest in her eyes disappeared as she dealt with the scene with perfect composure. 'Oh, good,' she said. 'You just on your way up, ma'am?'

Jamie ran to Winterson's leg and clung, somewhere beneath me. 'Bring Mama, Uncaburl,' he said, 'to see snowman. He wants to say goodnight.'

I began to protest, but Winterson had other ideas. 'Right,' he said. 'So if you let go of my leg, young whipper-snapper, and hold the door open for us, we'll go. Come on, lead the way.'

So we did, followed by hounds, striding, trotting and sailing high along the stone passageways, across the great hall and out to the front porch that overlooked the snow-covered terrace. The formal garden lay beyond like a fairyland of blue shadows and heavy-laden trees, and the cold air filled my lungs, making my hair prickle and my eyes water.

'Not too cold for you?' said Winterson, softly.

'No, not at all. It's beautiful.'

Mrs Goode tucked the blanket deep into my neck, her expression suitably serious. Jamie ran to greet the snowman who stood twice his height, wearing an old beaver hat. 'See, Mama!' he called. 'He's got Uncaburl's best hat on.'

'It was either that or one of my neckcloths,' the donor explained. 'There was little choice in the matter, really. What d'ye think, ma'am?'

'He's a splendid snowman,' I called. 'Shall we say goodnight to him before we go in?' It was like being a family, I thought. Mother, father and child, so different from the previous artificial relationship of pseudo-father and pseudo-uncle with me somewhere between.

But close behind that thought came the warning. Beware. This is getting too dangerous. Held in his arms, safe and warm, assuming another ambiguous role, it's going to be so easy to forget the brothers' scheme, forged years ago without a by-your-leave. You owe this man no favours, the warning said, coldly, bitterly.

Back in my room upstairs, the blankets were peeled off.

'Whose nightgown is this?' I said, noticing for the first time the unfamiliar broderie-anglais yoke. I had made all my own night attire.

'Mrs Murgatroyd found it for me,' said Debbie, holding the sheet open. 'I only managed to pack one, and that's gone to the laundry.'

'Then get this thing off me,' I said. 'Heaven only knows who's worn it before me. I'll have my own back, if you please.' I could well imagine who had worn it, and who had been hurriedly slipped out of it, too. One of his mistresses.

Wrestling it over my head, Debbie treated me to some mutterings about the whims and fancies of con-valescents, but the enchantment of the previous hour had faded and, as Debbie opened the bedroom door to retrieve my gown, I heard the chimes of the long-case clock before the parlour door closed upon them. He would be in there thinking, no doubt, that he had won that round hands down.

My recovery took only a few days, since I was healthy and strong and eager to resume my life in York. I used those few days well, though, playing around Winterson's spacious house with Jamie and Mrs Goode, having snowball fights in the garden, playing hide and seek, watching the racehorses, walking in the snow and skating on the lake. Each night my beloved infant would fall asleep with apple cheeks, exhausted and happy in his own rosy paradise, and I fell asleep in the hope that the thaw would set in overnight while my heart was still my own.

I kept to my side of the agreement to assume a convincing friendship with our host, which was little different from what I had always done whenever Jamie was there to see. But as for sitting with him in private again, that I did not do, but found some excuse to be elsewhere. It was not so much that I wished to evade any future tactics he might be planning, but that I had a campaign of my own that did not include letting him think I was softening. Not one bit. Good manners I could manage when I had to, but pretend a sincere friendship I would not.

At last, after a day of shovelling, of dripping eaves and light sleety rain, the way was cleared between Abbots Mere and York, and I knew that Goody and I would have our work cut out convincing Jamie that going home could be better than staying. A coach ride being out of the question, Jamie rode with Uncaburl to lead the way, helping to ease the transition, while the rest of us followed behind with two grooms. Whether Uncaburl said anything to his ward about accepting the situation, far from ideal in Jamie's eyes, I do not know, but there were no tantrums.

Jamie was carried around the house, straddled across

Uncaburl's waist, to reacquaint him with his own room, his rocking horse and Noah's Ark. How they had missed him, his guardian said, promising him another visit to Abbots Mere before long.

'And a pony?' said Jamie. 'You did say a pony, Uncaburl.'

'When the winter has gone away, there will be a pony for you.'

'He's too young,' I whispered as we went downstairs. 'I told you.'

'I know you did, but he's desperate to learn and that's the best time to do it. Trust me. I'll find something suitable. He'll be safe with me.'

'What am I to do about my own transport, my lord? Am I allowed to borrow one of the horses from the stable at Stonegate, as I did before?'

Mrs Goode and Jamie had gone ahead to the kitchen, leaving Winterson and me in my pretty pale-green panelled dining room. I poured a glass of port and handed it to him, aware that I was occupying his house and beholden to him for everything in it, even my mode of transport. My question about the horses was meant to point to the fact.

He placed the glass upon the table and came to stand before me where I could breathe in the freshness of his skin. 'Miss Follet,' he said, 'you may borrow any of the horses from Stonegate at any time, but don't take your phaeton out yet. It's not safe. If you want to go visiting, send me a message and I'll have a carriage sent for you. And don't go too far.'

'I see,' I said, flatly.

'No, you don't see, do you? You think I'm trying to

curb you. But this is only while the roads are treacherous. There's twelve inches of snow underfoot, and when all that thaws there'll be floods everywhere and the Ouse will burst its banks. The ground is still frozen solid. The water will take weeks to drain away. So don't take any foolish risks.'

'Yes, I *do* see. I'm sorry. I shall be careful with Jamie.'

'I want you to be careful with you too, Miss Follet.'

'Yes, of course.' As Jamie's mother, I had to stay in one piece.

'Oh, for pity's sake, woman. Must you see everything I say in the wrong light? Could *you* not thaw, occasionally?'

I had no answer to that, none that I dared speak. But something in my face must have given me away just long enough for him to see beneath the ice and, before I could sidestep, his hands gripped my upper arms, pulling me to him and sliding round to my back like steel bands, bending me and knocking my breath away.

'I could thaw you,' he whispered. 'I did it before and I could do it again. You've done your best to keep a distance between us. Don't think I've not noticed. But the time will come…'

'No, it won't,' I whispered back, finding it hard to breathe. 'The time will never come, my lord. Now let me go before we're discovered.'

His arms dropped. He seemed to struggle against some emotion that closed his eyes and tilted his head back with a noisy sigh that made me long to comfort him, to touch his lips with my own. He turned away to the table, picked up his glass and downed the contents in one gulp. Then, smacking the glass down, he threw open the door into the hall and called for his coat with quite unnecessary loudness.

I should have felt well satisfied by that but, for some reason, I felt quite the opposite, strangely upset and subdued, and wondering how much longer I would be able to stay on course.

Chapter Six

Not for my own peace of mind, nor indeed for his, could I allow him to go like that. We were not sworn enemies and, although his own behaviour had been less than gentlemanly, I must try to learn how far to push him. It was something I had not needed to do with Linas.

Caring not what Mrs Goode or Debbie might think, I quickly threw on the outdoor clothes I had just shed and went out again, half-running along Blake Street to the corner of Stonegate where I believed he would have gone. I was right. His horses were still in the courtyard, his grooms surprised to see me so soon. One of them ran to open the kitchen door for me.

He was there, hatless, in conversation with Linas's housekeeper, the first to notice my entrance. She turned in surprise. 'Miss Follet! Good morning, ma'am.'

He came towards me at once, his eyes anxious. 'Is something wrong?'

I felt that my impulsiveness was getting me into as

big a mess as my long-held resentments, for even now I had not rehearsed what to say to him. 'Yes,' I said. 'I forgot something.' It would do for a beginning.

As if he felt something of my discomfort, he escorted me up to the hall where the smell of paint, the general mess of displaced furniture and bare flooring indicated that a grand spring clean was already under way. The changeover was as good a time as any, and already the new coats of white and pale grey paint had brought a clean light to the walls.

'In here,' he said, holding open the door to Linas's study. It too was in some disorder, the bookcases half emptied, the mantelshelf bare, the few chairs shrouded with holland covers. 'Will this do?' he said, closing the door behind us. 'What is it? What did you forget?'

'My manners,' I replied. 'I've come…well…to beg your pardon. It was unpardonable of me to allow you to leave my house without thanking you for your good care of us, and for the second load of supplies, and for your kindness to me and Jamie. Thank you, my lord. I am not as ungrateful as I appeared to be just now. Of course, your own manners leave much to be improved on, but I am the one who should apologise. Which I do.'

He listened attentively, though I saw his lips twitch as if a laughing protest was being held in check, though his acceptance was never in doubt. 'Let's face it,' he said, 'you've been under some considerable strain lately, Miss Follet, so I think an occasional bout of queer stirrups can easily be forgiven. Think no more of it. As for what you choose to call my kindness, it has given me pleasure to be where I was most needed. That's exactly how I hoped it would be, though without the illness. My house is always open to you whenever you need it, and for any reason. Or for no reason. It can be your second home, if you wish it.'

This time, I would not allow my scepticism to spoil his generosity, so I nodded and thanked him politely and said I believed that's what Jamie already had in mind. Which made us both smile. I felt we'd made some progress.

His hand rested upon a pile of leather-bound volumes too large for bedtime reading, his palm fondly sweeping. He saw me watching, though thankfully without being able to see into my mind. '*History of Arts and Sciences*,' he said. 'I shall keep these, but I don't know about this lot.' He patted a smaller pile of note-books that had been well used. Linas had been an avid note-taker. 'I don't have time to go through them. Would you care to take them? They might be of interest, or they might not.'

I had an obligation to do what I could. 'Yes, I'll take them home. They're probably household accounts, in which case they'll be helpful.'

'Anything else?'

'Er...else?'

Suddenly, we'd begun to talk more like friends instead of fencers looking for an opening to make a hit. He would be spending some time here, and perhaps I ought to be making the most of that convenience instead of bemoaning it. There had to be some advantages somewhere. Perhaps, I thought, I'd been too hasty in my determination to exclude him.

'Yes,' he said. 'I mean...things.' He cast an eye over the piled-up desk. 'There must surely have been other gifts apart from those few you mentioned before? You should have them. If you tell me where they are…?'

I hesitated, then decided he should know how things stood. Mistresses, after all, are not on the same footing as wives. 'The things I collected before were bought by me, my lord, not Linas. They were only here for my use when I stayed, that's all.'

'Oh. Not gifts?'

'No, not gifts. Linas rarely bothered with gifts, did he?'

'So…your black mare was not a gift?'

'The horses and the phaeton belonged to Linas, not to me. They go with the house. I'm not complaining, my lord. That's how he preferred it. I think he was never quite convinced that I would stay. Perhaps he was influenced by your opinion that I'm unreliable. Who knows? So thank you for the offer. I could say, this, this and this, but that would be grasping and dishonest. There is nothing here that belongs to me.'

He stood very still while I spoke, looking hard at me with eyes widening, then frowning with concern. It was clear he was both surprised and puzzled. 'And gifts from you to Linas? Was that the same?'

Since I was being scrupulously honest, it was not. I shrugged, trying to make light of it. 'Embroidered nightcaps, silk nightshirts made by me, silk evening shirts ditto, kid gloves, a tambour-embroidered red-wool dressing gown that I made for him, with matching slippers and cap, monogrammed handkerchiefs and satin embroidered braces, and that striped lustre waistcoat you admired. None of them will fit me, I'm afraid. The monogrammed table linen had better stay where it is.

And the cushions, too. And the chair-seats and fire-screen.'

'Good grief!'

'Oh, don't be concerned. That's just the way it was. Linas knew he didn't need to pay me in the way that mistresses are usually paid because for one thing I never asked him to. I had a house to live in and a way of earning a legitimate living, and that's all I ever wanted, and all *he* needed from me was affection and attention, and for me to nurse him. And Jamie, of course. It worked both ways, didn't it? I don't think I let him down, my lord.'

Slowly, his gaze swung away to rest lazily upon the white scene outside and on the dazzle of windows opposite. 'No,' he said, 'I don't think you did either. If anything, the shoe was on the other foot, Miss Follet.'

'Anyway,' I said, 'it's never much use going over old ground again and again, is it? It's too late. Linas was very poorly and he did what he could. I only tell you this to settle once and for all what belongs to whom. Fortunately, he didn't need to buy my clothes, or Jamie's either. That's one thing I could manage to pay for.'

'You are the best-dressed woman I know. You must have saved him hundreds, over the years.'

'Well, now that's gone to Jamie, hasn't it? But when I said it's no use going over old ground, I meant *our* old ground too. I've had my say about that now, and you have listened and I believe you understand my feelings better than you did before. But we must try to put it all behind us and move on, although I would not want anyone to assume that I am now one of your mistresses simply because I was your brother's, and because Jamie and I must visit you. That's never going to be the case, my lord.'

'I agree. It's never going to be the case because I shall never ask you to be my mistress, Miss Follet. You may be assured on that.'

'Oh, then we are agreed. What a relief. So now we can perhaps deal more comfortably together without all those strings attached. Like business partners for Jamie's welfare and no more embarrassing references to…well…you know.'

Again, he appeared to be having difficulty in hiding a smile, though I had not thought my proposal to be so very entertaining. 'Just put it out of our minds, eh?' he said, touching his nose with a knuckle.

'Completely and for ever. I am not a saint, so I cannot say that I have forgiveness in my heart, but nor do I intend to harp on the subject till the string breaks. It could become tedious.'

He turned back to the window, I think to hide his face. 'Well, then,' he said, 'I suppose I must be devoutly thankful for a thaw, if nothing else. I was afraid the big freeze might last well into the spring.'

There was barely enough time for me to appreciate the analogy before the door opened rather abruptly to the sound of a high voice preceding its owner as if in mid-conversation. 'Oh! And so *this* is the dreary study that needs…oh!' she squeaked. 'Miss Follet…er… I had *no* idea you were here. Am I interrupting something?'

'Yes,' said Winterson, coldly. 'You are.'

'No,' I said, 'not at all, Veronique *dear*. This *is* the dreary study that needs a lick of paint. I always used to knock before I entered.'

Credit where credit's due, I recovered myself superbly. Faster than she did from my reply. But I could see her great baby-blue eyes greedily taking in my dishevelled appearance, my hair straying over my ears, my unbuttoned pelisse-coat and woolly scarf, hardly a walking advertisement for Follet and Sanders. She, on the other hand, wore a well-tailored crimson thing that drained her milky complexion and clashed gaudily with her yellow hair.

Picking up Linas's notebooks, I glanced up to see Winterson's displeasure. 'Thank you for these,' I said, forcing my frosty smile into his eyes. 'I would not like them to fall into the wrong hands. He was always *most* fastidious about who he allowed into his study, wasn't he? Good day to you, *dear* Veronique. So good to see you looking…er…well.'

Winterson found his tongue. 'Miss Follet,' he said, following me to the door, 'I'll come with you—'

'No, thank you, my lord. You must stay and entertain your guest.'

He opened the front door for me, but I was out through the crack and down the watery steps too fast for him to protest, and I felt him watching me stalk through the slush without a backward glance like an offended black-headed gull.

To say that I had made a complete fool of myself was well short of the truth: proposing a truce, putting my gripes behind me, attempting to lift our fragile relationship on to a more level plane, thinking in my stupidity that perhaps I'd been a mite too harsh, after his faultless hospitality. What *could* I have been thinking about? Had I really expected things to change because I'd thought it was time they did?

I had never 'deared' Lady Veronique Slatterly before, but if she was going to insist on getting under my feet at every end and turn, as I had no doubt she would, then there would be no more 'ladyshipping' from my lips. The thought of her paddling about in Linas's house made me sad and angry, and the thought of Winterson entertaining her there, perhaps in the same bed that Linas and I had once shared, made me angrier still. She must, I thought, have been waiting for Winterson to arrive. Timed to perfection. And why had he tried to hide his cynical smile? Why had he not simply laughed out loud at my absurdity?

Of course I had no hard and fast evidence that Veronique Slatterly *was* his mistress; it was an assumption I made in view of her frequent appearances at Abbots Mere and her simpering, clinging possessiveness of Winterson as if she were already the lady in residence. It was hard to know for sure, his attitude to her being not quite lover-like enough to reveal any deep affection, nor was it *quite* dismissive enough to keep her away for good. However abrupt he was with her—and he could be very abrupt, when he chose—it did not stop her from returning for more of those periods when he seemed content to tolerate, if not actually enjoy, her company.

She had wealth and good connections, plenty of rakes and rattles for friends and a fond father who owned a very successful racing stable near York. His jockeys were drawn from a keen circle of well-born young men who swarmed around the fair and voluptuous Veronique with a view, I supposed, to taking a share of what was on offer. Yes, I had seen the kind of favours she allowed, intimacies she didn't bother to hide from me since she probably assumed I had done the same, at some stage. Such were the problems of being a man's mistress rather than his wife. I dare say she thought that that kind of behaviour would make Winterson all the keener.

However, she had a title and I was still, in her eyes, a mantua-maker's assistant with ideas beyond her station. But because I now had close ties to Winterson's family, which she did not, she saw me as a threat to her ambition to become his wife. I would like her to have understood, once and for all, how unnecessary her fears were, but the cool civility he had always extended to me was far from the uncertain reception she often had to put up with from him and, although that seemed not to deter her, it did little to help my cause either.

From a woman's point of view, I was not in the least afraid of her but, as a mother, I *was* afraid of what she might try to do to my darling innocent Jamie while he was staying with his guardian. She would continue to think what she liked about my place in the grand scheme of things, but without Linas to help me keep out of her way, I would now have to remove the gloves and reveal my claws. Fortunately, I have never been afraid of taking matters into my own hands.

After two weeks away from home I had plenty of catching up to do and so, following some soul-searching concerning my responsibilities to Jamie, the business, and myself, I put aside what had happened, determined to move on. It was not as easy as it sounds.

One of my first calls was to the shop on the other side of Blake Street where I had to leap over gushing streams of melt-water running along the gulleys. Prue never complained about my absences, but I could see she needed all the help she could get. 'Orders?' she said. 'I should say so. The St Valentine's Day ball is only one week away and we've got fittings every day until then, and one worker off ill. We shall have to take an apprentice if we're to be ready on time. We need more lace too. Would there be any in those bundles Mr Follet brought?'

'You've not opened them yet?'

'No, I was waiting for you. Look, they're over here.' With an effort, she pushed two very large bales across the table towards me, too heavy to carry. Wrapped in waxed canvas and tied with twine, they contained separate packages of fabric, none of them of the ordinary sort I bought from the Manchester warehouses, but the finest sheer jaconet muslins, silks shot with gold threads, printed calicoes from India, brocades and silken ribbons, gold and silver braids, priceless bales of Alençon, black Chantilly, blonde and Valenciennes laces. Here were the finest embroidered kid gloves by the dozen, furs and fans, silk stockings and velvets, Kashmir shawls and nets like cobwebs that English women hankered after. Forbidden fruits. Exotic and rare—its value was immense.

Lifting and sorting, gasping at each new revelation, we were both dumbstruck by the quantity and quality, for this was by far the most valuable consignment Pierre had ever brought us. 'Where on *earth* is he getting it all from?' I whispered, holding up a length of tulle. 'This is...*priceless*!'

Prue was a realist. 'Not exactly priceless,' she said,

lifting to one side a heap of narrow lace edgings. 'Lyons velvet will sell at fourteen shillings the yard, and we can get three shillings for this French merino. And look at these braids, Helene. Three and fourpence a yard for that one, four and sixpence for that.'

'But how is he paying for all this, Prue? That's what I need to know. The money we put aside from the last load couldn't possibly have bought so much, not even at French prices. Look at this. We've never had an ikat-dyed muslin like this before, have we?'

'Nor Russian sable either. This'll make a lovely collar and cuffs for that grey velvet pelisse of yours. And take a look at this grosgrain, and these Pekins.' She held up an armful of silk that shone with a seductive lustre; the pale stripes on a paler background was what our younger customers could not get enough of.

'I can't understand it,' I said, trying not to sound too critical. 'He's actually buying more goods than we've given him money for, Prue.'

She frowned at me. It was probably the first time we had ever discussed the whys and wherefores of our dealings with Pierre. He bought the goods, we sold them, and the money was shared between us with one share allocated for the next consignment. The profits so far had been generous, benefiting all of us although, in theory, he could only buy what the previous share would cover. 'Does he go over to France for them?' she said. 'Personally, I mean.'

'I have no idea. He may do, but I think it's more likely that he uses an agent to bargain with the suppliers in France and to have a cargo waiting to be picked up by an English boat. Somehow.'

'I thought it was the French boats that brought it across the Channel.'

'Well, you may be right. I don't really know. All I *do* know is that Pierre works on his own and appears to deal only in fabrics. My father used his own boats, but Pierre is not in that league now.'

'Who knows what a Frenchman will get up to?' She smiled. 'Perhaps the less we know about it, the better. We've never bothered before, so why should we start now? Where's my notebook? I must make a record of this before we use it. Shall you write a notice for the window?'

'Yes. I'll advertise for an apprentice, too.'

'You'll be wanting something for the Valentine ball too, Helene. We ought to have thought about that before now, you know.'

'It wouldn't look good, Prue. I'm in mourning. I shan't be going this year.'

There was something in the way she looked at me, standing stock-still as if I had caused the pain in her eyes. 'Not going?' she whispered. 'Can you afford not to go? You know what a difference it makes to our order book when you're seen wearing one of our gowns at the Assembly Rooms. And this is one of the most popular balls in the whole calendar.'

'I know that, Prue. But I've always had a respectable partner until now, haven't I? So how d'ye think it'll look, only weeks after Linas has gone, and me cavorting around without him? What d'ye think they'll say? That I'm already on the look out for a replacement? Have some sense, Prue.'

She took my rebuke like a friend. 'What about Mr

Monkton's brother? You've just spent two weeks at his home. Would he not oblige?'

'Obliging doesn't come into it,' I said, crossly. 'I would not ask him. And anyway, he's in mourning too, so he won't be going, so that's that. Nor do I relish the idea of being taken for *his* mistress, which is *exactly*,' I snapped as she rolled her eyes heavenwards, 'what would be said if he were to partner me. You know how people talk. They're probably talking already.'

'And *you* would not be so hot under the collar, Miss Helen Follet, if you didn't already think more about Lord Winterson than you let on. You may be able to cut a wheedle with some folk and bamboozle others into thinking that you hold him in aversion, young lady, but I haven't been a dressmaker all these years without discovering where women wear their hearts as well as their hats. But if you're quite determined to play the martyr, then don't let me stop you, only don't ask why we have so few orders from February until Easter, will you?'

'Oh, Prue!' I wailed, thoroughly exasperated. 'Do try to understand.'

'I do,' she said. 'Better than you think. Now be quick and write that notice for the window, then let's get some work done, shall we?'

So I wrote:

Madame Helene, of Follet and Sanders, Blake Street, begs to inform the Nobility, Gentry and Ladies visiting York that her Show Rooms are now open with a choice selection of Millinery from Paris, Gloves and Bonnets from one guinea.

Mechelin, Lisle and Valenciennes laces, Real
Brussels lace, Bobbin net veils and squares, also
satins, bombasins, velvets and sheer muslins.
Dresses for Weddings and Mourning made in the
first style and a perfect fit insured. Executed with
dispatch.

An Indoor Apprentice Wanted.

Placing the notice inside the window, I wondered if
we might have an application from a fourteen-year-old
whose life had taken an unexpected turn, as mine had.

The day was busy with clients released by the thaw
from the big freeze, all expecting their orders to be
ready in record time as if we, not they, had time to
make up. The 'Nelson Fashion' was all the rage since
the victor's tragic death at Trafalgar in the previous
October. Before that, it had been the Lady Hamilton
style, an empire line in white satin, gauze and muslin
with the hair cut close around the ears, and no hat.
Now, the demand was for imitations of Emma's white
satin trimmed with gold, silver or lace, and a turban embroidered with 'Nelson' topped with white plumes.

The newest February edition of *Bell's Court and
Fashionable Magazine* showed the most recent 'Trafalgar Dress', which so far I had kept out of the shop. Our
embroiderers were working day and night ornamenting
every border with festoons and coronets, Nelson's
name, ships and flags, anchors and badges, and even a
newfangled stitch that took far too long. Black-edged
fans, ribbons and shawls, handkerchiefs and headgear,
reticules and gloves: one could dress from head to toe
à la Nelson.

I took *Bell's Court* home with me, with Prue's last parting shot resounding in my conscience about the Valentine's ball and the renewed surge of patronage that would be ours as a result of my wearing one of her gowns. Always in the very latest mode, my ballgowns had been the best possible advertisement ever since I'd been allowed to wear them. Now, they were my own property, and who was I to complain when our wealthiest clients requested copies? To a provincial business like ours, that was worth much.

With little Jamie snuggling on my lap, we leafed through the pages of drawings, giving each of the toffee-nosed models an appropriate name. 'That one,' said the little fellow, wiping his nose on the sleeve of his night-shirt, 'is Miss Mooney. She's all in white. Mama, wear that one.' He tapped the long feather boa. 'Worm,' he said, yawning. He looked good enough to eat—warm, soft and sleepy-eyed.

'What does Goody think?' I said, glancing at his nurse. It was not the first time I had asked her opinion about such things, but on this occasion she appeared to see that it was not so much the style we were discussing as the propriety of me attending a ball.

'Mmm,' she said, smiling gently, confirming what I thought. 'It's tricky, isn't it, ma'am? A mourning ballgown for a function one is hardly expected to attend. *However*,' she continued, 'there's the obligation to one's business partner, for one thing. For another, a fashionable ballgown could be contrived to reflect mourning for *both* Lord Nelson *and* for a loved one. And for another, it is quite possible to attend a ball without taking part in the dancing. Many ladies go only to be seen and to socialise, ma'am, as I'm sure you're aware. It would not be remarked upon, in your case.'

'So,' I said. 'Is it to be black, or white?'

'Both,' she replied, smiling at my acceptance. 'Keep it ambiguous, I always say. Shall I take Master Jamie up now?'

I was glad, in a way, that the decision had almost been made for me. I say 'almost' because, in my heart, I welcomed a chance to dress up and spend an evening in good company, meeting old acquaintances and shedding my cares for a few glamorous hours. I could tell myself that I was doing Prue a favour, but the truth was that Linas's death had cut me adrift again, unsettling me in a way that nothing else had done, not even my father's sudden death. Could there have been something in what Prue said about wearing my heart for all to see? Was that *really* what I'd been doing?

Chapter Seven

In that first week of the thaw, I felt as if my concerns were quietly breeding, growing all the more irritating for my inability to decide what to do about them. It was not like me to be so undecided.

For my mother's progressive illness I could do little except visit her as often as I was able and hope to be there when she needed me. On the more immediate problem of Pierre, I would have welcomed some informed advice rather than the heavily biased opinion Prue had offered me. She was, quite naturally, in favour of leaving things as they were, but I could see all too clearly that to do so was running a serious risk not only to ourselves and our business, but also to Jamie. While Linas lived, the risk had somehow seemed less of a threat.

Smuggling was illegal, I knew that. Along with thousands of otherwise law-abiding people, I was breaking the law. But Pierre's last consignment had indicated what I had not suspected before, that he was dealing in more than exotic fabrics, and that perhaps he was doing it for my sake, hoping to place me in his debt. If that was so, now was the time to call a halt before it was too late.

If it had been left entirely to me, I would have dealt with the problem at a sedate pace, in my own time. But once again Fate took a hand in things, setting the machinery in motion and taking no account of the inappropriate timing. We were leaning over the stone balustrade of the Ouse Bridge, Jamie, Mrs Goode, Debbie and I, to watch the swollen brown waters shoot below us at an incredible speed, the swirling satin surface wrinkling only inches away from the top of each arch. All along the banks as far as we could see, the flood had reached across the staithes and the new tree-lined walk, pushing back into the lanes on both sides, flooding houses. Debris and boats piled up together with tree trunks tossed like matchsticks upon the roaring torrent. Jamie, clinging tightly to my neck, was fascinated. On the bridge behind us, horses and carriages splashed through the water and mud, some of them loaded with baggage and furniture. A voice broke through the general din. 'Miss Follet, this is too dangerous. The water is still rising.'

Contrarily, my emotions wavered between elation and defiance, for he was one of the concerns I didn't know what to do about. My small son, however, suffered from no such conflict. 'Uncaburl!' he yelped, struggling against me, leaning out heavily with arms like reaching tentacles. 'Uncaburl, hold me.' The changeover was happening, whether I liked it or not.

I watched Jamie cling to him with a look of triumph on his little face. 'We're in no danger,' I said, not best pleased at having to justify myself.

'No, of course not. But I think you should come away now.'

His calmness, I knew, was for Jamie's sake, but when he turned and strolled off with my child in his arms, knowing that I would follow come hell or high water, it was as if he knew exactly how to lead me in any direction without the slightest fear of argument, either now or in the future. 'Where are you going?' I called, beckoning to Mrs Goode and Debbie.

He had the grace to wait for me, then. And he was smiling. Both of them were. Conspiring. Father and son, as alike as two peas. My heart flipped and twisted, acknowledging the deep yearning of my womb to be filled with more babies, more warm, defenceless, soft pink creatures to suckle, to adore. His babies. More Jamies to replenish me and make me whole and fruitful, to depend on me alone. I am not usually so tearful, but at that moment he must have caught a quick watery flash along my lower eyelid before I could catch it with a finger.

His smile vanished. 'It's all right,' he said, very quietly. 'Just stay close. We'll keep to the higher ground, I think. Coney Street will soon be awash so we'll go along Davygate instead. I have some visitors who want to see you.'

'Who?' I croaked. 'The last visitor you had I didn't want to meet.'

'Mutual friends. They went to Blake Street first, then to me at Stonegate. So I came to find you.'

'You found us, Uncaburl!' Jamie cried, proudly.

'Yes, little one.'

There was no more conversation as we walked in

single file through the watery streets, slippery with slush and silt, we women picking up our skirts although it was too late to make much difference. Approaching the space known as Thursday Market where many lanes met, the aroma of roasting coffee wafted out through the open doors of coffee houses where men came and went. My eyes were on the conditions underfoot, but Jamie was like an eagle on a cliff. 'Uncapare!' he yelled. 'Mama, look! It's Uncapare!'

I looked up, sure of some mistake. I would have to apologise. Two men had just emerged from the Davygate Coffee House ahead of us and were walking in our direction, their heads bent, deep in conversation. One of them was unmistakably Pierre Follet. Here, in York. And I would be obliged to introduce him. This was just the kind of thing I could have done without.

Hearing his name, Pierre looked up, first in astonishment and then with indecision, then with a quick word to send his companion off hastily in the opposite direction. His eyes darted uncertainly over Jamie in the care of a stranger, changing to relief and warmth as he saw my smile. *Between us*, his answering smile said, *we can bluff this out*.

As usual, I greeted him with a kiss to both cheeks and was pleased when he placed a kiss gallantly upon my hand. I was even more pleased when he spoke in French, which I had no doubt Winterson would understand. Pierre's drab coat and grey knee-breeches reeked of tobacco smoke.

Leaning out of his nest, Jamie insisted on hugging Pierre's head, thereby enforcing some kind of informal introduction between the two 'uncas'. Knowing that I would be on safe ground here, I took the plunge. 'Will you allow me to introduce my cousin to you, my lord? Monsieur Follet lives with my family in Bridlington. Pierre, this is Lord Winterson, Mr Monkton's brother.' I saw no reason to go into detail about the exact relationship, using the term 'cousin' in its loosest form. My father's family had been known as Follethorpe for three generations, now.

'Monsieur,' said Winterson. Speaking in faultless French, he asked Pierre if he was staying in York long, how bad were the roads to Brid, and was there any better news of Miss Follet's mother? It was a catch, I knew, to see how Pierre would describe her health, though I resented Winterson using such a device to expose his doubts.

Pierre put on a grave face. 'Madame Follet has been very unwell for more than a year, my lord,' he said. 'I've come to call on her usual apothecary on Petergate. He's preparing something stronger to deal with the pain.'

'Did you intend to pay us a visit before you return?' I said.

'Not this time, *ma chère*. Forgive me. Time is short.'

Jamie pouted. 'Come with us, Uncapare,' he pleaded. 'We're going to Papa's house.'

Sitting aloft in Winterson's arms, their faces a few inches apart, only a blind man could have missed the likeness between father and son, even with that age difference. In one respect, it was unfortunate that Jamie still referred to Stonegate as 'Papa's house' for that would take some time to change. But for him to say it to Pierre, who knew that Winterson now owned it, was particularly ill fated and guaranteed to set the cat among the pigeons.

Pierre's eyes darted between them, comparing, recognising each similarity, for although he had never met Linas, he knew that the twin brothers were not identical. This was disastrous. His refusal came as no surprise. 'Ah…*petit Jamie*,' he said, 'I must take some medicine to Nana Damzell. She's waiting for it. Next time, yes?'

Jamie nodded. I took the cue, gratefully. 'Send me word, Pierre, won't you? Give her my love. And the boys too.'

'Indeed I will.' He bowed, but for me there was no smile, only a cool, guarded glint in his eyes that I recognised and felt deeply, like a reproach. For Jamie, he had a smile and a kiss to the tiny waving fingers. For Winterson, he had a brief nod and, 'My lord', before he turned away.

'Safe journey, *monsieur*,' called Winterson. 'You'll be home before dark, I hope?'

Waving a careless hand, Pierre slewed round. 'Oh…easily,' he called back. Instantly, he saw his mistake reflected in my eyes, but he could do nothing about it but shrug and walk on. It was already mid-day, and no one could have covered the forty miles to Brid before darkness fell, especially in those conditions. Foss Beck Common was a possibility. We watched him go, swinging away down the cobbled street and disappearing round the corner, ignoring Jamie's waves. I felt a cold chill grasp at my arms and shoulders.

'Well, well,' Winterson drawled. 'What an interesting family you have, Miss Follet.'

'Oh, not *now*,' I said, under my breath. 'Let's go and visit the visitors. One fiasco at a time, *please*.'

Even so, as we drew level with the coffee house
from which Pierre had come, Winterson slowed down
to take a long look through the bow window where,
inside, a grey fog of smoke hung over the tables of bent
heads poring over newspapers and broadsheets, pens
and papers, copper coffee pots, cups and the inevitable
clutter of plates and clay pipes. It was the kind of place
I had never associated with Pierre, an outdoor man. Yet
he had admitted to contacts in York and surely that was
the kind of venue where he would pick up news of his
homeland. In a coffee house, his nationality would
arouse little comment when so many Frenchmen had
fled to the safety of England in the pre-Napoleon years.
Yet I would like to have known why he had time to
spend there, and who was the companion he didn't
want us to meet.

I would rather have gone back to Blake Street instead
of the disorder of Stonegate, but I was pleasantly
relieved to find that Winterson's visitors were high on
Jamie's list of favourites. 'Uncamedith!' he cried,
hurling himself at the young curate's black-stockinged
legs, clinging like a limpet. 'Where's Aunt Cynthie?'

Effectively hobbled, Medworth Monkton picked the
limpet off, laughing. 'Upstairs, young man, telling the
workmen off for sitting down on the job. As usual.'

If Linas had been the worn-out racehorse and his
twin the well-toned hunter, then the younger Medworth
could have been compared to a sturdy northern fell-
pony, strong and energetic and with a forelock of dark
hair that had apparently refused all attempts to imitate
Brutus. Pleasant looking he was, too, but lacking the
heart-stopping masculine virility of his elder brother

that riveted the eyes of women and made their minds wander off the subject, whatever that was. They stood together, the three of them, and though Medworth held Jamie, it was as obvious as night follows day which one was the father.

We stood in the dining room, breathing in the odour of new paint, where the walls had been lightened with spring tones of pale yellow and white, though the floor was still bare and the windows curtainless. Already, the improvement was startling, the room had expanded.

Medworth's wife, a merry motherly lady two or three years older than her husband, came down to join us with a sparkle in her eyes and the rosy cheeks of one who has just given someone else's workmen a dressing down. Warmly, she embraced me and told me how she had advised Winterson that a deep red carpet would be best in a dining room to absorb any spillages, a suggestion that appeared to meet with no particular enthusiasm. They were a happily outspoken pair, beloved by their parishoners as much for their kindness as for their lack of pretensions. Cynthia was expecting their third child, otherwise, she told us, they would have defied convention and bought tickets for the St Valentine's Day ball at the weekend. 'I may have been able to manage a stately gavotte,' she said rather wistfully, lifting a holland cover off one of the chairs, 'but not an eightsome reel. Oh, I *do* admire these seats, Burl dear. I wonder…?'

'Miss Follet's handiwork,' said Winterson. 'And no, dear sister-in-law, I shall not be replacing them. However, I *shall* take your place at the ball in order to accompany Miss Follet. You may sit on one in your delicate state, Cynthia. I have no objection to that.' He took the holland cover from her and threw it aside.

'Burl Winterson,' she giggled, sitting down.

He must have felt my stare, for he turned suddenly to catch my expression with an equally challenging one of his own, daring me to take issue with him, there and then, in front of his brother.

The truth was that Mrs Monkton's delicate state was a complete surprise to me, and instead of offering them my felicitations, I was once more overtaken by the yearning, now tinged with envy, and it was all I could do to keep my hands away from my flat belly to still the ache of emptiness. 'No,' I said, 'I don't think…I still have reservations…I'm not sure.'

'About…?' said Winterson.

'About whether it's the right thing for me to do.'

'Well, my dear,' said his brother, 'you must do whatever you feel is correct. But let me say this: Linas would not have wanted us all to go into months of mourning for him. For you to be seen in public at this time will not cause even the lift of an eyebrow from his family, and indeed, Burl's decision to accompany you will prevent comments from anyone.'

'Yes. Thank you. But I didn't think it would be seemly to dance.'

Looking across at his wife's nodding approval, Mr Monkton's beaming face softened even more. 'Wife,' he said, 'I don't know why we didn't think of that our-selves. We *could* go, for an hour or two, for a game of cribbage? A chat with friends? Just to be seen? How d'ye like that idea? No dancing?'

Cynthia was a farmer's daughter with the healthy

glow of a ripe apple and eyes like pips, her hair a curly mouse brown, her wide smile only one step away from laughter. 'We'll go and purchase tickets before we return home,' she said, 'and heaven only knows what I'm going to wear. I suppose it will have to be black?'

I assumed that she would want to talk of gowns, but I was mistaken. It was little Claude's third birthday the following week, and she wanted Jamie to spend the day with them at Osbaldswick. Would I take him and Goody over there after breakfast on Tuesday? Still, I could not help feeling relieved when they eventually departed, leaving a strained silence behind them.

It was almost lunch-time and Jamie would be hungry, and I could not keep him and the women waiting while Winterson and I hammered out the dents made to my family's façade by Pierre. Or tackled the vexed question of the ball and his sudden decision to escort me there.

'What d'ye think of the red-carpet idea?' he said as we returned to the dining room.

'Not much. Deep gold, perhaps, or pale green. That is, if you really intend to keep the chair covers as they are.'

'I wouldn't dream of changing them. Same for the curtains?'

'No. White brocade curtains with gold bobble-fringe, to match the gilding on the architrave.' I'd had years to think about it.

'White? Really?'

'Yes, really. Echoes the ceiling and frieze. Reflects the light. Widens the narrow windows. It's always been so dull in here. That's why I made the floral covers in pastel shades. But why not ask Lady Slatterly's opinion? She'll be the one dining in here most, surely?'

'Tch! You *have* got a bee in your bonnet about her, haven't you? There's really no need, you know.'

'The hem of my skirt is wet,' I returned. 'I must get Jamie and go.'

'I shall call round to see you later on.'

'I shall be in the workrooms all afternoon. I have clients to see.'

'Then I'll call round this evening.'

'You're staying in York tonight?'

'If need be. And no, the lady will not be here with me.'

A quick retort flew unbidden to my lips as if my heart felt the need to deny its caring. But the issue of beds, Linas's and mine, was too personal to discuss in the same breath as the Slatterly woman, and I dare not trust my voice to speak without revealing the unsoundness of my feelings. 'Perhaps tomorrow might be better,' I said, lamely, hoping he'd insist.

'This evening. After dinner.' His hand rested on the doorknob as he waited for me to reach him, though I could not meet his eyes. 'What is it?' he said, softly, deeply. 'Did she upset you?'

I knew he referred to his sister-in-law, yet there was no truthful answer to his query. With one hand on my forehead, I hid my eyes, shaking my head rather than give him an unconvincing no.

'Then what? Is it too soon for me to be making changes here? Does it distress you?'

'No, it's not that. Earlier…when Jamie and you were…together.' The words tumbled out, revealing what I ought to have kept to myself. It was foolish of me. It was not his problem, but mine, yet he appeared to understand without more being said.

'Well, yes. That small point did not escape your cousin, any more than it has escaped Medworth.'

My hand moved down to my mouth. Medworth too. 'Then Jamie must not be seen with you, my lord. You must see that,' I whispered.

'That's not the answer, is it? You know it isn't.'

'Then what is?'

Jamie's wail reached us through the door, and the brass knob in Winterson's hand began to vibrate urgently. Slowly, still looking at me, Winterson opened the door just enough to allow the angry little fellow to edge through, his face red with indignation. *'Uncaburl!'* he yelled.

'Whoa!' Winterson said, sternly. 'Manners, young man, if you please.'

On the very edge of a tantrum, Jamie stopped and looked up. 'Sorry, Uncaburl,' he wavered. 'Mama. I'm hungry. I'm *very* hungry.'

Holding out my arms, I enclosed and lifted him, feeling his warmth melt into me, and through half-closed eyes I was unable to hide the all-consuming craving for fulfilment that had been with me for days.

It had been a tiring but enjoyable afternoon spent in talk of little else but fabrics and designs, colours and styling details, the clients ranging from a dowager marchioness to the adolescent daughter of York's wealthy gentry attending her first ball. I was back home in time to tuck Jamie into bed and tell him a story, sending him to sleep before the happily-ever-after.

Finding no good reason to dress up for Winterson's informal visit, I changed into a loose gown of soft violet cloth with a frilled collar and wrists over which I wore a grey sleeveless waistcoat, floor-length and shadowy-patterned, my hair only just held up by a large tor-toiseshell comb. He had recently called me 'my beauty' as if I were a horse being told to lift up its other hoof, but my disconcertingly honest mirror told me only that I had lost weight and looked rather tired. I was bound to agree.

He arrived well before I had finished picking at my cold supper on a tray, shrinking my small but pretty parlour even more, and settling himself upon my blue velvet couch that could seat three of us and only one of him. 'Would you prefer to use the drawing room?' I said, thinking more of the distance I could keep.

'No, it's cosier in here. Finish your supper, ma'am.'

Winterson had brought regular news of his ailing brother's progress to my drawing room, but there had never been a time when we'd discussed our relation-ship, or Jamie's future, or my relatives, or anything as ephemeral as a local ball. 'You could have given me some warning,' I said to his opening of the subject. 'It would have given me time to—'

'To cry off. Yes, that's what I thought. Thank you,' he said, receiving a glass of port and placing it on the small table. 'But I had no intention of allowing you to go without an escort. Linas would not have approved.'

'Shall we not bring Linas into everything?' I said. 'Have you given any thought to how it will look on Saturday when I arrive with you, his brother? Can you not anticipate the speculation, my lord?'

The slow blink, like an owl, then that deeply chilling

note of sarcasm he was so good at. 'From one who has suggested keeping Linas out of it, that is a singular question, Miss Follet. Have *you* thought how it will look for us to arrive separately on Saturday and have nothing whatever to do with each other? Jamie's mother and guardian not on speaking terms? What will be the conclusions drawn from that, do you imagine?'

My silence answered his question while I pondered on his ability to see further ahead than me, who specialised in looking backwards.

'Have you forgotten?' he said, more gently.

'No. I have not forgotten.'

The Valentine Ball at the Assembly Rooms here on Blake Street was where I had met, first him, then Linas. We had danced together, he and I, saying very little, but aware of a powerful charge between us that dear Linas had no means to rival. We had been the centre of attention that evening. Yet it was Linas who pursued me, and Linas that I chose to cleave to because he needed me most and because I was not in a position to refuse his offer. I was under no illusions, after that, about Winterson's fleeting interest in me, which was no more nor less, I suppose, than his interest in many another. But for me, the disturbance in my heart was more profound than anything that had gone before, and so painful that I could hardly have called it love when I was obliged to see him regularly, for Linas's sake, and to suffer his coolness. Now, he asked if I'd forgotten, as if I might as easily have forgotten my name.

'We need not dance,' he said, 'unless you wish it, but it's best for all of us, as a family, if we are seen to unite on these occasions. And it's quite out of the question for you to go alone, yet I think you *should* go. So I shall call for you at eight and I shall escort you home afterwards.'

'The Assembly Rooms are only four doors away.'

'I know. If it's very wet, I'll have a chair brought for you. Now, eat your supper, and then you can tell me about your French cousin who thinks he can reach Brid in three hours over flooded roads.'

'I think I'd rather not, thank you. There's little I can tell you. He's a distant cousin, and I have no idea what he was doing in a coffee house except drinking coffee and reading the newspapers.'

'Then perhaps I may be forgiven for constructing a few facts of my own. The apothecary on Petergate where Monsieur Follet obtained your mother's medication informs me that her name is Mrs Follethorpe and that the French gentleman calls in regularly, about once every month. Which begs the question, in my mind, whether you and the French cousin are more to each other than that.'

So, he had already made enquiries. 'The apothecary had no right to give you that information,' I said, angrily pushing the tray away.

'Perhaps not. But he's as open to persuasion as the next man.'

'Well, then, let me put you out of your misery, my inquisitive lord. I changed my name to Follet when I came to seek work in York for no other reason than to protect my father's name. If he'd lived, he'd probably not have objected, since he always saw Pierre and me as future partners. As it turned out, he died only a few weeks after we left Bridlington. And, yes, it's quite obvious that my family don't live there, for reasons which I cannot discuss with you. Pierre is no more or less to me than a devoted relative who has helped our family through difficult times.'

'That's the first time I've ever heard you speak of your father. Could he be, by any chance, the famed Leonard Follethorpe, one-time mayor of Bridlington? No need to look so surprised. I *am* a Justice of the Peace, remember, which requires me to know what's going on in the area.' When I made no reply, he continued. 'So, if my knowledge is correct, and I'm reasonably sure it is, may I offer you some advice? The notice appearing in your shop window advertising French laces and other forbidden things from across the Channel may not be the good idea you believe it to be. If I were you, ma'am, I would keep quiet about that kind of merchandise when there are men walking the streets of York whose job it is to winkle out receivers of Free Trade goods. If they were to suspect that you and Mrs Sanders were involved, you would be asked to provide some very explicit answers ranging back over several years. You are an unmarried mother, don't forget, and very vulnerable.'

'Jamie,' I whispered.

'Yes, our Jamie. You cannot afford to take risks, Helene. Can you?'

'I had already reached that conclusion.'

'Of course. I cannot believe you would do anything so dangerous unless there was a very good reason for it.'

'There is.'

'Yet it occurs to me, as it will also have done to you,

that if you are able to do so well from the sale of these luxury goods, your family ought to be living in some style by now. Are they?'

'No. Far from it.'

'Then perhaps it's time the business was looked into and stopped.'

'I don't know how to stop it.'

'Simple. You say "stop".'

'It's *not* simple. Prue depends on it. My family depend on it. And I depend on it. How d'ye think I've been able to manage all these years?'

'I had already begun to wonder.'

'Well, now you know. I'm in deep trouble and, if I were you, I'd have no more to do with me.'

'Too late,' he said, quietly. 'It's much too late for that.'

Chapter Eight

We sat for some time without speaking although the silence was loud with sound, the crackling fire, the clock, the thud of my heart.

Reaching for his glass, he held it up to the lamplight, took a sip and replaced it on the table next to the pile of notebooks I'd still had no time to read. 'Mmm,' he said. 'What you need, Miss Follet, is some protection. It's not usual for a lady of your standing to live without a chaperon. When Linas was close I suppose it mattered less, but I think you should give the matter some thought.'

'I already have. I would have liked my mother to come here so that I could care for her, but she won't consider it.'

'That's not quite what I had in mind.'

'I have Mrs Goode, and Debbie.'

'Yet you went out alone to visit your family in atrocious conditions. You cannot continue to do that kind of thing. It's asking for trouble.'

'Then what am I to do? Advertise?'

Leaning forward, he extended one long arm towards me so that his forefinger just touched mine as it drooped over the arm of my chair. The shock of its tender impact caught at my mind and held it still. 'No,' he said, 'not yet. Not till we've explored the other possibilities. Next time you visit your family, I shall go with you. We'll take Jamie too, and show them what Monsieur Follet saw. You cannot keep that from them for ever, you know. And while we're there, we'll tackle the other problem too. Now don't start your objections too soon. You need some help in this, and I'm the one to do it. None of you can keep on living off illegal gains.'

I drew my hand away from the contact, too full of contradictions to accept whatever he was offering, too determined not to be won over at the touch of one finger. 'That's not possible,' I said. 'They'll think… well…'

'Yes, they *will* think. And as Jamie gets older, everybody else is going to think too. Surely your own family should be the first to know how things are between us, Helene. Not from gossip, but from us.'

'What d'ye mean? How *what* is between us? You're not suggesting telling them what happened, are you?'

'I'm suggesting telling them what's *going* to happen. They'll be able to see for themselves what's happened, won't they? Your French cousin, for instance, who has hopes of owning you, one day. Isn't it better he should know sooner rather than later that he doesn't stand a ghost of a chance? And your mother too? Isn't it best that she knows, before it's too late to tell her? It's time we began to put things in order, lass.'

If I was confused before, I was even more confused after his attempt at clarification. 'Pierre? My mother? Tell them what—that Jamie isn't Linas's?'

'That you are to marry Jamie's father and guardian. And if you don't want to tell them, then I will. Or would you prefer Jamie to discover what it means to be illegitimate? It won't be long now, the way he's chattering.'

'And that's what you call exploring the possibilities, is it?'

'Yes, Miss Follet, it is. So before you give me all the reasons why you can't accept that plan, consider instead the deep trouble you just mentioned. I'm offering you a respectable way out of it. I can take on the responsibility for your family without resorting to the illegal methods that are keeping you all in danger. You're playing with fire, and that's no way to conduct a business. Mrs Sanders will have to understand that.'

Naturally, I had my doubts whether either Pierre *or* Prue would understand, but Winterson knew nothing of Pierre's part in the smuggling, nor would I tell him. The talk of marriage, however, had taken me off guard, although I could appreciate that the offer was for Jamie's sake more than for any romantic reason. He put me right on that, too.

'Consider this also,' he said. 'If I'd chosen to go down on one knee and beg you to be my wife, you'd have stuck your neat little nose in the air and said not in a million years, wouldn't you? Eh?'

'Yes. Very likely.'

'So that's why I'm ignoring the romantic bit and *telling* you that you'd better start getting used to the idea. Fix any reason to it you like. Our son, illegitimacy, Linas, me, family likenesses, gossip, whatever.'

'Yes, whatever. But you've missed out an important snag, of course.'

'Which is?'

'That I am not good at sharing a man, my lord. Your kind of life and mine would not mix. You have mistresses, I believe? Well, I don't suppose anything would change there, would it? That would be asking too much of both of us.'

With a sigh, he leaned forwards again to rest his arms along his thighs as he looked at me with a frown of impatience at my recurring theme. Or so I thought. 'Then allow me to explain, my beauty, once and for all,' he said in a voice devoid of tenderness.

'Oh, there's really no need,' I snapped, nettled by the reading of my mind. 'I expect you used Linas's bed. Or did she prefer the one in my room?'

'Huh! Listen to me, Helene. In return for land, I train some of Lord Slatterly's racehorses. It's a reciprocal arrangement that benefits both of us, so he'd take it very hard if I told his beloved only daughter to keep away. She comes and goes, but I cannot stop her if she thinks she stands a chance with me. She doesn't, and she never has. Not once. Her friends all make use of her, but I prefer not to. In fact, I'm probably the only one who doesn't, and I only allow her to stay at my home when there's a party of friends there too. Never alone. No matter what she may say or imply, that's the truth of the matter. She's already wheedled her way through the back door of Stonegate, so I've given strict instructions that she must not be admitted while I'm out, under any circumstances. You, on the other hand, are always to be welcomed.

'But the day you saw her there was also the day you told me you were willing to put the past behind us and be friends, for Jamie's sake. Helene, I'm offering you more than that. I'm offering you both a new life. All together.'

'I didn't expect…that. It's further than I'm prepared to go, although I can see the advantages and I'm aware that a woman in my position can hardly afford to turn down such an offer without good cause. Especially when it comes from her child's father. But you see, my lord, ever since I discovered how you and your brother planned to make use of me as if I were a heifer of sound stock expected to produce a healthy bull-calf, the whole business of marriage has turned rather sour on me. My inclination now is to remain chaste until I can decide for myself when to continue my own breeding programme. I had not meant to keep harping on that string, but I seem not to have made it clear that I mean to stay as independent as I was when I first came to York. I find it suits me better. Yes, I know it may sound selfish, but I really cannot allow my three-year-old son to choose a husband for me.'

By the time I'd finished, I was trembling with the effort and with trepidation, too, for he was not a man to take a woman's snub lightly, having offered so much. So I rose rather quickly from my chair with the intention of putting myself beyond his reach. And his anger.

He moved much faster than I did, and I was caught under the arm and pulled back against him, off balance, my vision blurred by the lamplight and shadows, by the sharp conflict of wills and, in my case, by an explosion of petulance. 'Let go…let *go*!' I cried, struggling furiously inside his arms. 'I don't want…no…I don't *want* this! You're hurting. Let *go*!'

It was all the same, fighting him, loving him, wanting the hard pressure of his body against mine. Even the pain. Even his anger. But I could hear by his breathing, by his soft whispers and by the nudging gentleness of his lips that he was *not* angry, but enjoying my struggles. His hands restrained me, forcing me to be still while his forehead came to rest upon mine. We stood, head to head, me panting with vexation and he with eyes alight, amused to see my hair slowly slithering down my cheek, the tortoiseshell comb hanging on by a tooth.

His nose rested beside mine as he spoke, gentling me. 'That's my beauty. You think I wouldn't guess how you'd react to that? Eh? How you'd give me another roasting as soon as you had half a chance? Superb woman. Hush now. Not a heifer, sweetheart. Never a heifer. Nothing like. You were always a classy thoroughbred, temperamental, distrustful. You've not been handled well, have you? I shall have to remedy some wicked habits, but I can do it. I can make you sweet-tempered again, my lovely witch. And I shall get close to you again.'

'I shall not marry you.'

'Yes, you will. Of your own accord. You'll see.'

His hand raked through my hair to grasp a handful of it, tipping my face to fit against his mouth, closing my eyes as he did in my dreams, sinking me deep into the overlapping sensations that nightly craved consummation. I could not allow him to take me further, rendering worthless all I had striven for over the years. He had once called me unreliable, an insult that still rankled for, of all my copious faults, unreliability had never been one. Murmured so sweetly, his descriptions of me both excited and hardened my heart, for if anyone was responsible for my distrust of men, it was he. I would not make it easy for him, although my boast to choose my own time to breed was an empty threat he must have recognised. If I wanted to keep this roof over my head, I would be obliged to choose its owner above all others.

'Let me go,' I whispered. 'We are never going to agree on this.'

'You think not? Well, I can wait. You'll come to me.'

'Can you wait another four years, then?'

His head jerked back and he was once again the proud powerful hunter with eyes that glinted like polished jet. 'Don't play the waiting game,' he warned, 'unless you're prepared to damage yourself and our son while you revenge yourself on me. Time is too precious for that, Helene, and your heart is not really as hard as all that, is it?' As he answered me, his hand slipped beneath the grey waistcoat, pausing over my crazy heart to feel its beat before straying to one side, cupping my breast, reminding me once again how easily I had given myself to him that night.

Rather than try to find an answer, I prised his hand away, murmuring, 'Have we explored the other possibilities, my lord? Or is that it?'

'There were no others worth exploring, Helene. In spite of your cynicism, we *are* talking about Jamie's future here. Just remember, will you?'

'There was never any danger of me forgetting,' I said.

Again, it was the tone of my voice that betrayed my peevish heart that would have kept its wound for ever open, if need be, at whatever cost. But I was a mother first and foremost, beyond the anguish caused to my womanly pride, and I could no more have put Jamie's well-being in jeopardy at the expense of my self-esteem than expose him to a cage of lions. He was my life, and here was I, about to reject the best possible future for him, only to wreak vengeance for perceived wrongs. What was I about? Could I afford to ignore the olive branch he was offering to put things right between us? He had even tried to clear up my concerns about the Slatterly woman.

'Helene, look at me,' he said, lifting my chin.

I *did* look at him, and loved and hated him, wanted him, wanted to hurt him, wanted him to persist with me, to see my ritual objections for what they were and not to concede defeat. I wanted him to storm my barriers and crash through to the core that was his for the taking. I had always wanted him. I had lived, wanting him, for years with his brother and child. My body ached for him night and day without ceasing. So I looked up at him, not wanting to hear him accept one single word of my hostility. 'Don't speak,' I whispered, placing a finger upon his lips, 'until I've tried to excuse myself.'

'There's no need,' he said, behind my fingertip.

I wanted to kiss him. I wanted him to kiss me senseless.

'I know I've been breaking the law. It's a way of life for the people along our coast, and when I was given the chance to make some money for my family, I took it, just as I sold my body, and worked here in York, and scrounged to feed them and clothe myself. Now, you're offering me a respectable way out for which I am grateful. But they depend on me. The success of the shop has been built on it. You may forfeit Lord Slatterly's goodwill if you were to give his daughter the cold shoulder, but I shall certainly lose my partner's goodwill if I suddenly stop providing her with our most lucrative lines. You say you're willing to share the responsibility for my family, my lord, but they wouldn't allow it, and nor would I. Linas played no part in their lives, and nor must you. As for your offer of marriage… well, it's taken me unawares, and I must delay my answer to that. Jamie's birth certificate cannot be altered: he was born out of wedlock with Linas as his father, but I dare say memories will fade. At this moment, he needs a father more than ever he did.'

'He needs brothers and sisters, too,' he said, watching my eyes turn away, my lips part for the sigh that followed.

That was the last weapon left to me, after marriage, the one thing I could hold on to longest in my quest for retribution, though which of us would feel most pain was open to question. How long could I hold out against him? How long would his patience last? He was right about Jamie needing siblings, but one could not ignore the element of self-seeking that went with it. His kisses were telling me that.

He read my expression correctly. 'No, you're right,' he said. 'One thing at a time. We've made some progress, and I have to be content with that.' He lifted a fistful of my hair and held it on top of my head, with strands wandering into my eyes. 'Beautiful black witch,' he murmured. 'I lie. I'm not content, but it will have to do. As for your family and business, let me deal with that. Trust me?'

'I may not always agree with you, my lord, but I cannot fault *your* reliability.'

'*That* was taken out of context. One day, I'll explain it to you. The day after tomorrow is the ball and my parents will be over here for the weekend. Will you bring Jamie to see them on Sunday? For a family lunch?'

'Yes, we'll come. Thank you.'

'Good. Then I'll send a carriage for you.' Taking my hand from his chest, he touched my knuckles with his lips. 'Go to bed early and don't lose any more sleep over it. We had to come to an understanding sooner or later, did we not, Miss Follet?'

'For all our sakes,' I said.

But too much had happened for my thoughts to quit the future and lie quiet in the present, and sleep came nowhere near till the town-crier had called out the hour for the third time and Debbie had brought some warm milk to calm me. One thing that gave me some peace of mind, however, was that I had not shared his beautiful body with the Slatterly woman.

Next morning, with Winterson's caution still uppermost in my mind, I went straight to the shop to remove the incriminating notice from the window. Quite what had possessed me to put it there in the first place I will never understand—it was what we had always done without thinking of the possible consequences. Prue was not there, though she had been in.

'She's left a message for you, ma'am,' said Betty, the senior seamstress.

Propped up against a pile of calicoes was a hastily written note, very much to the point. *Mother v. ill. Father in a state. Dare not leave them. Sorry. Prue.*

It was bad timing. Perhaps the cold had affected them. Her unscheduled absence, however, made it easier for me to take some positive action in advance of any snooping visits from the Customs and Excise Men, a fear that had stayed with me since Winterson's call. With Prue out of the way I would do as I pleased and remove the damning evidence while there was still time, and none of the sewing-women making the least objection when I explained what we would do.

The unused cellar was ankle-deep in flood water from the street outside, but as each package was placed in the niches set into the darkest wall, this proved to be the safest of all places, the only one too uninviting to be investigated fully.

As if some supernatural clockwork had been set in motion, we were visited that same afternoon by two dour gentlemen who asked with the greatest courtesy if they might inspect our property in the name of His Brittanic Majesty King George III. As if we had any choice.

Well acquainted with Customs Officers, I found little that was unfamiliar about these two, and nothing that ought to have caused the alarm I felt, or the fear, the appalling guilt, the sickly terror of being just in time, and the dread that something relevant had been missed out. I could only pray that the women would answer any questions calmly, for I'd had little time to brief them. 'Do you seek anything in particular, gentlemen?' I said. 'Where would you like to begin?'

Their eyes darted, missing nothing, but they were uncommunicative. They fingered the fabrics, lifted rolls, drapes and boxes, but we could all see they didn't know a poplin from a kerseymere. One lifted a length of heavy Argentan lace attached to the dress Betty was stitching. 'Where's this from?' he said, rubbing it between finger and thumb.

Betty hardly paused. 'Nottingham,' she said. 'And Maudie's sewing Bedford, and over there is the Limerick, and that pile you've been looking at is Devon, and that bobbin lace is from Buckinghamshire. It's known as...Bucks...point...' But with a lift of his eyebrows, the man had moved on.

'You have a loft, ma'am?' said the other man.

'Yes, indeed we do. The ladder is over there in the corner.'

He clambered up, but came down again immediately. 'There's nothing there but chairs,' he said, pained.

'No, that's very true.'

'Why not?'

'Because we can't get up there, can we?' I replied with a hint of impatience. 'Everything we sell is on show to our customers, not in a loft.'

The pulling out of drawers, hampers and baskets went on, bolts of fabrics were toppled to expose walls that had to be tapped, with ears pressed against them. 'You have cellars?' the man said, frowning at the floor.

'Yes, the trapdoor is in the kitchen, but we don't keep anything down there. It's too damp.'

Nevertheless, they took one look down into the murky hole, saw their lamps reflected on the water and closed the lid with a grunt of acceptance. 'What's through there, ma'am?' said the man, indicating the fitting rooms.

'My customers, sir. By all means take a look, but please don't go into the fitting rooms without a warning, or I might never see them again.'

'So where do *these* fabrics come from, exactly?'

From the drawer of my desk I brought out a sheaf of receipts and pointed out to him the recent dates. 'Mostly from Manchester, but some from Sampson and Snape's warehouses in London, some from Paisley near Glasgow. Shawls, see? Some from Norwich, too, stockings from Leicester and Derby, gloves from Worcester…' I spread the receipts out before him '…and silks and muslins from…'

'Yes…yes, thank you, ma'am.'

'…Blackburn, and cottons from…'

'Thank you, yes. What about the bonnets?'

'The millinery is made to order, sir. To match an outfit. The Lord Nelson turban is very *à la mode*, at the moment.' I took one off the wooden stand and passed it to him.

Gingerly, he took it off me, pulled a face and passed it to his colleague. 'Nothing much Frenchified about that, Horace,' he muttered.

'Nah, c'mon, we've seen enough.' Horace passed the turban back, like a bucket. 'But you had a notice in your window saying something about these things being straight from Paris, didn't you?'

'Yes.' I smiled. 'Ladies always fall for that, sir. They

see the French modes in our fashion journals, so anything with a French name is bound to draw them in. A little deception, I know, but they understand.'

'Bit of a wild goose chase, Horace.'

Horace looked at me with—I thought—a trace of sympathy. 'I heard that Mr Linas Monkton passed on recently, ma'am. Very sad, that was. A lady such as yourself needs protection in these times. And a little lad, too, I believe. Pardon me, ma'am. No offence.'

'None taken, sir,' I said, indulging in a moment of relief that the dreaded inspection had passed without incident. 'But I *do* have some protection. Mr Monkton's family are very supportive. Lord Winterson is my son's guardian, and he keeps a very close eye on my business affairs.' It was a boast I never expected to make. I felt them both stiffen, heard them gulp, saw their eyes blink and widen with concern.

'Lor…ahem!…Lord Winterson?'

'Aye. He's a J.P., Horace, is Lord Winterson. Better be going, eh?'

'Thank you, gentlemen. I shall tell him you did your job thoroughly and with courtesy. Good day to you both.'

The light outside was fading and a fine rain was beginning to spatter against the glass as I closed the door and leaned my forehead on the cool wall. A dizziness passed over me, reminding me that I had eaten no lunch that day. The danger was gone, the goods were safe, and I had used Winterson's name to protect myself from further investigation, which, to be honest, I ought not to have done. But the blissful feeling of security I had experienced as I spoke the name out loud seemed to outweigh all other considerations.

Coming along the passage to meet me, Betty took me into her arms to quell my shaking. 'We all knew, ma'am,' she said. 'None of us ever said nowt, but we knew. Come and have a nice cup o' tea.'

There was a slightly hysterical edge to our giggles as we nibbled our biscuits, the tea being just as likely to be smuggled by the tea merchant as our fabrics were by us. And the sugar by the grocer, for that matter.

Underlying that light-heartedness, though, ran another thread of concern about how we should all manage without the goods that had kept us in business for so long. It was not a problem I could discuss in the workroom, yet our handling that morning of the consignment brought by Pierre had only strengthened my suspicions that he must be playing some secret game of his own that I was not being allowed to share. His appearance in York, ostensibly to purchase my mother's medication, was in itself unusual, for I had taken enough to last her a month on my last visit, some of which had been double-strength for emergencies.

And who was the furtive scruffy character he'd been with in the coffee house? And why, for the second occasion, had Pierre found no time to call on me at home? Was his excuse a genuine one? Recalling Winterson's decision to accompany me to Foss Beck to meet my family, I wondered whether that would solve any of the problems or simply create new ones, in the light of Pierre's attachment to me. Though the outcome was hardly in question, I was still unwilling to be the cause of any bitterness between them. Perhaps the best thing, I thought, would be for me to go there alone, despite Winterson's instructions.

Chapter Nine

❦

The terrible floods that followed the thaw brought tragedy just as severe as the crippling cold, and now instead of freezing to death, people fell victim to diseases borne upon the waters that carried effluent from broken cesspits into even the most respectable houses. Tavern taprooms were awash, the Guildhall cellars were flooded and, on my Friday visit to Lop Lane to see how Prue was managing, I discovered that the rats escaping from the water had gnawed their way through her store cupboard, eating everything remotely toothsome. Both her father and mother had gone down with the sickness by the time I arrived, and Prue herself was at her wits' end with worry. It was not the time to tell her about the Customs and Excise Men.

The apothecary on Petergate was running low on the standard remedies for such a prevalent complaint and had quite sold out of mallow-root and seeds for a decoction that rarely failed, in my experience. All he could offer me was powdered bistort root, a syrup of dried roses, and distilled mint-water which, although soothing, were not what I would call outstandingly effective. I purchased all three and took them back to Lop Lane, then I set off to scour the other apothecaries, returning an hour later with a quantity of Dr James's Fever Powders, Analeptic Pills, and a bottle of Dr Benjamin Godfrey's Cordial that I'd seen advertised in the *York Mercury*, hoping that one of them would ease the distressing symptoms. I also sent round some candles and firewood, bread and milk, cheese, soup, clean bed linen and blankets in return for the soiled ones that poor Prue had been forced to use, underlining once again the difference in our circumstances.

She had once been my employer, but now I was reminded of how hard she must be finding it to care for two ailing parents in their dilapidated town house while keeping up the appearance of a thriving business. In some ways, my responsibilities were similar, but in my accommodation I was far more fortunate than Prue, and I longed to help her out instead of giving her the bad news about the smuggled goods that only waited to be told. Nor did it help my conscience much when Debbie assisted me with a final fitting of the ballgown I'd been making all week. If Prue had not insisted that I show it off for the sake of the business, I doubt I would have spent my time so indulgently.

Nevertheless, when Saturday came I could hardly contain a *frisson* of excitement as Debbie clipped a pair of small pearls on to my earlobes and then, finding little else for her fingers to adjust, she twisted long tendrils of my hair like corkscrews and arranged them in front of my ears. She had threaded ropes of seed pearls through my coiled hair, but I would wear no other jewellery except a small pearl and moonstone brooch to clasp the folds of my gown upon one shoulder.

I had made the dress of white crape, a sheer silk gauze with a crimped surface that produced a matte effect, underneath which the soft sheen of a white satin undergown showed through when I moved. Narrow black satin ribbons crossed over the short bodice to outline my breasts, tying at the back in a bunch, the same ribbons edging the skirt above a narrow hem of black lace. It was a plain easy-to-wear style to suit many shapes and sizes, its greatest extravagance being in the rich drape of silk over satin, like moonshine behind a film of clouds edged with the darkness of night. To add another touch of luxury, I carried a black lace fan edged with black feathers, one of two sent by Pierre in the latest consignment. White satin slippers with pearl-studded buckles, silk stockings, long white satin gloves and a reticule trimmed with black beads completed the ensemble.

Although I was more or less satisfied with my appearance, I was still apprehensive and unable to dismiss the memory of that time, years ago, when the enigmatic Burl Winterson had partnered me, living up to his reputation as a thief of women's hearts. We had met on subsequent occasions at the Assembly Rooms when I was with his brother, but never again had he stood up with me for more than one dance, which I thought more likely to be a duty than a pleasure.

* * *

He came at eight to collect me, waiting at the bottom
of the staircase to watch me descend, his eyes showing
the kind of appreciation he had never revealed previously, I suppose for Linas's sake. He held out a hand to
support me down the last stair, not knowing how the
steely strength of his arm imparted the kind of secure
confidence I'd never drawn from his brother. Then, I had
been the supporter. This time, he would be my protector.

'St Valentine's Day,' he said, quietly.

'Yes.'

'Six years ago, was it?'

'Yes, my lord. It's surprising how much can happen
to people in that time, isn't it? We've both changed,' I
said, hurriedly, in case he was about to suggest we
might start again at the beginning.

But he agreed with me. 'We have indeed,' he said,
'in many respects, although six years may also confirm
first impressions, Miss Follet. In your case, motherhood
has made you even lovelier than you were before, to my
mind.'

'For which I should offer you my thanks, my lord?'

His reply was a shade too prompt for civility. 'Yes,
I think you should. What kind of thanks did you have
in mind?'

He always took my sarcasm too literally. 'I'll think
of something suitably momentous, if you give me time,'
I said, looking round me. 'I have my pattens somewhere, to carry me over the mud.'

'You won't need them. I have a chair waiting
outside.' Taking the black velvet cape from Debbie, he

draped it over my shoulders, still smiling at my snappy retort, making my heart lurch at the closeness of his hands. If I had indeed been improved by motherhood, then fatherhood had brought him closer to physical perfection than ever, and the thought of walking into a ballroom beside such a handsome beast made me resolve to get the most out of the experience, not to spoil it with petty bickering.

I had seen him in evening dress many times before, always attracting attention by the perfect cut of his coat, skin-tight white knee-breeches and stockings, his neck swathed in a snow-white cravat that set off the healthy outdoor skin of his lean cheeks. His hair, I noticed, had been trimmed, though it still curled, thick and luxurious, over the white muslin. My fingers itched to sink into it. 'Thank you,' I said. 'That was thoughtful.'

'I would have had them bring it inside, but they'd have covered your hall floor with mud. So this is what we'll do.' So saying, he bade me place an arm around his neck, swooped me up into his arms and carried me down the steps to the sedan chair where I was placed in the cushioned interior without a speck of mud reaching the hem of my gown. Then, with the lid lowered and the door closed, I was swayed and jogged along the cobbles to the steps of the Assembly Rooms where a sea of colour dotted with black seethed upwards between the massive pillars into the portico, to the distant sound of a country dance in progress.

Chattering and squeals, shouts and giggles, wavings and trippings-up all contributed to the excitement of seeing and being seen, the promise of liaisons, the affirmation of connections, comparisons, flirtations. It rubbed off on me too, as my eyes singled out the most interesting fashions and a few I had personally designed, sometimes sadly disfigured by fussy accessories, others improved by slender bodies and graceful steps to give them life. Aventurine and crimson, claret and cherry, geranium, azure, citrus and cinnamon, rose, violet mingled with black and white, hairstyles *à la Grecque*, braided and wreathed *à la peruvienne* with ears of corn and feathers, turbans, lace caps and knots of hair like steeples. Sashes and shawls, sleeves of puckered net, necklines only a finger-width away from decency, bare shoulders and arms, looped trains and glimpses of silk-stockinged ankles all taken in by one sweeping glance as we followed the tide and waited to deposit our cloaks.

'Lady Osmotherly, lovely to see you looking so much recovered. Lady Percival, so delighted to see you again. Mrs Knopp, I hoped you'd be here.' I curtsied to the exact degree, endorsing their patronage of Follet and Sanders. They trusted me with their most intimate secrets and I was accepted by them as a friend. Here in York, as in many other provincial towns, the social structure was less rigid than in London, barriers between the great northern families with centuries of inherited wealth and the *nouveau riche* having often been breached in the unsettled years of war with our neighbouring France. I knew their daughters, had been on the receiving end of their ambitions and disappointments, and had been asked for advice along with hints on fashion, which, as often as not, placed me in the role of confidant. Shy smiles were exchanged across the jostling anteroom, smiles which then settled upon my well-known escort and back to me, approving or envying my choice. Little did they know what lay behind that choice.

After so many years of being held at a distance, it still came as something of a surprise to me that, when he wished it, Winterson could make me feel cherished and so necessary to his enjoyment. It was not what I was used to, nor was it what I'd seen of his offhand manner with other women and, although that never appeared to dampen their interest in him, it would certainly have inhibited mine if I'd been looking for a successor to Linas. What I had found acceptable in a lover six years ago and what I would accept now were two different things, small indefinable things like taking my cloak, offering me his arm, greeting my acquaintances and introducing me to his, none of which Linas had bothered with unless I prompted him.

Mr Medworth Monkton had been correct when he assured me that no one would remark on a show of solidarity in our ranks, he and Cynthia having arrived just ahead of us, already chatting animatedly to a group of friends who apparently saw nothing out of the ordinary in my being there with Linas's two brothers. Cynthia, wearing undiluted black from head to toe, was complimentary about my evening gown. 'I might have known,' she said, 'you'd create something out of the top drawer, Helene dear. That's a simply *glorious* gown. Do you not agree, my lord?'

'I always agree with you, dear sister-in-law,' he replied, gazing abstractedly over my shoulder into the assembly. 'Miss Follet is indeed a glorious creature.'

The last remark was made quietly as if half to himself and half to anyone who could catch the words and, as Cynthia's berry-eyes twinkled and widened, her husband drew her away with a hand on her elbow and a look of sheer mischief.

'A game of faro, m'dear, and perhaps a glass of iced water after the shock of hearing Burl wax lyrical, eh? Come, my love. It may be catching.' He winked at me, in parting.

'Shall we see you at supper?' I said.

'Of course. I'm already starving.' Cynthia laughed, moving off.

'I think you should be careful,' I murmured to Winterson.

'Of what?'

'Of where you direct your dry wit, my lord. Your sister-in-law is a dear lady and quite likely to take you seriously.'

'And you do not, Miss Follet?'

'I'm learning how to tell when you're talking moonshine.'

'Then keep learning. I was not talking moonshine, and that was not an example of what you choose to call my dry wit. And you had better refrain from talking cant while you're wearing that dress. The two don't mix. Come over here and watch the dancing for a while.' Squeezing my arm with his, he led me through the throng, nodding and smiling at friends till we stood behind the dancers. At the far end of the ballroom, the orchestra swayed and gently perspired, flanked by marbled pillars, the gold-topped Corinthian capitals of which clung to each side of the creamy-green room, lit by sparkling chandeliers that hung in crystal tiers above the moving pattern of figures.

Several times I moved away from him, but always found that he had come to rejoin me, and for an hour or so we were engaged in conversation with friends who accepted that neither of us intended to dance. But the talk returned again and again to the severe flooding that had devastated acres of good arable land, drowned many animals, ruined stores of hay and cut off entire villages for the second time in a month. The Vale of York with its wide river was now a disaster area, leaving few families untouched by its broken banks.

Prue, I was sure, would be happy to hear the compliments about the dress for, although it was not quite the done thing to comment, northern folk have fewer scruples about making known their likes and dislikes or issuing praise where they think it due. I didn't mind, sure we'd be seeing some new customers within the next week or two.

There was one, of course, whose compliments were less than direct. Lady Veronique Slatterly, looking like an overblown peony in a bright pink frilly creation and too much jewellery, wished to know more about the black lace fan. 'Now where on *earth* did you find that?' she said, looking me over as if I'd got it all wrong. 'It looks Parisian to me.'

'I didn't find it,' I said. 'It was given to me by my cousin Pierre. And it *is* Parisian.'

'Oh,' she said, looking dubious. 'You actually have French relatives, do you? I thought perhaps you used the name Follet only for professional purposes.' She glanced up at Winterson, who stepped in with an unexpected contribution.

'Miss Follet has no need of an assumed name. We met Monsieur Pierre Follet in York only a week ago, a generous man of about my own years, good looking, good breeding, still unattached and wealthy. Shall we introduce him to you, Veronique?'

Before she could hide it, a look passed across her eyes like a cloud that casts shadows across a hillside and moves on, and I sensed a desperation and a kind of loneliness that stems from having everything except the thing she most wants. Winterson's glib offer had hurt her, as did the patronising smiles of the group and, for once, she was stuck for an answer.

I put on my school-ma'am voice. 'If anyone offered to present such a paragon to me on the assumption that I would drop my handkerchief at any niffy-naffy fellow still on the shelf, and a Frenchman too, I would say he had maggots in his head, my lord. I'm sure Veronique would say the same. We're both more than capable of finding our own beaux, are we not?' I said, turning to her and placing my fingertips upon her arm.

'Yes,' she whispered. 'Indeed we are.' Her colour had heightened, and I felt she was close to tears.

I could not leave it at that. 'Shall we leave these coxcombs to their racing talk and repair to the supper room?' I said. 'I have an appetite.'

She nodded and turned away, missing my frown at Winterson and the hand I laid on his arm to prevent him from following.

Looking back over the past days, I could see how his recent account of Veronique's circumstances had affected the way I was beginning to respond to her, for I accepted his word that they had never been lovers, despite her wanting it to be so. Indeed, he had confirmed what his feelings were only a moment ago in that insensitive remark as he rushed to my defence with an unnecessary put-down. Perhaps, I thought, Veronique's intention had been merely to keep me on my toes with a few needling comments but, whatever the truth of the matter, she had revealed to me that there was more to her than the shallow golden-dolly. Here was a rather sad young woman searching for something that life was not providing her with. My theory, such as it was, was further strengthened in the supper room where we met Medworth and Cynthia Monkton still eating and socialising.

Standing sideways on to a lady dressed in violet and silver, Cynthia's profile accentuated her newly rounded shape clearly. Unlike others, she would never have attempted to disguise it. There was no need for introductions for they had met Veronique on many occasions at Abbots Mere, but her astonished glance at Cynthia's bulge brought back the cloud of discontent to her eyes that disappeared almost as quickly as before and, instead of the usual congratulations, she dithered as I myself had done only a few days earlier. Quickly averting her eyes, she stuttered something about the warmth, accepted a glass of punch from Medworth and gulped it down rather too quickly, pressing one hand beneath her bosom.

After some chatter, I drew Veronique aside in the hope that we might sit and talk together as friends, for once. But it was not to be, for we were joined by Winterson, who seemed determined to sit us down at a table and to share the food he had brought as if to make amends for his earlier tactlessness. If he saw anything unusual in our being together, he gave no sign of it.

Other things had begun to make more sense to me concerning Veronique's spite, her unconcealed jealousy of my position, especially while I'd been pregnant with Jamie. Did she share with me that yearning for a child? Had it become almost a sickness with her, as I well knew it could? Did she need some real friends? And would she accept me as one?

'I think,' I said to Winterson when she had been invited to dance, 'you might try a little more kindness. It wouldn't hurt, surely?'

Sitting back into the gilded chair, he crossed his long legs and treated me to one of those superior looks that tell a woman he'll humour her at the price of a brief skirmish. His eyes narrowed, cynical, amused, as if he enjoyed having to defend himself. 'Hurt whom?' he said.

'You. A gentle answer turneth away wrath, you know.'

Heads turned in our direction as he laughed out loud. 'Oh, don't go all biblical on me, Miss Follet,' he grinned. 'But to answer your question, yes, it *would* hurt, eventually. Give some people an inch and they'll take a yard. You be kind to the lady if you wish. It's in your nature. But if I did the same, she'd get the wrong end of the stick all over again, just when I think she's started to see that it's you I want, not her.'

'I shall pay no attention to that last remark.'

'Do as you please. It's true. I only dole out kindness as I do to my horses, as an inducement for something I want or as a reward for something I'm given, not as largesse to those who'd take advantage, as she most certainly would. So there you have it.'

It was not so much the sentiment alone that shocked me, for that was a typical response from the wealthy land-owning aristocracy who rarely saw the need to part with anything unless there was a sound reason for it. But to apply that to friendship did strike me as odd. 'Well,' I said, 'I never heard anything quite as cynical as that in all my born days, my lord. So am I to take it that the only reason you've ever had to offer *me* kindness is because you expected something in return? Never kindness for its own sake?'

'For both reasons I've just stated. You have what I want, and you've given me something too.'

'So if that were not the case, I take it you would have no other reason to offer me kindness.'

'But it *is* the case, Miss Follet. I cannot imagine seeing you without wanting you, nor can I forget what you once gave me.'

'This conversation is shocking,' I whispered, pushing it to its limits. 'And what happens when…if… you get what you want? You revert to unkindness, do you? Thank you for the warning.'

'No. When I've got what I want, I shall want more. I shall never stop wanting more.'

'How do you know that?'

'How do I know, woman? Do you need to ask? We—'

'Shh! No, don't say it. I *don't* need to ask. Nor do I need to ask you about charity, or compassion, or pity. Clearly you don't deal in those, either.'

'If we're talking about our mutual friend again,

charity she gets from her father by the cartload, compassion is for women to give, and pity she'd not thank you for. Or me. I know what she needs, and she's looking in the wrong direction for it. I offered to help, just now.'

'Yes, by stepping on her pride, before her friends. By being facetious at my expense. That was not well done, my lord,' I said, angrily. 'She was hurt by it. You understand little of women's needs, in spite of what you say.'

His reply came after a long silence during which he watched my anger simmer and my eyes avoid his. 'I understand your needs,' he said, softly. 'But I was taken once before in a direction I didn't want to go, and I'll be damned if I'll do it again. Yes, I have grown cynical, and perhaps unkind too. And I could have taken her at any time these last six years, Miss Follet, and landed myself high and dry for my kindness. For that's all it would've been.'

'I didn't mean that sort of kindness,' I said. 'And what do you mean about a direction you didn't want to go?'

'Remind me to tell you one day. It's a long story.'

I knew that it concerned me, but I would probe no further. 'I think,' I said, 'that we are talking about two different things. A woman's view of kindness has other connotations. Men calculate the cost beforehand. Women calculate afterwards, if at all.'

'By which time it's usually too late.'

'Yes. That's the nature of it.'

The strains of a gavotte from the ballroom signalled the end of the interval and our eyes held, in remembrance of another time when we had lost ourselves in our own and each other's needs as if differences did not exist. He had become hardened, unsympathetic, and I had grown wary and resentful, and now we needed to find a way of moving on without causing more pain.

'Dance with me,' he whispered.

My eyes must have reflected my doubts, but he did not accept my refusal. Standing abruptly, he held out a hand and raised me to my feet, leading me like a sleep-walker into the ballroom where we joined the end of the line, moving into the steps as we went, turning, parting, closing, balancing.

If there were stares of disapproval, neither of us noticed, only the slow and stately steps that moved us apart and together again, our bodies and hands just touching, like those six years condensed into six minutes. His eyes were brazen with desire, and mine were speaking of I know not what, except too much of my feelings. He was a superb dancer, bending and graceful, concentrating totally on his partner as if she were the only one, while other dancers glanced through their eyelashes and turned pinkish after being held by him. I knew then that I was losing control, that I was showing him what was in my secret heart because, with his outspoken talk of wanting me, he had found a way in.

The slow seductive ritual ended and, after that, we seemed to be marking time until we could catch a mutual signal to end the charade and go home. We talked again with friends, we drank more punch and ate more apple pie and cream, we laughed at poor jokes and came together again with Medworth and his fecund wife, and the desire to be like her in that one respect burgeoned within me again, as I believe it had with

Veronique too. Inside me, I quivered and sobbed with the effort of constraint while outwardly I displayed the ice-cool front that deceived everyone. Everyone, I think, except him.

Finally, when my almost frantic glance connected with his lazy blink, he made our excuses, found my cloak and his hat, and carried me over the muddy cobbles to my home, ignoring the smiles and stares of those who passed by. His taciturn silence warned me of what was on his mind, but it was on mine too, and past the stage of discussion.

'Lock the door and go to bed,' I told the astonished footman.

'Yes, ma'am.'

Thinking I would be late, I had told Debbie not to wait up, but she had left a single candle burning in my room where chocolate-brown shadows wrapped us in a blanket as dark as the lust that spilled over, even before we had pressed the door closed with our bodies, our mouths and hands already seeking. The room was warmed by a low fire, but neither of us noticed it in the heat of our desire, in the relief of being alone with our craving where no polite preliminaries were expected.

I have no notion how long before we paused, but by then his hands were slipping softly over my gown, his mouth lifting from my bare shoulder to whisper commands against my face, and I knew by his tone not to expect the same restraint this time from one who had waited over-long for what he wanted. I would not plead for either gentleness or consideration after my own enforced celibacy, for I was no inexperienced girl with unrealistic dreams of tenderly sighing lovers. The desires of my heart owed nothing to all that.

My expectations were not far wrong.

'Take it off,' he growled.

'Help me.' I was breathless, trembling.

'Where...how?'

'At the back. Hooks and eyes. And a tape inside.'

Turning me round, he snapped the fastenings apart like the rattle of a drum, sliding it off my shoulders and over my feet, flinging aside my work of one week while shaking off his own tailcoat to keep it company. I have never in my life seen a man remove his own tailcoat so quickly.

I stood with my palms pressed to my breasts, a natural reaction, in the circumstances. But he took my wrists and slowly eased them apart, holding them wide against the door panel, and I could not help but turn my head aside as he leaned away to scrutinise my body, as a sculptor would. My eyes closed, and his lips awakened my breasts to his warm hungry wanderings until they closed over the nipples, engorging them, forcing a cry from deep in my throat.

'Untie my cravat,' he whispered.

'Let me go, then.'

His hands needed that excuse to explore my waist and hips, caressing while I struggled blindly with the knot at his throat. Eventually, my fumblings produced an end, which he pulled, throwing the long thing on to the growing heap with a laugh before taking my mouth in a kiss that made me reel, reminding me again of his words earlier that evening, uncompromising, almost vengeful. 'Look at me, Helene,' he whispered to my closed eyes.

High up on the chest the candle flame wavered beside us, illuminating his face like the setting sun on coastal rocks, deep shadows and rugged surfaces sloping to granite throat and shoulders. His eyes were more intense than ever I'd seen them, but when had he ever allowed me to see what he was thinking, until now?

'Don't hate me for this, as you did before,' he said. 'You were willing then, and you are willing now. But don't reward me with your hate.'

'I don't hate you,' I replied, taking his face between my hands. 'I'm being given the choice, this time. That's all I ask, to be given the right to choose. This night, I've chosen to take whatever you have to give, kindly or not, and to give as much in return. I shall not hate you for that.'

'Then that's all I dare hope for, sweetheart,' he said, blending the last word seamlessly into a searing kiss that sent me spinning into another kind of darkness. I felt myself being carried and laid upon the cool sheets of my bed where the long curtains blocked out the wavering light, but not the sight of a broad torso being revealed, like the muscle-bound marble of a Greek god. He was more perfect than my imagination had drawn him, more gracefully vigorous in movement, his bared legs more robust, his back rippling with manly strength, his deep chest just as my fingers remembered it, wide and downy in the centre. Half-intoxicated, I watched him blow out the candle flame, heard his soft movements, felt the mattress dip and then the wonderful soft warmth of him, setting me on fire with his first touch.

Somewhere at the back of my mind, I wondered if

he might intentionally be recreating the sightless sound-
less anonymity of that first time when our senses had
blended on another level. On that occasion, I recalled,
I had tried to fight him off, though not with half the
effort I might have done. Then, he had gentled me and
led me, half-swooning, into hours of loving that had
ebbed and flowed on a tide of sensations, dazzling and
seducing me with skilful wooing. He had been passionate then, but I had known nothing of his reasons
except, perhaps, as a solace for my unhappiness. I learnt
that it was not the case.

This time, knowing him just a little better, knowing
myself even more, my desire for him had grown so
great that I was ready to close my mind and to respond
without the restraints of reason or preference. Even ungentleness, I felt, would be preferable to the last four
years of emptiness.

His hand swept over me from throat to groin and my
body responded like a wild thing, uncontrolled, fiercely
demanding the attention it had lacked, arching into him
to know the touch of his skin upon every surface. My
lips opened upon his face to feel with my teeth and
tongue, to fill all my senses with his taste and scent. My
fingers raked deep into his hair, letting the thick silk slip
through them like water, and my thighs yearned and
opened for him as his kisses reached my throat.

He made me wait, holding my pestering hands away
with a deep laugh. 'Not yet, my beauty. Not yet,' he
whispered. Tracking downwards, he nudged and licked,
knowing that I would soften and wait, though I doubt
he knew how his leisurely suckling would make me
weep, and beg him to take me. He changed to the other

breast, teasing the deserted one with tenderly milking fingers. But I could bear it no longer, letting out the wail held too long in my lungs. 'Burl…please!'

As if he'd been waiting only to hear me call his name, he placed an arm beneath my hips, holding me as he'd done that first time to feel the hard throbbing length of him before slipping wetly inside, dilating me with each slow and powerful thrust that changed my tears to panting sighs and moans of ecstasy. Then, I was neither Helen nor Helene, but the primitive spirit of womanhood, earth and growing things. My womb was greedy for him, inviting and fruitful. My hands caressed, urging on his teeming virility. He was everything I remembered. And more.

I think we had both expected…wanted…it to last longer, but we had failed to take into account the tensions of the evening and all that had gone before under cover of our animosity. Neither of us could delay the growing thunder that roared through our beautiful rhythm, and Burl's response owed something to that ungentleness I'd been prepared for which, when it came, brought quivers of delight from deep down in my roots.

'Sweetheart…hold on!' he gasped, thinking that I might protest.

My fingers dug into his back as he bent deeper into me, though I had not intended the damage to his skin to be as noticeable as it was, later. 'Yes,' I told him, 'yes…oh, yes! Go on!' Flying along with my body, my mind rode the storm, plunging and surfacing, clinging to the calm that followed, floating with him upon that delicious pulsing beat that always fades too soon.

Like babes, we slept in each other's arms, spooning

back to front with his hand between my breasts and his face in my loosened hair and a tangle of pearls. Hours later, I think, I woke to hear the wind howl and gust at the windows, to feel a warm body at my back just as it had been that first time. His hand was stroking my thigh, slipping down between them, fondling.

We might have recreated that original scene, but now we were strangers no more, our appetites renewed by sleep and no impediments of kinship to add guilt. He must have been awake some time for he was impatient, already pulling me roughly under him without preamble. I felt justified in making a sharp protest, feeling that some wooing would not come amiss at this stage, even from a lover hungry for consummation. So I bit the nearest part of him, which was his chin, making him rear back and give me a chance to roll away, squirming and flailing my arms, doing no damage whatever.

Following me across the bed, he swung his feet to the floor with a purposeful thud, swept me round by the legs to face him and placed himself between them, quite out of reach of my arms. Until then, I must admit it had not occurred to me that there were other ways of doing this, but he taught me something that night about how, if lovers are of the same mind, enjoyment can be taken how, when and where they will.

Naturally, I refused to make it easy for him at first, protesting that a February night calls for some form of covering if one is not to suffer from exposure. But that problem was soon solved and my protests curtailed, for it was the most exciting and unique experience that ended very suddenly in an explosion that left us both

gasping and laughing. He pulled me upright, cradling
and rocking me while he knelt between my knees with
his head on my breast and my hair covering his face.
'My fierce beauty,' he whispered. 'I think I can just
about handle you. Eh, lass? After a few battle scars.'

'Brute,' I murmured. 'Mannerless brute.'

His arms tightened, and I felt the deep chuckle
within his chest.

But I was far from serious, for laughter was also new
to me in this context. It had never been a laughing
matter with his brother, a solemn, silent and usually
hasty affair, more like, with politeness and reserve
followed by instant sleep, no talk, no aftercare, no
banter, compliments or approval. Now, in the space of
one night, I had wept and laughed, retaliated with my
own kind of manhandling, and experienced more joy
and pleasure than in all those years as Linas's mistress.

Inevitably, in the langour that follows exhaustion,
there was teasing mixed with the adulation; accusations from me of smugness, counter-accusations from
him of impetuosity, then the half-expected mention of
marriage which, he suggested, would tame me. Another
bairn was what I needed, he said, yawning and pulling
my hips closer to his.

We lay together, wrapped against the howling gale,
me with my face beneath his chin. 'Is that what this is
all about?' I said. 'Getting me with child again?'

'You are remarkably innocent, Miss Follet. What
did you *think* this was all about? Not for our mutual enjoyment, surely?'

'You know what I mean. This night. Coercion, is it?'

'Don't spoil it, sweetheart.'

'All right. I agreed not to blame you. So three months from now I'll ask you again.'

'You won't need to. Three months from now you'll be my wife.'

'No, I won't.'

'Little goose. Go to sleep.'

I did not sleep immediately, as he did, but lay thinking how easy it had been for me to overturn all my intentions to keep him at a distance. Now, despite my impassioned contradiction, I knew that I was committed, that it was only a matter of time before I would be obliged to agree to his proposal, if one could call it that. The only card I had left to play concerned the timing, for I was sure that tonight's loving would be as potent as the last. Well, I would make the next few months spread out until I could keep him guessing no longer, having little reason to agree with him there and then.

Other concerns plagued me too. Although I realised that women married knowing much less about their husbands than I did about Burl Winterson, it was what I *knew* about him that made me think I was heading for disaster. The evening's talk about the way he limited his kindnesses should not have surprised me as it did, for until recently his uninterest in me had been a prime example of it, as had his visit to me that one night. He had wanted something, and got it. Now, he wanted Jamie and me to make an instant family, hence the sudden revival of interest of which this lovemaking was a part. He had admitted it without batting an eyelid. Was I supposed to feel flattered? Gratified? Piqued? Insulted? Would it all grind to a halt when it was accomplished, or would he keep on wanting more of me, as he'd said? It was a gamble, but was I really in a position to care as much as I did? If I had cared less for him, perhaps I would have reached a decision more easily.

The following morning I was woken before Jamie's habitual assault by a large figure in dark silhouette whose arms were braced on each side of me, his voice softly whispering. 'I don't want to leave you without a word, sweetheart, as I did before,' he was saying. 'Wake up and listen.' He was dressed and ready to go.

'Mmm? Yes?'

'I must go. My parents are at Abbots Mere and I want to be there before they're up. I'll send a carriage for you and Jamie.'

'No need. I can drive the phaeton.'

'It's blowing a gale. You can't ride out in this.'

'But I must go to Prue's first.'

'On a Sunday? Why?'

'She's in a fix. Both her parents have the dysentry.'

'For pity's sake, lass, keep away, then. It's contagious.'

'I must go. I shall not get too close.'

'Send one of the servants. Please. Think of Jamie.'

'Yes, if you insist. I'll send someone else.'

'Promise?'

'I promise. I'll be ready by mid-day.'

'Good. Wrap up warm. D'ye want to stay overnight?'

I smiled. 'Thank you, but no. I must be at the shop early tomorrow.'

His nod was curt, but understanding. For a short separation, his kiss was long and deep, and I felt my body stirring even before it was awake.

Moments later, Jamie came to join me, as usual. 'The bed's nice and warm, Mama,' he said, snuggling up. 'Did Debbie sleep with you?'

'No, darling. We're going to have lunch with Uncle Burl today.'

'Ooh, goodie! I wish Uncaburl was my papa. Shall we ask him?'

'No, darling. Not yet. It's too soon after Papa went, you see. We shall have to be content to have Uncle Burl as your guardian for a while. That's almost the same thing.'

'But I want to live with Uncaburl, Mama, like Claude lives with his papa. Claude's friend says I haven't got a papa.'

I could feel the little fellow's hurt and bewilderment. 'I'm sure Claude's friend didn't mean to be so ill mannered,' I whispered, stroking his dark curls. 'Perhaps he doesn't understand.'

'He does, Mama. He said I never had one. He said you were not Papa's wife. You were, weren't you, Mama?'

'It's no business of Claude's friend whether people's parents are married or not. If he mentions it again, I shall speak to Uncle Medworth.'

'Uncamedith knows.'

'He knows? About the rudeness? What did he say?'

'Said he had more 'portant things to think about.'

Chapter Ten

Much as I disliked sending a deputy to see how Prue and her parents were, I felt obliged to keep my promise, if only to avoid exposing Jamie to the infection, even at second hand. Debbie had no fear of catching anything, she assured me, though I insisted she tie a scarf over her face before she left the house. Having delivered the basket of food, she was back home inside the hour with the news that the old couple were still very poorly, the various potions having made little difference. Their growing weakness was a cause of serious worry, but Prue, she said, was managing well enough.

I had agreed to be ready for Winterson's coach by noon, and it was my desire not to disappoint Jamie or to keep the coachman and his horses waiting in the pelting rain that prevented me from listening to my conscience. Prue needed a doctor, yet I told myself that one more day might see an improvement. So it was with the firm intention of sending my own Dr Biggs round there first thing in the morning that I set off with Jamie and

Mrs Goode for Sunday lunch at Abbots Mere along roads that were, in parts, axle deep in water.

Jamie had no trouble pretending he was sailing a boat through lanes and past cottages while the rain clattered incessantly upon the roof of the coach and bounced off the horses' backs. Branches had been brought down during the night, and every dip of the land was reduced to a lake where seagulls wheeled, reflecting the leaden sky and rippled by the wind.

By contrast, Abbots Mere was a warm haven lit by oil lamps, candelabra and blazing log fires, with the tantalising aroma of roast beef and Yorkshire puddings reaching the stone-paved hall. The sound of laughter reached us too, and I felt the familiar shiver of apprehension before going in to meet Winterson's parents for the first time since the funeral.

I had taken care to dress appropriately in a charcoal-grey silk velvet sleeveless pelisse over a long-sleeved gown of silver grey sarsenet. No jewellery. No ornament. My hair tied up with black satin ribbons that hung down my back. Nothing to show how I felt after a night spent in the arms of their eldest son so soon after his twin's death. Nothing to betray the hypocrisy, either.

'You look beautiful, Miss Follet,' Winterson whispered. 'Are you well?'

I knew what he was asking. 'Yes, my lord, I thank you,' I replied demurely. 'I am indeed well, if a little fatigued.'

'Really?' he said. His eyes laughed into mine. 'Oh, dear. Unaccustomed exercise, is it?'

'Shh!' I said. 'Jamie dear, here's Claude come to find you.'

I followed on behind, using Jamie to interrupt the

conversation quite naturally before his grandparents turned to greet me. Not that they were in any sense an awe-inspiring couple. Far from it. But there had once been a reserve in their manner towards me, as mistress instead of wife, that had only recently been replaced by a genuine warmth and, I think, with some admiration and gratitude for my dedication to their son. According to him, they had been more than relieved by the appearance of a grandson, which had perhaps worked in my favour too, and now they had smiles for me as well as for Jamie.

Lord and Lady Stillingfleete were a handsome couple. He had been a major in a top cavalry regiment when he'd married Lady Frances Milton, the celebrated beauty. She was still lovely, stately, slender and white-haired with particularly brilliant dark brown eyes able to convey in one glance the precise degree of her approval. Although I had now no need to doubt that, I could not help but wonder if those discerning eyes would see behind my Sunday face to the previous night's lust that had spilled out with an unstoppable energy, or the tell-tale signs that might still linger upon me, somewhere. I hitched up the fur-trimmed collar of my pelisse to reach my earlobes, just in case, then wished I had not for, on rising from my curtsy, I saw Lord Stillingfleete's eyes leave his son's and return to mine. 'Miss Follet, come to the fire, m'dear,' he said, and I knew that he had interpreted the gesture correctly.

Heaven knows, I'd had plenty of practice, but I would never have made a first-rate actress. I did not go to the fire, but to Medworth and Cynthia, hiding my blush in their greeting and the duet of chatter about the perilous journey from Osbaldwick, all the while aware of how the grandparents watched my Jamie like a pair of eagles, linking his dark good looks to their eldest son, as anyone must. They had not seen him for several months, and he had changed with each passing week. Their expressions, shifting from child to father, were easy to read, and the realisation seemed to catch them unawares in a moment of rigidity. Immediately, they recovered themselves, transferring some of their attention to little Claude, who was attempting to ride one of Winterson's unwilling wolfhounds. To my mind, the child needed a firmer hand than Medworth's, who appeared to find something to applaud in every silly thing his son did.

Winterson lifted him off and dismissed the hounds from the room with one word, for Claude was over-weight as well as over-indulged. Fortunately, the youngest one had been left at home, or we might have been treated to more bids for attention.

In some ways, the Sunday lunch was an ordeal that demanded a greater-than-usual effort on my part. Winterson's family were never difficult to converse with, but I found myself having to work hard to keep my thoughts on track when my eyes were drawn like magnets to the one for whom I hungered much more than roast beef or pheasant, salmon or winter veg-etables. Having given no thought to how I might feel if that solo night should ever be repeated—for I had not believed it would—I was confused by the meld of emotions and by the way my body had not recovered from the hours of arousal after so many years of neglect. No matter how I tried to hold them back, the memories of his magnificent body lying warm upon me blanked out the middles and ends of so many of my sentences that it began to look as if I might be sickening for something. More than once did Winterson come to my rescue, smiling at my dreaminess and reading my eyes like a book.

Unusually, the children were allowed to eat at the table with the adults, a treat I approved of on occasions like this. It was gratifying to see how well my Jamie behaved compared to Claude, who messed about with his food and kept his mama so completely occupied with him that she was scarce able to eat her own lunch. Medworth seemed totally unaware of any problem.

Apple pie, creamy rice pudding with nutmeg, and spotted dick with custard was the perfect conclusion to a family meal on a day of such darkness and unrelenting rain, though we sat in the rosy glow of a fire that filled the room with the sweet aroma of burning apple boughs.

'I had the men clearing the ditches when you were last here,' I heard Winterson telling his father, 'but the snow, then the floods have filled them up completely. Some of the fields will take months to recover.'

'Then you may have to reclaim more of your wasteland.'

The two men took their glasses of port to the long window that overlooked the flooded terrace. Beyond, the swollen river had lost its banks, rushing and seething like a brown menacing monster across the field.

'I've already decided on that,' Winterson replied. 'Do you care to come and see what I intend? The plans are in the study.'

'Aye. I'll come and tell ye where ye're going wrong, lad.'

They smiled and sauntered off, leaving Cynthia to sink deeply into one of the leather sofas and Lady Stillingfleete to do the same in a high-backed chair, already halfway to a siesta. True to her name, Mrs Goode had taken the boys into a window-seat where they lounged against her knees and the book she was reading to them, and I was left with Medworth, who was already fretting about being home in time for his evening service. Pulling out a wad of papers from his coat pocket, he noisily smoothed them out upon the table, pulled a candlestick forwards, and began to read his sermon to himself.

I moved away, relieved by the suspension of polite exchanges across the dining table that had covered every topic from food to floods, fashion to farming. I was not myself, I realised, nor would I ever be the same again. Riddled by conflicts, my life was changing like the landscape by forces outside my control, and I would have to heed my intractable head or my vanquished heart, neither of which was reliable.

I had not intended to follow the one who monopolised my thoughts, and certainly not to snoop, but the sound of his voice and the need to be near him drew me along the panelled passageway towards the oak-lined study where he daily met his steward and bailiff to plan the estate work. The door remained open wide enough for me to see a table covered with maps, and over by the window stood Winterson and his father with their backs to me, hands clasped behind, their shoulders almost touching.

Lord Stillingfleete was speaking with some emphasis. 'You'll have to marry her, Burl. Damn it lad, I'm not blaming you one bit. She's a high-flyer, but it's as plain as a pikestaff and it'll be even plainer as Jamie gets older. *Then* you'll have some explaining to do. Better to put things on a legal footing now than hang about for more years. What's stopping you?'

'*She* is, Father. She's bitter about what happened. Linas gave her a raw deal, you know, and it's going to take me some time to win her trust.'

'Well, I cannot insist on knowing what you and he agreed, for it's none of my business, but time is what you don't have, Burl. Do something about it before the gossip starts. If your mother and I can see it, so will others.'

'I am doing, sir. But she'll come to me in her own time, not mine.'

'She's in love with you. We can see that, too.'

'Yes, I believe she may be.'

'Isn't that enough? The lad needs a father more than a guardian.'

'Yes, sir. She knows that, too. Give me time to…'

They turned away and I had to step well back into the passage and retrace my steps while my guilty heart thudded an angry rhythm of its own. *She's in love with you… Isn't that enough?… You'll have to marry her, Burl.* Standing with my back pressed against the panelling, I could feel each heartbeat rebelling against everything the two of them had said. They had no conception of how things stood with me, nor how many shades of grey came between their black and white. To his father, the matter was simple: marry her before people start to talk. I could almost taste the perversity that rose into my mouth, ready to shout my objections. Well, at least he appeared to understand that I would marry in my own good time and in no one else's.

Making a slight sound, a cough and an exclamation about the chill, I once again approached the open door, tapped, and entered. With shoulders hunched, they were braced over the maps on the table, looking up in surprise and with some questioning in their eyes. Women rarely visited men's offices. 'May I come in?' I said. 'I don't mean to disturb you.'

'Of course,' Winterson said, smiling. 'I'm showing my father where the worst of the floods are.' With one finger he drew an oval around the river and its surrounding plains. 'It'll be weeks before we can plough these fields again, and we've lost acres of grazing before the land will recover.'

I peered at the areas shaded with grey, land belonging to the Abbots Mere estate, other fields shaded a darker grey presumably belonging to Lord Slatterly which Winterson had the use of. A large area to the east was enclosed by a wide red line. 'And that?' I said, knowing the answer.

Lord Stillingfleete replied. 'Foss Beck. Been wasted ever since I can remember. No one goes there. It's time it was looked at, Burl.'

'Yes, as soon as I can reach it I'll go there. We can't afford to hang on to unused land any longer. I believe there are some ruined buildings on it.'

'They'll have to be demolished. You could use the stone for barns.'

The shock in my voice made them both look sharply at me. 'You...you *own* this place...Foss Beck?' I said.

'It's been part of the estate for centuries. It was a thriving village once with its own manor house and a priest for the church, but I believe it was hit by the plague more than once, so that was the end of it. There must be quite a few fields worth reclaiming.'

'But surely, if it's deserted, it must have reverted to common land where anyone can—'

'Not anyone, Miss Follet,' said Lord Stillingfleete. 'That might have been the case if it had once been legal common, but it never was. Over the years we've turned a blind eye to some land that was less profitable, or inaccessible, but at times like this we have to work them and make them yield again. New methods, you know. Fertilisers, crop rotation, new hardier strains of wheat. And new sheep breeds, too. Burl needs to get his hands on it, especially after a winter like this.'

I was staggered. Numbed with shock. My family had lived there in hiding since I was fourteen, expecting to renovate the buildings, dragging every ounce of goodness from their small crofts, eking out an existence. Where would they live if the old house was levelled, their garden ploughed over? Ought I to expose them now, before it was too late? Should I reveal their reason for living there, and who it *really* was who had borne the Stillingfleete heir, a criminal's daughter whose relatives lived illegally on the Abbots Mere estate, her father buried there?

But the two of them bent to the map again, the query dealt with, and I could say nothing of my dread as a sickness filled my lungs, blotting out each panic-stricken response as it arose. I would have to go and tell my family immediately. They must be warned of what was about to happen to their livelihood.

Though the rain had not abated all day, we were back home on Blake Street before darkness fell completely. Winterson had found the chance to speak a few words with me alone and had demanded to know what ailed me. Was it fatigue, or something more?

No more than that, I lied, wondering how convinced he was. It seemed to satisfy him. He would be in town in a day or two, he said, and I think when he kissed me that he expected some pleasurable response rather than the vague nod that was all I could manage. Perhaps if his parents had not been staying, I might have told him what a catastrophe he was planning but, as it was, his fierce kiss was accompanied by the distant howls and screams of his over-tired nephew, reminding me of my promise to take Jamie to his birthday party on Tuesday. Straight away, I saw that I could make that the day for my visit to Foss Beck while Jamie and his nurse were at Osbaldwick, which was fortunately in the same direction.

As Medworth's carriage moved off, I made sure that Winterson knew about the invitation. 'See you on Tuesday,' I called, waving.

It took what remained of my dwindling resolution not to change my mind about staying at Abbots Mere overnight when I could think of little else but wanting him. But to have done so would have convinced his parents that Winterson had already taken Linas's place as my lover, which was certainly not the cut-and-dried case it would appear to be, especially when I'd told him only recently that I would not allow that to happen. Yet it had not taken him long to find a way round my objections, and the last thing I wanted was for Lord and Lady Stillingfleete to label me as fickle.

For his father to recommend to Winterson that he

should marry me, a mere milliner and mantua-maker, was in itself remarkable when the pedigree of future daughters-in-law must be well documented and above reproach. Nothing so lofty could be said of mine, unfortunately, although Jamie's appearance had certainly helped in that respect. For one thing, he was the Stillingfleete heir and, for another, he was unmistakably Burl's offspring rather than Linas's, a fact that was unlikely to be admitted, but which could certainly be ignored, once his parents married. And for that event, I felt no immediate obligation to comply, after the way I'd been used by them.

I slept alone, and fitfully, plotting the course of the previous night's lovemaking while posing a hundred questions that could be answered in multiples, some of them concerning the fate of my family, who deserved better than poverty and obscurity and, on my part, denial.

My first duty next morning was to visit Prue with Debbie, carrying armfuls of clean bedding and food. But it was a doctor they needed most, and I called upon my own man, Dr Biggs, bidding him return with me, which he did, shaking his bald head sadly at the emaciated old couple too weak to move, and at the mess caused by the flood water in which they were obliged to remain. With all the stubborn pride of old folk, they refused even to consider accepting my offer to have them at Blake Street. Between us, we did what we could for them, yet I felt I was paying the good doctor for little else but a potion to ease their pain and a prognosis of only a few days more.

In Prue's absence, the shop continued to function just as if she was there, for now we had gained a very presentable young apprentice who had taken on many of the daily chores that used up precious time. She was a neat and willing girl, glad of the chance to join our company and so, with Betty as deputy manager and myself to keep an eye on our list of patrons, new designs and accounts, we were able to fulfil all our orders to everyone's satisfaction.

That evening I called at Stonegate to order the phaeton and pair to be brought round to Blake Street early next morning, come rain or shine. I also bade Goody prepare for an overnight stay at Medworth's house, since I would be unable to collect Jamie from the party before dark. What a nuisance those short days were. But looking back on those decisions, I can see how unclearly I was thinking, how desperately I was trying to juggle my responsibilities, and how spineless I was being by not explaining to my child that I was going to see Nana Damzell yet again, without him. I even chose not to tell him that he'd be staying overnight at Osbaldwick, sure that, between them, Cynthia and Goody would fill the gap left my by absence. Yes, I admit it; I was afraid of provoking another tantrum. We have a saying, in Yorkshire: 'What the eye doesn't see, the heart won't grieve over.' Applied to Jamie, it was patently nonsensical.

Cynthia's colourful description of the floods between York and the little village of Osbaldwick was not, for once, as exaggerated as I had thought. Although not of the high-perch design, the body of my phaeton was set well above the large back wheels and yet, even at that elevation, the water came within an inch of the floorboard, the horses wading belly-high through flooded tracks. Unusually, Goody was heard to comment that, if dear Mr Monkton could have bestirred himself to send his carriage for us, we would not be subjected to such danger, all for a birthday party. Personally, I was relieved he had not, since I was carrying hidden supplies for my family at Foss Beck.

As soon as I could politely excuse myself from those gathered for the party, and with Jamie too occupied to notice, I went on my way eastwards out of Osbaldwick. Cynthia, so easy going, assured me that he and Mrs Goode were welcome to stay until I could collect them some time before dark the next day. However, not having ventured in this direction since the snowfall, I had not appreciated how serious the flooding was, kicking myself for not paying closer attention to Winterson's maps. For mile after mile I drove the phaeton through the flooded lanes, even the higher ground being thick with mud and rubble, the ruts made by other wheels being too deep to get out of.

I became increasingly concerned, for the skies darkened menacingly as rain began to sleet across the open moors, forcing the hardy sheep to huddle together for shelter. From rocky outcrops, water poured in angry brown torrents into deep gulleys, then across the track, the underground culverts being unable to cope with the volume. Then, and only then, did it occur to me that the usual dainty trickle of water at Foss Beck into the trout stream below would certainly now be as swollen as these.

I was right. The whole mercy mission was a complete disaster, for when at last I managed to reach

Foss Beck Manor, the house was up to its second storey in water, completely cut off from the world, and from me. My shouts to the boys had to be conducted across a new lake while I dripped with rain, the phaeton leaning into the mud, the horses exhausted. The news from my brothers was that Pierre had left them, gone who knew where, after angry words. My instructions to make Mother and her companions ready to leave as soon as I could get a boat to them were greeted not with thanks, but with caution, my brothers unable to agree with me that she would go anywhere, even with me. At that, I grew angry and yelled at them to insist, telling them that I would be back the next day, though heaven only knew how I'd get back home that night in those dreadful conditions.

My journey home was no better, for the dark was falling and the horses were unable to find the road in the deepening water and, when the phaeton jolted to a standstill with a lurch to one side, I knew that to walk the rest of the way was my only option. Shivering with the cold, I began to unbuckle the horses from the phaeton. Then, through the howl of the wind, I heard a shout that made them whinny in reply, my own reaction being both joyful and concerned at some gruff traveller's annoyance that my phaeton was in the way. No one would want to turn back or wrestle with a broken vehicle, having got so far. Paralysed with cold and wet, I stood with my ankles locked into the mud and my shoes buried somewhere behind me, my teeth chattering like castanets.

Flickering lamps appeared, a coach-width apart. Two

large horses loomed up with a dumpling-shaped coachman above them, with doors beyond that opened on both sides discharging men who called instructions and waded towards the horses as if this was all in a day's work. One tall familiar figure strode forwards out of the grey wetness, leaving a wake to wash against the banks. His arms reached out, ready to catch me. 'Hell!' he called.

Hell, or Helene? I wondered. Either would do.

'I'm s-s-stuck,' I gasped, flapping my arms to keep my balance.

Grim and gloriously handsome, with rain dripping from his hair and face, he caught my wrist, bending towards me and ducking his head under my captured arm. 'Right,' he said. 'I want you to lie over my shoulder…go on…bend…that's it. I'm going to pull.'

I thought he meant the arm held hard upon his chest, but then I felt my feet move through the mud and my body hoisted high into the wind where I hung over the swirling water like a sea bird, a very limp and emotional sea bird that mewed with relief to be wrapped untidily around the neck of its beloved. 'Burl,' I sobbed into his broad back, 'you came for me.'

'Yes, and the sooner you stop galloping over here like an angel of mercy, woman, the better it will be for all of us. How the devil did you think you were going to reach Foss Beck when it's under water?'

'You knew?'

'Of *course* I knew,' he snapped. 'It's my property and it's my business to know who lives on it. I'm not as nicked in the nob as all that. There.' He lowered me carefully to the ground. 'Stand there and wait.' Pulling a rug from the carriage, he shook it out and parcelled me securely inside it, lifting me up on to the seat where the hollow patter of rain made a welcome break from the squall outside.

'I don't think you're nicked in the nob,' I muttered.

'Then you should try thinking with your head instead of your heart, little fool, or I might be performing this wild goose chase once a month.' The door closed, and I was too exhausted to be affronted, to answer back, or even to think of a snappy reply.

As I saw it, I'd had little choice when to go, or by what method. As for the angel-of-mercy bit, that was what a man *would* think, especially one who sees a kindness as a chance to bargain. I lay there helplessly with my head on the velvet armrest, shivering and dizzy, half-listening to the comings and goings outside, the thud and splash of hooves as the horses were released.

He grunted and closed the door, then quickly opened it again to cover my muddy feet with the rug. 'Leave the phaeton,' I heard him call. 'We'll come back for it tomorrow. Come on, lads. Let's be away. Jump on.'

My deliverance was made all the sweeter when he climbed in, lifting me into his arms to hold me across him with my legs along the seat and my head resting against his wet greatcoat. 'I can do nothing about the wet,' he murmured, 'but I'm sorely tempted to beat the hell out of you, one day.'

'Please don't,' I whispered.

I felt his warm lips touch my forehead, then the softness of his handkerchief wiping my eyes and cheeks, the tightening of his arms to snuggle me closer to him. Rocked and lurched, my aching limbs succumbed to the warm dampness of his embrace while my mind wrestled weakly with an ever-growing mountain of problems. 'I have to collect Jamie from Osbaldwick,' I mumbled. Already my plans had become confused.

'No, you don't. Jamie is at home with Mrs Goode.'

'Home? How did he get there? Did Medworth…?'

'No. I took them. Then I set out to look for you. Don't you ever tell anyone where you're going these days?'

'I told cook we wouldn't be home for dinner.'

'Extremely thoughtful of you. But that's not quite the same, is it?'

'It's the best I could do. I didn't know you'd be at Claude's party too.'

'Just as well I was,' he muttered under his breath.

But I heard, and sensed that there was more to this than a kindly lift home for my son and his nurse. 'Why?' I said, raising my head. 'What's happened?'

'Nothing,' he said, pressing me back onto his chest. 'Jamie is perfectly safe at home, and probably fast asleep. As I suspect you would like to be.'

I sighed. If Jamie was safe, that was all I could ask for. I knew, however, that once I was home and dry, I would have some explaining to do, for this amazing man was not only Jamie's guardian, but mine too, and he was taking the role very seriously indeed.

I have no recollection how long it took us to reach York, though I realised it could not have been as long as the outward journey. The rain had stopped by the time we reached Blake Street, and it was the regular rumble of cobblestones under the wheels and the hard clop-clop of hooves that woke me to the clammy warmth of my situation. Never had I been so thankful to be home, to be ministered to by my maid and house-keeper, to bathe in a hot tub, dress in warm robes and then to partake of soup and rolls by the fireside with my feet tucked into my best fur muff, mostly for effect. My hair was left loose to dry, the rainwater having done it no harm and probably some good.

My Jamie was indeed sleeping soundly and, on careful inspection, showed no signs of injury. Neverthe-less, as I sipped at my soup, I questioned Mrs Goode about their few hours at Osbaldwick, expecting to get no less than the full unadulterated female version rather than Winterson's, which would probably not suit me half so well. He had promised to return in a couple of hours. There was no time to lose.

'No, ma'am,' said Mrs Goode as soon as the door closed behind the footman, 'it was not exactly a tantrum, but Jamie has a little temper, as we both know, and he's taken rather a strong dislike to Claude's little friend.'

I groaned. 'Oh, not the *friend* again. What was it this time?'

'The same insult as before, ma'am. Only this time, Jamie was not in a mood to ignore it. They were all chasing the ducks over by the mill-pond, with Mr Monkton and a friend of his standing nearby, talking. Then, before we knew it, the two boys were wrestling and pummelling, rolling straight into the pond where the reeds are. It's flooded, you see. Personally, I would not have let them anywhere near it.'

My soup spoon hit the dish with a clatter. 'Oh, no!'

'I'm afraid so, ma'am. Mr Monkton and his friend didn't even notice what was happening. But Lord Winterson had just arrived in his carriage. I think he was expecting to see you and take you back home,' she added, coyly. 'His three hounds raced across the field to the mill-pond and took a flying leap into the water. It was Jamie's shouts they heard, I think.'

I whispered from between my fingers. 'What then? Didn't Mr Monkton see *anything*?'

'No, ma'am. It was the wolfhounds the boys clung to. They're so strong. They pulled them to the edge, barking like mad, and Lord Winterson went running full tilt, and climbed down into the water and lifted them out. I was there by that time, and Mrs Monkton too. I'm to blame, ma'am. I ought to have been there with them.'

'No, my dear. Don't blame yourself. Not when other adults were there, on the spot. Was he very upset?'

'Jamie? Only a little, and not hurt. The other child was very frightened. Jamie told us in the coach what it was all about.'

'Ah. So Lord Winterson knows?'

'I felt it best to tell him of the first incident too. I hope I did the right thing, ma'am. Jamie was getting a bit mixed up about his parentage. Oh, dear,' she said, turning a rosy pink. 'I *do* beg your pardon.'

'No need, dear Goody,' I said. 'It is confusing for a three-year-old, particularly when someone comes along to challenge what he's been told. Did Mrs Monkton suggest you should go home?'

'Oh, no. It was Lord Winterson who said we should go. I think he was rather annoyed with Mr Monkton, and no one protested when we left, not even Jamie. And

I certainly didn't. What a chaotic household, begging your pardon again, ma'am.'

'So did Jamie's guardian take him to task for brawling in company?'

Goody's tight-lipped disapproval changed to a fleeting smile before her sober reply. 'Er…no, not exactly,' she said. 'But he *did* promise to teach him how to swim, in summer. And how to hit with the fist closed instead of open, tucking the thumb down.'

'How to *hit* someone? God's truth! What kind of a guardian is *that*?'

From the doorway, a deep voice replied. 'A useful one, I hope. I did knock, but you didn't hear.'

'Do come in, my lord,' I said. 'We were discussing the day's events.'

'Which is what I hope to do too.'

Mrs Goode rose and bobbed a curtsy. 'Good evening, my lord. Will you please excuse me, ma'am? I have things to attend to upstairs.'

'Indeed I will. Thank you for all your help. Goodnight.'

Typically discreet, she left us with a smile. Even though Winterson knew she was totally in my confidence, he closed the door behind her without suggesting that she might stay. 'Well,' he said. 'Two half-drowned Folletts in one day. That must be some kind of record. Do I get a medal?'

Chapter Eleven

The way he looked at me across the cosy parlour, arrogance spiced with a trace of uncertainty, I would have given him anything he asked. But he had told me to think with my head instead of my heart, and my reply was guarded, taking into account his request for rewards after a kindness done. 'Not a medal, but perhaps an hour of my company, my lord, for what it's worth. Will that do from one half-drowned Follet? That, and my thanks for the rescue? I've heard about the mill-pond incident, and I'm most truly grateful to you.'

With arms folded, he lounged against the door looking down his straight nose at me with eyes that roamed, halted, and roamed again, sparing me no little confusion. '*How* grateful?' he said.

Yes, anything he asked. 'Oh, dear,' I said, looking down at my hands. 'Are we to talk of rewards so soon? Did you ask Jamie, too?'

'No, he's too young. I prefer to ask his mother instead.'

My heart was misbehaving badly under his scrutiny.

He'd been to Stonegate to change his clothes and to clean up, for he was almost as soaked as I. Now, he was perfectly dressed in a mid-grey tailcoat of smooth superfine with an M-cut collar over a waistcoat, just showing, of silver cut-velvet. It shone like pearls when he moved. The broad shoulder upon which I'd been hoisted only hours before was now unblemished by the slightest wrinkle. His beautiful head appeared to be supported by the white folds of his cravat, and the dark hair showed ridges of dampness along finger-raked waves. He was, in fact, heart-stoppingly desirable. He was also in my room, alone with me, and expecting something.

'His mother,' I said, 'has been advised to use more common sense. Perhaps you could help her with that. Will you be seated, sir?'

'I hoped you'd ask me.'

'Forgive me. I've only just begun to thaw.'

He pushed himself off the door and came forwards, settling himself into the wing-chair that Mrs Goode had just vacated. 'So, if it's too soon to discuss rewards, Miss Follet, may I ask how you managed to reach your family at Foss Beck? Is your lady mother improving?'

'I didn't manage to see her. I didn't actually achieve anything I'd set out to achieve.'

'Which was?'

'You must be able to guess, after I'd heard how you intend to reclaim the site. If I'd known it was so badly flooded, I'd have taken help with me.'

'So why d'ya think I'd drawn a red line round it on the map?'

'Well, to mark it out for reclamation, I suppose.'

'Yes, when the floods subside. The red line enclosed the worst areas, to show my father which part is earmarked for the greatest attention.'

'Attention? You spoke of demolition as if no one lived there. If you knew my family lived there, why did you pretend not to?'

'Because, Miss Follet, I prefer my father not to know. Would you rather I told him? If I'd thought you intended to race there like a mad March hare without first discussing the problem with me, I'd have told you to wait till it was safe.'

'Much good the delay would have done when they're going to have to leave for one reason or another. The place is in a terrible state, and they're running short of food and fuel, animals drowned, hens stuck up on the roof. I promised my brothers I'd bring help tomorrow, so I *have* to make another attempt. Somehow. How long have you known?'

'About your family? Since your visit in the snow. I made enquiries. I knew someone was at Foss Beck, because my bailiff told me. He and my steward keep a close eye on all the estate.'

'My brothers intended to rebuild parts of it. They love the place.'

'Using the money from contraband?'

'Yes. They've saved and been thrifty. They work hard, too.'

'And the cousin, Pierre Follet? Is he to be rescued too?'

'Pierre has gone, so my brothers tell me.'

'Aah! Has he indeed? Where? Back to France?'

'Why do you say that?'

'I assumed, that's all.'

'I don't know. I shall find out when I get them here.'

'Where…here? In York? You mean, in this house?'

'Yes, if you'll allow it. It'll be a bit of a squash, but they'll be safe and dry, and well fed.'

'Tch! Angel of mercy on the rampage again?'

'I don't need your gibes, my lord. They're my family. We don't do rewards and bargains; we simply help each other for love's sake. You've done the same for yours.'

'Quite right, sweetheart. And I was not mocking you. Your principles are admirable. You put me to shame.'

Even so, I believed he *was* mocking me, but this was no time to make an issue of it when I needed his help.

'Would you care to tell me about them before we meet?' he said, gently.

'I can do better than that. If you were to help me rescue them tomorrow when you send men to retrieve the phaeton, you could meet them sooner.'

His promptness took me by surprise. 'That can be done. I will arrange to have them brought here, if that is what you wish.'

'Thank you. That would help. The floods are actually working in your favour, it seems. They've brought your plans forwards, haven't they?'

'Yes, that's about the size of it.'

'And since you have a policy of never doing anything for nothing, I suppose you'll expect them to pay you to be rescued.'

'You will be familiar, Miss Follet, with the Yorkshire adage, "Never do owt for nowt. And if tha ever does owt for nowt, do it for thi sen." Yes, I expect there'll be some kind of price to pay. After all, this is my house.'

'What kind of price do you have in mind, my lord?'

'I'll think of something. Leave it to me.'

'Gladly. But I hope it will be something they can afford. Once their livelihood is gone, they'll have few means, except for their savings.'

His fingertips pressed together, making a tall steeple. 'Then it will have to be something *you* can afford, won't it?' he said, quietly.

Inevitably, we had strayed on to dangerous ground. In a house of this size, it would be quite impossible for us all to live together for long, the three bedrooms being taken up by myself, Mrs Goode and Jamie, with servants' quarters for my cook, housekeeper, maid and footman, chambermaid and kitchen maid. My mother would need a room to share with her two old faithfuls, the two boys to share another. I had no idea where or how they would all fit in, unless I converted my parlour into a bedroom. But where was I going to find beds for them all? Where would I put all the stuff they would bring? If only Winterson would offer them the use of Stonegate. I could not ask him, but I needed more than a rescue for them. I needed another house.

'I don't suppose…?' I began, hesitantly.

'Yes?'

'That there's any chance…well…that they could be…er…re-housed somewhere? The boys are strong. They'll have to start earning. Somehow. I don't expect my mother to see the year out. She'll need my attention. Do you have a small property they could…er… borrow, until…?'

'Until?'

He was not about to make it easy for me. Why should

he? He had more than once suggested marriage and I had refused to consider it, expecting that he would keep trying. His father had urged him, only to be told that the final decision rested with me, to be made in my own time. Now, much sooner than I had intended, the time had come for me to offer myself as the price of my family's welfare. I would have to summon up the courage.

'Lord Winterson,' I said, watching his steepled fingers curl up cosily together, 'you once offered to marry me, for Jamie's sake. Do I take it that your offer still stands?'

'No,' he said, tonelessly.

'What?'

'I said no. I make no offer.'

'Oh, I see. Then you do not wish me to be your wife, after all.'

'I didn't say that.'

'Then what *did* you say?'

'I said that I make no offer, Miss Follet.'

'Isn't that the same thing?'

'Not at all. I have no objection to you making *me* an offer, nor does it stop me accepting it. After all, *you* are using marriage as a bargaining tool, are you not? So if you want that to be the price of my help to your family, then you must offer me that price and let us see if we can reach agreement.'

No doubt he caught something in my eye, some glance of controlled self-consciousness, for he continued before I could find a word to say. 'Yes, I know what you're thinking. You are recalling the time, only last weekend, when I said I shall never stop wanting you.

It's still true, but you must not confuse that sentiment with weakness. You see, you're just as bad as me when it comes to the price of a favour, are you not?'

'No,' I said, indignantly. 'We were talking then of kindnesses. Marriage is not a kindness.'

'You have experience of it, then?'

'No more than you, my lord.'

'Then we're both in the same wobbly boat. Do I take it that you're offering me your hand in marriage? Not for our own sakes, of course, but for more unselfish reasons.'

What deceits. What bickerings and bluff. Who did we hope to fool by this dissembling? I wondered. I adored him, and he must have known it, yet my pride was still unmended and I could not offer it to anyone in that condition. Only as an exchange of favours, so that we both knew what we were getting, this time. So that there was no talk of love, the superb abstract that cannot be weighed or valued. Nothing as fugitive or as fragile as love. No, nothing as dangerous as love that can be confused with so many other agonies. Yet there was a moment, a lull in the grand deception, when our eyes held as they had before, when our desires went naked and wanton into each other's souls, reaching in to dance madly, to mate, and to come as close to love as need be. His eyes darkened, and still I was too uncertain, too cautious to bare my heart to him in words.

'For those reasons, my lord, yes,' I lied. 'If you will find them somewhere suitable to live, with a patch of land where they can start again. They can stay with me until then, but I must keep my promise to rescue them tomorrow. Is it agreed between us?'

Leaning forward, he took both my trembling hands

into his. 'Jamie needs it. Your family needs it. What do *you* need, sweetheart? What is it you intend to withhold? What do you have left to hold on to except that hurt pride? Isn't it time you allowed me to fix it? Just remember this, that I may not know all there is to know about you, yet, I still know more than any other man exactly how that pride was damaged. And although it may be damaged, it's still in good working order. I will accept your offer, even on those terms. I will give them a place to live and make it habitable for them. I'll do whatever is necessary for their comfort. And for that, exactly what am I to expect?'

An end to this dreadful pretence, I wanted to cry, *for the pain of it is too terrible for me to bear much longer*. But how could I place my entire trust in such a man whose coldness had hurt me for so many years since that first meeting? Then, there was that one mad night. Then more bewildering indifference. And now this. What was I to believe? What could he expect from me except the same, on a longer time-scale? Passionate nights with intervals of icy coolness that would be as difficult for him to understand as it had been for me? Yes, at one time a certain pretence would have been necessary, for Linas's sake. But surely…oh, *surely* there could have been something to keep my heart from breaking. Had he thought that Jamie was *all* I wanted?

My hesitation was too much for him, and I felt his hands tighten over mine before sliding up to grasp my elbows, pulling me to my feet that were still trapped inside my muff. His grip moved up, his thumbs cruelly hooked beneath my arms, pulling me up to his mouth like a child with a puppet. My body swayed and bent.

His voice was hoarse with emotion, almost angry.
'Then I'll tell you what I expect, shall I? I expect everything you gave my brother, and more. You'll be in
my bed each night and at my board by day. You'll be a
friend to my friends and a mother to my children, my
companion and helpmeet. In all things obedient. Now,
is that what you can offer me, or have I missed something out, Miss Follet?'

Nothing material, I wanted to say. Only the mention
of love, which apparently he did not expect. The bargain
had only been waiting to be made, but I had not thought
it would come like this, so prematurely. It was, after all,
only a few short weeks since we'd begun to communicate. But my precious family were all I had, and I was
responsible for them.

'Well?' he whispered. 'Second thoughts, is it?'

'No. That *is* what I'm offering. Just that.'

His eyes searched mine for doubts, but found none.
'Your family must mean much to you. Then we have a
deal.'

I would have said yes, spit on my palm and shook
hands on it as farmers do at market, signed something,
exchanged some small token. But in the blink of an eye
his mouth was upon mine, taking my breath away with
a kiss as fierce as any I'd ever received, a kiss of victory
and possession that I was helpless to soften in any way.
His arms encircled my waist and shoulders, pushing
my arm up to hold his head against me, cheek to cheek,
and I heard his breathy whisper past my ear. 'Mine.
Mine. You belong to *me*, Helene Follet. Me alone. I
have you at last, woman.'

It was the talk of envy, jealousy, rivalry, not the words

of love or desire. It seemed to be repayment time. Collecting the winnings after an all-night game and a too-long wait. Though he had mentioned my needs, I could not expect him to dwell on them when his own were so great.

If my mind began to seek provisos, it was too late, but I had made no mention of the business, or my need to supplement what Linas had once provided. Presumably there would be no need for that in the future. So I did not mention it. One thing at a time, my common sense told me. Surprisingly, what my heart told me was very similar. *Comfort him*, it said. *He needs your comfort, for his pain is just as great as yours. It's up to you to find out why.*

Without a shred of understanding, I cradled his head inside the garland of my arms and rocked him gently like a mother, fondling his cheek and earlobe with my lips as if I knew where all this was coming from. We had both done our best to give, and to take what we believed was our due, and now the time had come to comfort each other for the price we had agreed. There was still so much explaining to be done, so much that I did not know about this business, long-held misconceptions about the relationship between two brothers. He had accepted my offer without demur, but I could sense the pain. Perhaps he felt an improper urgency so soon after his twin's demise. Or was there something else? Now was not the time to ask, for we were both tired, especially me.

In more normal circumstances, I would have gone early to bed and slept like a child, but this was not normal, nor could I imagine being held in his arms without wanting to belong to him in every sense, exhausted or not. It was not that I wished to reward him for coming to my rescue, for agreeing to help my family, or for offering me lifelong security. Nothing like that. He would have sensed the difference between a payment and a demand, I know. So while I aroused him with my lips, my hands delved beneath his tailcoat to find the hard muscle-bound valley of his back and to pull his shirt out of his breeches for a more intimate contact with his skin. Shamelessly demanding, I was, flaunting my honesty.

There was no pretence with him, either. No mock surprise or prudish rebuke of my brazenness, but a deep gasp of excitement from his throat as he bent to pick me up and swing me into his arms, dipping me at the door so that I could open it. Across the hall and up the stairs with no one to witness the abduction, only Debbie emerged from somewhere to open and then to close my bedroom door behind us without a word.

Then, since I had initiated the undressing, he allowed me to act as his valet, though with more haste and less reverence than he was used to, and punctuated by my kisses to every newly exposed area I could reach. How can one describe the soft tang of male skin, the scent of masculine intentions, or the air that breathes sexuality, anticipation and mastery? I had not managed to disguise my love from his father, and apparently I had not done so from him, either. Yet while I indulged myself in this way, exploring and fondling his body by the light of the fire, even down to his toes, I sensed no complacency or conceit in him that the affair had gone so soon in his favour, but rather an appreciation of the gentle ministrations after my earlier indignation.

My own garments were loose and easily undone, quickly slipped off my shoulders as I unbuckled, unbuttoned and untied him from complicated flaps and folds. I think I was bared before he was, kissed at intervals and caressed constantly until, at last, we could no longer delay the pleasure of the full-length contact our bodies demanded. Lifting me again, he carried me across to the bed where, with my arms still around his neck, he repeated the words he'd spoken earlier. 'Mine. *Mine*. No going back, sweetheart.'

I had carried my own version of that sentiment, though now it was already too late to put it into practice. In my dreams of retribution, I had thought to withhold myself, to blow hot and cold, to confuse him with my inconsistency. That was before the reality of our last night together, and now this—it would take more strength than I had to play the coquette with him.

In deference to my nightmarish day and extreme tiredness, his loving was exquisitely tender and undemanding, full of sweetness when his lips brushed across my eyelids, when he told me I was all a man could desire and how I was all *he* had ever desired enough to want to marry. Which, of course, I had difficulty believing, since he had not desired me enough to pursue me all those years ago, but had let his brother take up the hunt. I let it go, for his lips and hands lured me into other more immediate responses, and I was discovering a new kind of enjoyment in being dog-tired and being made love to by a sympathetic lover. He knew exactly how to comfort me better than I knew how to comfort him, how to bring me with patience to a star-bursting climax before taking his own pleasure as the stars fell earthwards. He knew to wipe me down and attend to the ease of my weary frame and, in his arms, I fell asleep almost immediately while thinking how different again this was from any previous experience. I ought not to have compared them, I know, for therein lay the root of unfairness. But I did.

It was still pitch dark when we woke, simultaneously stirring in each other's embrace, entwining, hungry for more sensation, our mouths seeking through a screen of my hair. Full length I lay upon him with my tresses making a tent over his face. His hands cupped my behind, pulling me into position, then rolling with me so that, in one quick flip, I was beneath him, possessed again, mindless with excitement and still only half-awake. There was no long languorous preparation this time, more like that first unreal night at Abbots Mere when no word was spoken, when we came together countless times, insatiable and desperate for consolation. It was like that now, as if making up for time lost, as if to remind ourselves and each other, even in half-sleep, that we had made a pact that could not be broken. He was powerful and purposeful and I matched him, urging him with my hands and lifting my hips to him, revelling in the knowledge that he would still be with me in the morning, and every morning to come.

Afterwards, comforted, I wondered whether that would be the right time to confirm his father's opinion that I was in love with him. But he had not spoken of love, only desire, and my pride was, as he had said, still in good working order. Time enough for talk of love, I decided. There would be as many difficult days ahead as there had been in the past, and some riddles to be solved about the exact nature of Lord Winterson's conquest. About my family's future, I was not half so sure.

Our breakfast together, taken well before Jamie was astir, was served by my footman as if Lord Winterson's presence there was now a foregone conclusion.

'I shall not be taking you with me,' he said, scraping up the last crumb of scrambled egg from his plate.

'Was that to your satisfaction?' I said. 'Not quite the way your Mrs Adamson does it.'

'The company more than makes up for it. Did you hear what I said?'

'I heard. But I don't see how you can do it without me. My mother is hardly going to deliver herself into the hands of complete strangers with all her goods and chattels. I wouldn't.'

'No, I dare say you would not. But she's had time to prepare herself, and I'm not exactly a complete stranger. You must have mentioned me from time to time, and your brothers will surely persuade her to trust me. Anyway, you said she was ailing.'

'So you think she'll quit like a lamb? It would not do to underestimate my mother's fighting spirit, my lord.'

'Like mother, like daughter, then.' Even passing his coffee cup to me for a refill was done gracefully, with a slide of his eyes over me as I poured.

'Please let me come,' I said. 'The shop will look after itself.'

His hand closed softly over mine. 'I know,' he said. 'You are a model of efficiency, but how will you prepare to receive guests if you're not here? They'll need places to put their things, places to sleep, bedding, food, whatever. You're needed here, sweetheart. Give Jamie some jobs to do.'

'Jamie? What can *he* do?'

'More than you think. Let him help. He enjoys it.'

I frowned, not best pleased to be told how to mother the child I'd reared more or less alone for three years.

Ignoring the stony response, he continued. 'I've sent to Abbots Mere for all the men and carts, and a boat to get them across the water. They'll bring all we need to do the job. And a carriage for the ladies. I shall pick up your phaeton, too.'

'And check that the supplies are still in it, if you please.'

'I'll bring them back. Now, just trust me, will you? I have to go. I expect it will take all day. You'd better clear out some of those storerooms at the back of the house. We shall need them.'

'You'll be dining here, too?'

'Probably not. My parents are still at Abbots Mere, so I'd better go back. Will you miss me?'

'Yes,' I said, before I could think about it.

His hand squeezed and released me, sliding down my fingers and changing the direction of my breath. He could have taken me on the floor. Anywhere. I argued no more, for he was quite right. I was needed here. Jamie needed me, after a day apart. Prue needed me, particularly.

The rain had stopped in favour of blue sky and fluffy

clouds pushed by a stiff breeze, bringing some colour back into the day. Our bargain had changed me too, though it was hard to say how except that I had reached another turning point, this time more permanent than any before it. My mother would think it was love at last, and she'd be delighted. And I dare say we'd be able, without too much effort, to convince her that she was right.

What had happened, however, was too important to be filed tidily away in a back drawer of my mind while I took on the day's duties, and there were times when I ought not to have been staring blankly out of the bedroom window, or trying to part Jamie's thick waves on the wrong side of his head.

'Mama!' he protested, clutching at the comb. 'What on *earth* are you doing with me?'

Mrs Goode, watching the process, tipped her head to indicate the problem, but her smile caught Jamie's eye and their indulgence was like a warm hug. After that, there appeared to be a mutual understanding that the whole messy business of too many guests was rather beyond me and that they ought, out of kindness, to send me off on some less mind-taxing mission. Nana Damzell, said Jamie, should have his room, and he would sleep with Goody. And since the sacrifice meant so much to him, neither of us denied him. After a talk with Mrs Carson and Mrs Neape, my housekeeper and cook, I left to visit Prue whom I'd not seen since Monday.

Prue was not a demonstrative lady, but on this occasion she wept in my arms as I smoothed her back and tried to find some comforting words to say, which turned out to be very unoriginal. 'Dear…dear Prue,' I said. 'I'm so sorry. So very sorry. Is there anything I can do? There must be something?'

'No, you've done more than enough, Helene. But thank you,' she said, drawing away. 'They were both very peaceful at the end, thanks to your help. They're at rest now, thank God.'

'Still together, Prue,' I said, feeling the sting of conscience that I had not sent for the doctor sooner, when I ought to have done. Would it have made any difference? That was something we would never know.

'Mother first, then Pop. Within the hour. After forty-four years.'

'When will you…they…?'

'Day after tomorrow. St Thomas's at Osbaldwick. They were born in that village, christened and married there too. Always went to St Thomas's.'

'I didn't know that. Did Mr Monkton visit them, Prue?'

'Nay,' she said with a huff of disapproval. 'Not him. I sent a message, but he never came to see them. Too busy, I reckon. It's only two miles beyond Walmgate, but young curates have more interesting things to do than visit their dying parishoners, these days. The undertakers are making all the arrangements for me.'

'Let me pay for it, Prue. Please. I shall be there with you, and the staff, and I shall close the shop on Friday.'

'Yes, I'd like that. They'll be very proud, will Ma and Pop.' She blew her nose and straightened her white lace cap. 'They were so weak, you know.'

'Yes, love. Quite a few others have been taken in the same way.'

'Aye. It's been a wicked winter so far.'

I went straight from Lop Lane to the shop to inform the staff, and to warn them that on Friday we would all be attending the funeral. I stayed for an hour to design some morning gowns for Lady Mirfield's seventeen-year-old overweight daughter, then returned home to find the place in the process of being rearranged, adjusted and turned upside down to find enough basic requirements for the invasion. What I had just heard about Medworth Monkton's indifference to Prue's request had both puzzled and shocked me, having always believed him to be the most diligent of curates. Could it have been Claude's birthday party that had prevented him? If not that, then what?

I had not been home above half an hour, spent stuffing pillows into cotton cases, when my footman came to say that Mr Medworth Monkton was downstairs in the drawing room, hoping for a few words with me. Which rather amazed me, considering that, in my mind, I had just been having a few well-chosen words with *him* about his parochial duties.

As always, his greeting was courteous and friendly towards me, despite my unorthodox links to his family. He had never been judgemental. In fact, if I were to criticise him at all, it would be on his ambivalence on matters which one might expect a man of God to have some kind of opinion. Sitting on the fence is all very well, and comfortable, but for those of us who welcome some direction from time to time, Medworth was probably not the one to ask. Not a highly practical man either, regardless of the medley of livestock he kept. Apart from being a good husband and a friendly scholarly curate, it was hard to know what else he was.

His bow was meticulous, his acceptance of a seat precisely timed to my being seated, his coat and breeches surprisingly free of animal hairs that show up so well on black. *His* hair, however, was as unruly as ever. Yet in the strong low winter light, I recognised a handsomeness akin to his brother's in the distinct jaw and nose that I had not been aware of before.

'Are you in town on business?' I said, thinking he might even now be on his way to Lop Lane. Better late than never.

'I came, Miss Follet, to ask about little Jamie and to apologise most sincerely for the accident. I was instructed,' he said, releasing a sheepish grin, 'to stay with the boys in the field. But one of my old friends insisted on distracting me with his chatter, and I'm afraid…well…I failed in my duty.'

It was kindly meant, and fair, to explain what happened for, since then, my opinion of his guardianship, temporary or not, was only lukewarm. 'Thank you,' I said. 'There's no harm done, Mr Monkton. Jamie is perfectly recovered. Your brother is going to teach him to swim.'

'Ah! How like Winterson to see the positive side. Excellent. He rarely lets a chance slip past him, does he?'

There was something in the tone of his question that seemed to have more behind it than polite rhetoric, followed by a smile that failed to lighten his eyes with the usual boyish mischief. Had he really come here to ask about Jamie, or was there something else?

'I don't know. I know much less about Lord Winterson than I did about his twin brother, you see. You know him better than I do.' I heard the artfulness of my reply. I was going to marry the man. 'But I do know that he makes an excellent guardian for my son.'

'Mmm, yes. Well, I suppose that will remain true as long as Jamie is too young to understand. I cannot help wondering, though, what will happen when Jamie reaches…er…the age of questioning.' Dropping his voice to a conspiratorial whisper, he observed me from beneath his brows, waiting for an appropriate reaction.

'Jamie has already reached the age of questioning, Mr Monkton, as you may recall when he told you of the remark made to him by Claude's little friend. That, you see, was the cause of the fracas at the mill-pond. Perhaps something ought to have been said at the time, don't you think?' My heartbeat had stepped up its pace in anticipation of a new phase in the conversation that had begun so amicably.

His eyes dropped away from mine as he nodded, and I could see that he had sucked in his bottom lip and let it out again, grimacing. 'Which is exactly the point I'm making, Miss Follet. That it's best to say something at the time, before it's too late.'

'Too late for what? About Jamie's parentage? I think that will all become clear in time, sir.'

'Er…well, not *that*, particularly. As you point out, that will be resolved eventually, I'm sure. It's the problem of my brother's lifestyle that concerns me most, and how it's going to affect a young impressionable boy like Jamie. Even though you claim to know so little about my brother, you must know what I'm referring to, Miss Follet. You yourself have been a part of it for some years now.'

Astonishment and indignation seethed in my breast, but I would not allow him to see. Instead, I smiled. 'Dear Mr Monkton,' I said, calmly, 'you must allow me to put your mind at rest, for I can see how misinformed you are about the kind of life I lead. I have *never* been part of Lord Winterson's…well… lifestyle, for want of a better expression. As for Jamie being affected by his guardian's behaviour, all I can say is that if Lord Winterson is only *half* as diligent, dutiful, loving, generous and caring to Jamie in the next three years as he has been in the last, I shall have nothing whatever to worry about. Nor will you.' Come to think of it, I had never spoken to anyone about Winterson in such terms, though there could never have been a better opportunity to say what I felt to one of his own family.

As if my praise of his brother gave him satisfaction, he nodded again, although the contortions of his mouth indicated that the matter would not be allowed to rest there. 'It does happen,' he said, 'that parenthood often brings out the best in even the most unusual circumstances, and it heartens me more than I can say to know that my brother has begun his duties so well. But I must refer you to my original concern, Miss Follet, about the kind of questions Jamie is sure to seek answers to in the future.'

'Do you have something specific in mind, sir?'

'Well, for one thing, about Winterson's love-child and its relationship to *him*. About who its mother is, and why—'

'Mr Monkton, please hold on a minute. You go too

fast for me. What exactly...*who* exactly are you talking about? Which mother?'

Sitting bolt upright, he pulled his chin deep into his collar like a runaway horse responding to the curb. His eyelids fluttered, but whether in mock or actual surprise I do not know. The whole conversation had an air of unreality about it, for I found it increasingly disturbing that a man usually so devoid of opinions should have come down so strongly against something that had not yet happened. Or had it?

His frown was childishly embarrassed, and one cheek went into a spasm as if it was all too painful for him. 'Oh, dear, what have I said?' he whispered. 'I thought you'd *know*. You seemed to be in each other's confidence.'

Confidence, I supposed, was his euphemism for pockets.

'Yes, what *have* you said, Mr Monkton? What is it you thought I'd know?'

'Er...about Lady Slatterly...and my brother.'

I don't know how I found the breath to say, 'What about them?'

'You saw that she was not quite herself at the ball, last weekend?'

'I had noticed it.'

'Did it not occur...? No, I see that it did not. My brother and she have always been very close, you know. It should hardly come as a surprise.'

'To know...?'

'That she's in,' he whispered, '*a delicate condition*.'

I must congratulate myself. I kept my voice level. 'It doesn't really surprise me at all, Mr Monkton, to know that Veronique is in the family way.' Yes, I felt justified, at that point, in using a little spicy vulgarity to bring the wretched man down to earth. 'In that, you are absolutely right. What *does* surprise me is that it hasn't happened sooner, after all the chances she's had.'

'I see,' he said, glancing wildly from side to side. My outspokenness had shaken him. 'But what about Winterson? That will surely not surprise you either, knowing something of his tendencies.'

I did not intend to give him the satisfaction of an answer to that. 'May I ask how you come to know this, sir? There are no visible signs of it yet. Is it not regarded as confidential at this early stage?'

He could not look at me, the father of three. Coyness had set in. 'The fashions, you know. They're very concealing, are they not?'

High waists, gathers and drapes, shawls and winter wraps. Yes, it was true. His own wife's bulge could be seen only from the side. Then I recalled Veronique's reaction as we joined them in the supper room, and there was I, thinking she was broody, like me. Breeding she was. Not broody. 'They are indeed, sir, but that doesn't answer my question. How do *you* come to know about Lady Slatterly's condition?'

'Old friends, Miss Follet. Veronique...er, Lady Slatterly has always found it easy to confide in me, both as curate and as Winterson's brother. She came to me some time ago for my advice.'

Advice? From Medworth? Now that *was* clutching at straws.

'In confidence, of course? How many others have you told, sir?'

He had the grace to look away, and I began to dislike him intensely. 'The point in my telling *you*, my dear Miss Follet, is that you and my brother have a legal share in Jamie's custody. A trust, as it were. And if that trust has been broken by one party, I feel it my bounden duty to inform the other of it, whether that breaks a confidence or not. I did hope that Winterson would have admitted his part in this affair by now, if only to discuss with you what steps he intends to take regarding his responsibilities. Marriage to Lady Slatterly would, of course, be the obvious solution, and this is why I am expressing some concern about the possible confusion in Jamie's mind concerning his exact relationships.'

'So you are certain about her condition. Are you equally certain who the father is, Mr Monkton?'

He adopted his pained expression again, as if I had challenged his veracity instead of Veronique's. 'I have her word on it,' he said, puffing out his chest a little, 'which I trust implicitly.'

'Then you are not as wise as you have always appeared to be, sir. You must surely be aware, in your role as confidante to the lady, that she's probably had more lovers than he? How can she possibly know who the father is? Has she kept notes?'

Wincing at my forthright turn of phrase, he was obviously rattled by my lack of conviction. 'She is absolutely certain of it, Miss Follet. I really do apologise for being the bearer of this distressing news, but I assumed, wrongly, I see, that my brother would have told you how things stand between him and Lady Slatterly. I came only to offer you the benefit of my advice and support, coming so soon after our mutual loss.'

'Your advice…ah…what would that be, in confidence, of course?'

His glance flickered uncomfortably in my direction as if I were a restless congregation. 'I find it is rarely successful to confront my brother with a problem head-on. He would deny it, naturally, as would most men in his position. As I said, he has an uncanny way of turning negatives into positives. No, perhaps the best way to handle the situation would be to distance yourself from him just a little more and then to allow him to broach the subject when he's decided what to do about it. Perhaps he already has, but I think it's much better for him to bear the bad tidings.'

'Of great joy.'

He did not, as Winterson had done, laugh and tell me not to go all biblical on him. Instead, he said, 'I beg your pardon?'

'You mean that, after all you've told me, I am now to pretend total ignorance of the matter? Then I'm supposed to appear shocked? On the other hand, is it really any of my business what your brother and Lady Slatterly get up to together? It would be if he were my husband, but he isn't, is he? And by the time Jamie is old enough to ask some searching questions about his half-relatives, he'll be old enough to be given some searching answers, I expect. He's quite intelligent. Regarding his own parentage, we have put in place a solution to that problem, such as it is. About other people's parentage, sir, I shall advise him to do as the rest of us try to do.'

'And that is?'

'Why, to mind our own business, of course, and

never… ever…to break a confidence unless it's a matter of life or death. And this isn't, is it?'

'It may be of great importance to young Jamie, Miss Follet.'

'Is that why you told him you had more important things to think about when one of your guests insulted him?'

That, apparently, was enough confrontation for the young curate of Osbaldwick who had already stayed longer than the regulation fifteen minutes. Standing up, he prepared to make his bow, though he could not resist a parting shot as he did so. 'I shall pray for you, Miss Follet. I came here as a friend out of the goodness of my heart to help you see your way out of an embarrassing situation. I suppose I must be relieved to find that you need no such help, but I shall always be available whenever you do.'

'That is very kind of you, Mr Monkton, and greatly appreciated. As you suspect, I am not in the least embarrassed by anything you've told me, though I imagine Lady Slatterly might be. Now, just remind me again, will you? Am I to tell your brother you called on me? Or not?'

His look of deep reproach convinced me that the interview had not gone according to plan, which had been to drive a wedge between me and his brother, as large a wedge as he could devise, and as plausible too. Everyone in the family, and plenty outside it, knew how Veronique Slatterly felt about Winterson, and who was I to blame her? But I knew also that, whether he was the father of her child or not, she would lose no time in laying her pregnancy at his door in the hope that, with enough pressure from all sides, he would do 'the honourable thing'.

But I had Winterson's categoric denial of any association, and whatever delinquencies he might be guilty of, dishonesty was not one of them. Quite the reverse. Too much honesty had kept us apart for years. I would not believe what Medworth was telling me. I would refuse to be upset by it. Nor would I challenge Winterson with this tale, as I knew full well Medworth wanted me to. Why else would he have come here to tell me? Why would he have come these two miles if he *expected* I'd already been told, when he couldn't be bothered to travel the same distance to administer God's grace to two of his dying parishoners? He was already halfway down the street before I remembered to ask him what had kept him from his duty to Prue's parents.

I would like to have felt as carefree as I seemed, but Medworth's visit had disturbed me deeply, both for its implications and the reasons why he should wish to cause a rift when he'd done no such thing during my association with Linas. There must have been other occasions when Winterson was thought to have fathered someone's child, yet nothing had ever been said to confirm it, or hold him to account. Furthermore, Linas's last few months had been spent in his brother's care at Abbots Mere, and I found it inconceivable that, during such a sad time of intensive nursing, Winterson would have been taking advantage of Veronique's generosity after so many years of refusals. The idea was ludicrous. No, I could not and *would* not believe it.

All the same, what if it was true?

Chapter Twelve

Those short dark February days, the cold, then the floods, seemed at the time more like a breeding ground for low spirits than the onset of spring when the first spears of snowdrops would normally have appeared, and birds building nests. In many respects I had much to be thankful for after a disastrous start, with my future set to become more secure than it had ever been, Jamie's problems alleviated and my family about to be relocated, albeit not a solution guaranteed to gladden them. In my do-gooding mode, it had hardly occurred to me that they might have other ideas when alternatives were so few, so I consoled myself with thoughts of their pleasure at the efforts I had made for them.

Jamie was ecstatic at the thought of having his own dear Nana Damzell, Greg and Finch to stay with us at last. His excited chatter and impractical suggestions made us smile; if it turned cold again, he said, his uncles could sleep with him and Goody in her large bed. But I did as Winterson suggested and allowed him to help, fearing that it would surely take me weeks to find anything as a result. And while the little fellow ran errands from kitchen to attic, I could not dismiss the absurdity of Medworth's errand and the plight of poor Veronique and what, if anything, I ought to say to Winterson about it.

As one problem was resolved, another had come to take its place, all set to strike at my most vulnerable parts. Knowing what I did of Winterson, how would I ever be sure? Was this what I would have to get used to, as the price of my uncontrollable love for him? The idea made me turn cold and sick, even while I smiled at Jamie's excitement. But just as disconcerting was Medworth's unusual officiousness and his alarming lapse of ethics that could hardly bode well for the future, especially when I had always regarded him as a firm ally. What a good thing I had never confided in him about my relationship with his brothers.

From a clear cold sky the light had begun to fade as we stood near the front windows to watch for signs of returning travellers. Behind us, last-minute adjustments were being made to the dinner table where places had been laid for eight people, candles and lamps lit, posies of ivy and hellebore arranged. Servants had been briefed, logs stacked in the hearth and jugs of ale brought up from the cellar, and wine too. My mother was fond of the sweet sauternes that Pierre obtained for her.

Jamie gave a yelp and wriggled like a worm off the window-seat, pulling the cushions with him. 'Uncaburl! Uncaburl!' His cries of welcome faded as he headed towards the hall. Through the gloom, I could make out no accompanying carts or carriage, so assumed he must have ridden on ahead to prepare us for their approach. I held a hand to my shawl-covered bodice to still the fluttering beneath, as the loud crack of the door-knocker was cut short, then the high yelp echoed by the deeper one followed by Jamie's chattery briefing. The limpet-like cling of his embrace as Winterson tried to rid himself of hat and gloves brought a laughing protest. 'Hold on, young man. I didn't come here to be smothered.' Trying to catch my eye round the little head, Winterson held him on one arm as he came to me, unexpectedly bending for a kiss to both cheeks.

His skin was fresh and cold, and I could smell the sweet scent of the moors upon it. 'Welcome, my lord,' I said. 'We've been awaiting you.'

'So I see,' he whispered, greeting me with eyes that held mine fractionally longer than etiquette required of a man, soothing the fears that had dogged me since Medworth's visit. 'Jamie,' he said, turning to the excited child, 'be still. Your mama and I must talk before I go home.'

I knew then, by the seriousness of his expression, that my plans for my family's immediate future had fallen through and that the reason for his lone visit was because they were not on their way here, as we had expected. Conflicting emotions passed through me as we went from the hall into the well-prepared dining room, and thankfulness that he was not about to leave me alone to deal with Jamie's inevitable disappointment.

Perhaps sensing the unwelcome news, Mrs Goode poured a glass of brandy and placed it beside his elbow as he sat Jamie upon his knee and cuddled him, a Jamie who had suddenly become astonishingly composed.

'What is it?' I said. 'A change of plan? Things have worsened? Is it my mother?'

'According to your brothers,' Winterson said, 'your mother is in better health than she's been for some time. But you warned me about her fighting spirit. She's quite a lady, isn't she? And, no, things have not worsened.'

Anticipating, I felt the dead weight of failure. 'She wouldn't budge, then. Tch! So stubborn. I might have known it.'

'Wait. Don't jump to conclusions. I spent most of my time there talking with her and your brothers, and the rest of it in the boat looking round the buildings and the parts they've been farming.'

'And the devastation, too?'

'More at what they've achieved than what's been spoiled. Yes, there's still plenty of water coming over the foss, but less than before. The water levels have actually begun to drop. We got the boat across to the house, but I could see that they had no intention of moving, and, to be honest, Miss Follet, I believe they've made the right decision.'

'But didn't you tell them you'd decided to reclaim the land and demolish the buildings?'

'I didn't see the point. I took my bailiff and steward along with me to meet your brothers, and we could all see that it makes more sense to leave the Follethorpes there to farm it. We were very impressed by what we saw. They've done extremely well, considering the lack of help over the years and the unfavourable conditions they've lived in.'

'They had Pierre to help them. What happened?'

'He left after a…a difference of opinion.'

'Tell me the truth. He and my brothers always had a difference of opinion. What was so special about this one?'

Tenderly, he cradled Jamie's head against his chest, sliding his hand across the hair so like his own. Jamie's fist was already moving up towards his mouth, thumb first, his eyelids heavy with sleep. 'You,' said Winterson, very quietly. 'It was after Monsieur Follet had seen us together near the coffee house. Remember?'

How could I forget the look on Pierre's face? 'Yes,' I said.

'Well, he went back home and voiced some rather harsh comments.'

'Yes, I can imagine.'

'Your brothers were not aware. They'd never seen me until today. Now they can understand it, but when your cousin began to…'

'To throw insults about?'

'Yes, they told him he'd better leave. So he did. There and then. I don't know anything about their relationship, but neither of your brothers seems too concerned about his departure. Except for one thing.'

'You mean the loss of what he used to bring from Brid?'

'Worse. Prepare yourself for bad news. He took the savings with him.'

'Oh, no! All? Everything?' My sounds of despair widened Jamie's eyes for a second until his lids drooped again.

'Every penny. The lot.'

My sigh was deep and genuinely painful, for this I felt to be partly my fault. But whatever he thought of me, how *could* he have done that to my mother for whom he professed to care and to be grateful for those years of safety? 'Where has he gone? How are they managing? What does Mama have to say about his treachery?'

'I believe your mother is secretly relieved to have an end to the wrangling and bad feeling, Miss Follet. And I must say that young Finch makes an impressive head of the Follethorpe house. We saw very much eye to eye, your brothers and I. As to the loss of funds, well, none of them is too pleased about that because it was a considerable amount they'd put aside for renovations and living costs. They told me how you'd helped them financially at great personal cost to yourself. They're very proud of you, you know. That's why they refused to tolerate your cousin's criticisms.'

'Family loyalties. It works both ways,' I said.

'But they don't know where Monsieur Follet has gone. They've had other things to think about since he went. We rescued your phaeton, by the way, and delivered the supplies to your mother. She sends her thanks.'

'Thank you. But what happens now?' I said, trying to understand the implications of all this. 'Did you mean it when you said they should be left there to farm the land, just as they have been doing?'

'Not just as they have been doing. The place needs money spending on it, and a lot of extra hands to make it profitable.'

'But now they haven't *got* the money. *Or* the extra hands. *Have* they?'

'Shh!' he whispered, looking down at the sleeping bundle on his lap. Adjusting his position, he held Jamie closer to touch the cool forehead with his lips. For some moments, the conversation was suspended, then Mrs Goode caught my eye.

'Shall I take him up, ma'am?'

'No,' Winterson said, looking up at me with a smile. 'Wait a while. He's tired out. You allowed him to help you, then?'

'Practically non-stop. We're the exhausted ones.'

His smile broadened. 'Well, there's a lot to be done at Foss Beck. The men and I are going back there on Friday to take a longer look at what there is and what we may be able to do with it. By that time the water levels will have gone down further and we'll be able to see more. The house needs a lot of attention, and there'll be some of the other houses I can put tenants into, to help on the farm. If we start straight away, we could have it up and running by early summer.'

'I think,' I said, 'you should allow Mrs Goode to take Jamie up.' Without questioning, he passed the sleeping little body over to his nurse. 'I'll be up shortly,' I told her.

'Yes, ma'am. Goodnight, my lord.'

Winterson closed the door behind them and returned to his chair, anticipating me as I took a breath to begin my interrogation about these far-fetched plans of his. To silence me, he took my hands into his. 'Everything has changed, sweetheart,' he said, gently. 'I can see how you've slaved all day to prepare for them, but you had not allowed for their preferences, had you? You might have realised your mother would refuse to leave.'

'It's my father,' I said, gulping as the tears began to

prickle. 'She's said it before, but I really didn't think she'd be quite so obstinate. Besides, if you were to go ahead and demolish—'

'But I'm not, lass. I shall not demolish the place. They know that.'

'Did they tell you what happened, years ago, at Bridlington?'

'Of course. I didn't say that I already knew, naturally, but that business about being arrested for an offence your father committed all those years ago is utter nonsense. The law doesn't work that way. They've been badly misinformed.'

'What…misinformed…about…?'

'About having to stay hidden for fear of arrest. They're not in any danger. Never have been. If a wanted man dies, sweetheart, that's the end of the matter. Whoever told them otherwise is completely wrong. Or bluffing.'

'It was Pierre who insisted they must stay hidden.'

'Then it's just as well he's gone, even if he did take the money too.'

'Maybe he thought he was the one who'd earned it. And if he was not too familiar with English law, he might have assumed…'

'Rubbish!' he laughed softly, kissing my knuckles. 'French law is no different on that point. I intend to make some enquiries about your cousin.'

'Then there's something else you ought to know, Burl,' I said, feeling the warm imprint of his lips on my skin, such a simple tender gesture worth more to me than twenty springtimes.

A smile spread into his eyes and crinkled their

corners like fine tissue. 'You're calling me Burl,' he said. 'Say it again.'

'Burl. Sounds like pearl.'

'Sounds like angel voices to me. Go on.'

'Flirt. I was saying there's something…'

'Something I ought to know. He wanted to marry you. I know that.'

'No, about the shop. When the floods started. We had a visit.' I told him how the Customs and Excise Men had searched but found nothing, while his expression grew more and more concerned.

'Do you happen to know why they singled you out?'

'One of them mentioned my advertisement in the window. The one you saw. I thought that was what had aroused their suspicions, but I wondered just now if Pierre might have wanted to alert them after he'd seen us in town. But he wouldn't. He was never vindictive.'

'Vindictive enough to steal the family savings. I shall find out what I can. I know the Customs Controller. He'll tell me why you were investigated and who the men were.'

'You believe someone might have tipped them off?'

'Oh, not necessarily. Leave it to me.'

It was something he enjoyed saying, these days. Leave it to me. So I did. 'You said my family need stay in hiding no longer,' I said.

'There was never any need for it except that, without realising it, they had parked themselves on my land. Just as well they were quiet about that.'

'For which offence you will require compensation, in the Winterson tradition?'

'I thought we'd already settled that,' he said, letting go of my hands to take up the glass of brandy. 'Haven't we?'

'As you said, things have changed. You've decided not to force them out and not to find them alternative accommodation. But how are you expecting them to put the buildings and fields to rights without their funds?'

'Haven't I told you? I thought I had.'

'No, you haven't, my lord.'

'You *must* be exhausted,' he commented, drily. 'Is *this* contraband too?'

'No. It's one Linas used to drink. And I'm not so exhausted that I cannot remember what you said, or didn't say, a moment ago.'

'About?'

'Renovations. Restorations. Reclamations. All that.'

'Ah, I see. You wish to know exactly what you're getting on your side of the bargain, Miss Follet, now that they won't be here and homeless after all. Well, I didn't share the details of our bargain with your brothers, but...'

'I should hope not!'

'...but I did discuss with them, which *you* failed to do, what their preferences would be. In an ideal world, that is.'

'It was pouring with rain, and I had to shout across a lake.'

'Nevertheless, I find it more democratic to—'

'Oh, get on with it!'

'—not to take things too much for granted. So we sat down together over a bowl of *superb* vegetable broth and dumplings, to discuss their needs.'

'Their needs, or yours?'

'Theirs first, then mine. And if you insist on interrupting me, Miss Follet, I shall be here all night. Is that your intention?'

'Please, I won't interrupt. Just tell me.'

'Thank you. I was trying to.' Picking up the brandy, he sipped again and carefully replaced it, smiling, teasing. 'There was no mention of compensation, sweetheart,' he said. 'The property belongs to the Stillingfleete estate and it will be Stillingfleete money that will completely renovate and redecorate the house, install running water and proper cooking facilities, sanitation, everything they need. Your brothers have agreed to manage the extended farm for a monthly salary, and to work the fields that my men will plough and sow. The other fields will hold new stock, sheep and a few milk-cows, more horses and better machinery, some poultry yards and perhaps pens for rearing pheasants in. We may need an assistant gamekeeper, I think.

'We'll also have to decide which barns to repair and which fields to turn to arable and pasture. We can drain most of the arable land, and redirect the beck so that the farm can't be flooded again. After that, we'll rebuild some of the cottages for the farmhands. Eventually, we might even start to use the old church again, if I can find a curate willing to take it on. It's in a bit of a mess, isn't it?'

I listened to this as if it was all a dream, and I was waiting to wake at the first sound of discord. 'I can hardly believe it,' I whispered. 'What did Mama have to say?'

'Sharp as a bag of nails. She wanted to know why I was bothering with it, and did I intend first to marry you and accept Jamie as my own, which she had no doubt of, since we're as alike as two peas.'

'She said *that*? Tch! Oh, she's too outspoken for words, my lord.'

'Not a bit of it. She has the right to know. I told her she'd have to reconcile herself to being my mother-in-law.' He grinned like a mischievous schoolboy. 'Oh, then she wept a little.'

'Oh, dear. Poor Mama. She's been so very unwell.'

'She's not been so very unwell since Cousin Pierre left. For one thing, she stopped taking that concoction he was bringing her from York once a month, and immediately she began to improve. The boys tell me—' He stopped himself, directing his attention to the brandy.

'Tell you what? Do they suspect Pierre of something?'

'Probably not. It seems a strange coincidence, that's all.'

'Well, bargain or no bargain, I believe I'm in your debt, my lord. What you've agreed to do for them is—'

'For you, lass. I'm doing it for you.'

'Why?'

'Because I've got you, and my son. It's as simple as that.'

Something echoed inside me. *And I have the man I love, even though I'm not so certain of his heart or our future together.* 'I still have trouble believing it. It's everything they've dreamed of, and much more than I deserve. I really don't think the bargain is so very equal, is it?'

'That's one thing we shall agree to disagree on, so let's forget about it. I cannot have a wife whose family live like outlaws in derelict houses on my property, can I? That would never do.'

My heart staggered a little. 'No, of course not,' I said, lightly. 'That wouldn't do at all.' Too hastily for a skilful recovery, I changed the subject, telling him about Prue's recent bereavement and the Friday funeral.

He was all sympathy. 'Friday is when I'll be going over to Foss Beck again, so why not have a day at Abbots Mere tomorrow while your house is being put back together again? Jamie can stay overnight, then on Friday he and Mrs Goode can spend the morning with my parents and I'll have a coach bring them back here in the afternoon. Besides, I have something for him that I believe he'll like.'

I stared into his smiling eyes. 'Something with four legs and a tail?'

'Indeed. A lovely little Exmoor mare that I've had my eye on. She'll be perfect for him. One owner, grown too tall.'

'He'll be over the moon.'

'It'll help him get over the disappointment of not having his Nana Damzell to stay. Bring them tomorrow after breakfast, and be sure he has some stout breeches and boots. Now,' he said, getting to his feet, 'I must be off. I'm sorry about your spoilt preparations, but it's all for the best. Forgive me?' He held out his arms and I went into them with an enthusiasm that appeared to take him by surprise, since it was much less to do with either thanks or forgiveness than with my need to feel the security of his embrace. I needed that more than he would ever know, after what I'd heard that afternoon.

'Hold me,' I whispered.

He did better than that. His kisses were heady and brandy-flavoured, and I knew it would be easy to persuade him to stay. We reached the hall, both of us searching for the perfect reason why he could not possibly leave. He took up his hat and gloves from the hall table, catching sight of three calling-cards on the silver tray, one of which he recognised. 'Medworth?' he said. 'When did *he* visit you?'

'Today.'

'You didn't say.'

'I forgot. Just a social call while he was in town. He wished to apologise for not safeguarding Jamie too well on Tuesday.'

'Did he, indeed? I should damn well think so, too. Heaven only knows what kind of rector he'll make when Slatterly grants him his new living, if he cannot tend his flock better than that.'

'Rector? New living? What does Lord Slatterly have to do with it?'

'I'm surprised he didn't tell you. I thought he'd told everybody. The living at Osbaldwick is in Slatterly's gift, you see. It was he who made Medworth curate there, to help the old rector out. But the old chap has retired at last and now Medworth is to step into his shoes at Easter. Wear your riding habits tomorrow, you and Mrs Goode, and I'll find two horses for you. We'll ride across the estate with my parents, shall we?'

'Er…yes. Will my phaeton be repaired by then?'

'It was not broken, Miss Follet. Just stuck in a deep rut with a stone jamming it. The boys will have it all cleaned up by morning.'

'So I need not have…?'

While the footman had gone to stand impassively by the door with one hand on the knob, Winterson could do little but nod. His mouth, however, was struggling against an impulse to laugh. 'Goodnight,' he said. 'Sleep well, Miss Follet.'

My first call was to the kitchen to apologise to Mrs Neape for being the bearer of such unwelcome news. We had devised the menus with great care, choosing all my family's favourites, beef steak pudding with fricassée of turnips, roast saddle of venison with redcurrant jelly, cheesecakes, that kind of thing. She was philosophical. It could all be eaten cold, she said, seeing my bitter disappointment, and we would have enough to keep us going for a week.

Mrs Carson was equally sympathetic and quite unruffled by the extra work involved. She had seen it all before and by this time tomorrow, she said, everything would be back in its usual place.

Still dazed by the unexpected generosity showered upon me and my family by Lord Winterson, I went up to see Jamie, who had slept through his undressing and was in his own bed between lace-edged sheets meant for Nana Damzell, hugging the empty embroidered nightdress-case that smelled of lavender. Mrs Goode and I swapped smiles and tiptoed out. 'Come down to the kitchen with me,' I said. 'We'll dine with cook and Mrs Carson tonight.'

Afterwards, I gave in to the urge to begin putting things back where they belonged, and it was late when I went to bed in a silent house that I had expected to be warmed by my brothers' laughter and my mother's chatter to her companions. But now they had seen Winterson at last and had made the connection for themselves, leaving me with no explaining to do. He had eaten their vegetable broth and dumplings, and they would understand how easy it was for me to love him and, about the complications, they would not need to know. Nor did I ever expect them to ask.

Yet for all the resolution of problems, I could not help but feel the worrying undercurrents that nagged me, not like the broodiness of recent days but more like a fear that there was something I ought to know, brought on, no doubt, by Medworth's perplexing visit. Certainly something unusual had been agreed between Winterson and his sickly twin, something that even his father had no wish to pry into. But what could be Medworth's purpose, I wondered, in trying to rock his brother's boat? Had he anticipated our marriage? Did he have a problem with the inheritance? Was there an underlying jealousy that he'd managed, until now, to keep to himself? There was, after all, some difference in status between village curate—even rector—and titled landowner-farmer, heir to the estate. And although he and Cynthia managed to exude an aura of rather chaotic domestic bliss, could there be more than that behind the scenes, as I knew there was behind most marital façades? The thought of watching him in action for the first time on Friday failed to provide me with any hope, and it was a long time before I slept.

Even then, I dreamt of enormous lakes, and boats, and huge mill-wheels thrashing the water, and my little Jamie yelling to me, over and over, that he could swim, and ride, and fly. I called to him, but he didn't hear me.

His initial disappointment was soon overcome by the promise of a day at Abbots Mere and a stay overnight, though it did not escape his notice that Mrs Goode and I wore our riding habits for our journey in the shining phaeton. That, we said, was easy enough to explain, for the temperature had fallen to below freezing during the night, and the fields, once white with reflected clouds, were now white with ice and frost, blinding us with flashes from the mirrored sun. But when he saw that Nana Frances and Grandpa were also dressed for riding, he felt obliged to make the plaintive enquiry, 'Am I going to ride with Uncaburl again, Mama?'

Winterson held out a hand. 'Come with me, Jamie. There's someone out here who needs to take a look at you.'

'Look at *me*, Uncaburl?' he said, clasping the large hand. 'Who wants to look at me?'

'A lady called Penny. She's out here.'

We followed, eager to catch the first rapturous expression on Jamie's face at his introduction to the dark brown mare, which to my mind was too large for him. A twelve-hand Shetland would have been far more suitable for a child of three. Jamie had no such reservations. Speechless with joy, he and the polite little mare formed an immediate bond of friendship, for he was confident from the beginning, without fear, taking the reins as he'd seen Winterson do, responsive to every instruction, determined to do everything correctly. His little feet hardly cleared the saddle-flaps, but the smile of pride in being a horseman at last helped to lift the burdens from my heart as nothing else could do. Watching them set off, side by side, one as tall as a church and the other reaching no further than the stallion's saddle was a sight to pull at my heartstrings, though I think only Goody noticed the glisten of a tear upon my cheek. I thought then that if Jamie were the one to receive his father's love, instead of both of us, I would not complain or allow it to embitter me.

There was something else to give me food for thought that morning, not having ridden out with Winterson and his guests since last autumn when Linas's health began to deteriorate. Then, I had been left much to my own devices by our host, except when I was with Linas or another guest, Winterson never singling me out for a word as he had done on that isolated day in April 1802, forgotten by my lover. Nevertheless, someone must have taken the trouble to remind Linas after that, for on the day after our return home that year, a red rose appeared on my hall table which I placed before me at breakfast, lunch and dinner until it withered. The same thing happened on my birthday the following three years. Linas was always undemonstrative, and I dare say that was his way of saying what he could not say in words.

The difference on that sharp frosty morning is worth recording if only for the happiness it gave me to be one of the group instead of an outsider tolerated only for her relationship with a brother. That day, I was made to feel like one whose opinions were valued, drawn into conversation, laughed with and teased, occasionally. Jamie, of course, preferred to take his instructions directly from Winterson rather than me.

'Bear up, Miss Follet,' said Lord Stillingfleete in an aside that everyone could hear, 'mothers are not supposed to know a thing about horses. Frances suffered in exactly the same way, convinced that Burl's first pony was far too large for him. It didn't do him any harm, in the end.'

'I seem to recall,' said Winterson, straight-faced, 'that a certain three-year-old *end* was rather sore for a day or two. As you say, I recovered.'

'Burl Winterson,' his mother reprimanded, 'there are ladies present.'

'Yes, Mama,' he said. 'Keep your hands together, Jamie.'

'I've lost my stirrup, Uncaburl.'

Winterson drew on the leading-rein. 'All right. Sort it out. Ready?'

'Yes.'

'My lord,' I said, 'is it time for Jamie to take a rest now?'

'Yes, and tomorrow he can practise riding bareback in the paddock.'

Mrs Goode's sidelong glance at me showed that her thoughts ran parallel to mine, that we had entered men's territory and that, from now on, Jamie's infancy was on the wane.

With a view to discussing what Jamie could and could not do tomorrow, I lingered near the pony's empty loose-box after the others had gone into the house, certain that Winterson would want a private word with me concerning Jamie's shifting allegiance and my sharing of him. New experiences, and not comfortable for a possessive mother.

He entered the stable, stopped, looked, and saw me. I had not expected to feel such breathless girlishness as he came slowly towards me, bare-headed, stripping off his gloves. Laying them with his whip along the top edge of the box, he steered me backwards by one arm into the thick brass-topped doorpost. 'I suppose you must go home this afternoon?' he said, not waiting for an answer. 'Because if I have to spend another night without you, Miss Follet, I may be obliged to make violent love to you here. Would you mind that?'

'Lord Winterson, *please*! I waited here to speak with you in private.' I was not as shocked as I pretended, and he knew it, but nor did I take his request at all seriously. *What is it about stables, I wonder?*

'Sorry. It's the figure-hugging jacket that brings out my baser instincts.'

'Then I'd better go and change into something looser.'

'No. Stay as you are. You did well just now. It's not easy for you, is it, to watch him pass into someone else's hands? But don't worry about tomorrow. My father will be there, and my head groom, and Mrs Goode. They won't overtire him. They'll show him how to groom the mare. He'll be quite safe.'

'Yes. Thank you. I know he will. He's beside himself with happiness.'

'He's going to be good.'

'Like his father,' I whispered, unable to avoid the ambiguity.

But his reply was to take me in his arms as I'd wanted him to, instinctively knowing which twin I referred to. 'You were thinking, out there, of those other times. I know. I could see it. But there's no need to, sweetheart. It's all in the past. Let it go.'

'I would, gladly, if I knew what it was all about.'

'One day we'll talk about it. Give me time. It's hard for me too.'

'I can wait. But don't turn cold on me again, Burl. Previously, if I'd had the courage, I could have walked away from it all. This time, I shall not be able to do that, shall I?'

'There'll be no walking away, lass. There'll be no cause. No more of those wild parties and loose women. Only people we both like.'

The wild parties were the least of my problems. 'Were there many loose women?' I asked.

'Only a few. No one I allowed you to meet.'

'That sounds, my lord, as if you cared who I met, which I find hard to believe. Half the time you didn't even know I was here.'

'Wrong, Miss Follet. I knew *exactly* where you were *all* the time. Particularly I knew where you were on the eighteenth day of April in 1802 during the hours of—'

'Stop! We must go in, or they'll come looking for us.' I pushed myself away from him, but he pulled me back roughly by my shoulders and I felt the hard sting of his hands as his kiss demonstrated how his desire had not cooled. If he recognised the reasoning behind my queries, he had given me no hint of it, and though I was tempted to share my concerns with him about the Slatterly woman, those few snatched moments were too precious to spoil when I had so little evidence to go on, and even that was at third hand.

So I savoured the warm seeking thrill of his lips as well as the pain of his hands, then the dizzying shock of release that made my walk across the cobbled stable-yard more dangerous than usual.

Hot chocolate and shortbread awaited us by the crackling fire, but I had sacrificed my sense of taste for the more powerful sense of yearning, and I might as well have been eating sawdust while I smiled and chatted as if nothing out of the ordinary was happening to me. He knew, I'm sure.

He knew enough of my strangely elevated status to escort me all round the house into places I had never had reason to visit before, opening up all the rooms to my inspection to show me, I presumed, what I would soon be mistress of. The kitchens, the extensive pantries and larders where game and poultry hung in furry bundles beside hams and sides of venison. Fresh fish waited for attention, baskets of eggs, shallow bowls of cream, shelves of cheeses and butter, wooden churns, racks of vegetables and bunches of pot-herbs. The beautiful frosted kitchen garden too, with glass succession-houses I had never seen before, and the wide lacy arms of fruit trees pinned against the walls. His roses, he told me, bloomed throughout winter and into spring.

He took me through the long gallery built in the sixteenth century for King Henry VIII's overnight stay at Abbots Mere. I had attended routs and balls here with Linas very occasionally, but Winterson must have guessed that I had never been introduced to their brooding ancestors who lined the oak-panelled walls. It was an omission he put to rights as we walked, finding yet another way to make up for his brother's lack of attention, which I knew better than anyone was more to do with his illness than deliberate neglect.

Perhaps, I thought as we joined the others, Winterson had at last begun to realise that it was not so much Linas's thoughtlessness that had hurt me most but his own icy detachment. For my part, it was not so much being mistress of that beautiful house that would soothe my pride, but knowing that, for whatever reason, Burl Winterson wanted me.

Chapter Thirteen

With no Jamie or his nurse for company, the evening felt oddly vacant. Yet although the house on Blake Street was almost back to normal, there were still a few things left to be rearranged and put away, and by bedtime I felt sure of being able to sleep soundly. The fresh air had done its work; riding was something I hoped to do more of, for Winterson had some very fine horses and some wonderful gallops too.

But as I lay in my bed thinking things over, I realised that the pile of Linas's notebooks I had last seen on the side table in the parlour had not been replaced. Nor could I recall where I had put them. They would be sure to turn up unexpectedly, somewhere.

Friday was the morning of Prue's parents' funeral and I was up early to the shop to place a notice in the window, to pull the blinds halfway down and to tie a large black satin bow over the coloured tassels. The wearing of black had almost become a habit with me, these days, and I longed to wear colours other than greys and violet. But propriety was everything to Follet and Sanders, so I did my best to be worthy of Prue by adding a long black feather boa to my ensemble, a plume of ostrich on my bonnet and a fine edge of the same around my wrists. With black braid frogging down the sleeves and a narrow panel of it down the front of my pelisse, I felt that she would approve. Even at a time like this, Prue Sanders would be critical of what her staff were wearing.

For the second day, the rooftops shone with white frost, and the cobbles had been sprinkled with straw to make them less treacherous as Debbie and I walked down to Stonegate to pick up the phaeton. Having no reason to call at the front entrance, our approach through the ginnel into the rear stableyard was the most direct way to approach the phaeton and the groom who would accompany us. Winterson's coachman was there talking to the green-and-grey liveried young man, showing me, by the way their conversation lingered, that something had disturbed them.

'Good morning,' I said. 'Are we ready?'

'Indeed we are, ma'am,' they said, touching their grey beavers.

'Something wrong?'

A quick glance at each other told me there was. 'Er…well…not exactly wrong, ma'am,' said the senior coachman, getting his word in first. 'Mr Treddle's had a bit of a problem at the house just now. His lordship gave us all instructions, you see, not to allow anyone in while he's away, excepting yourself, ma'am. So it's a bit tricky when…well…' He touched his nose with a

knuckle, striving to be respectful in his bluff Yorkshire way.

'When someone demands an entry? Anyone I
know?'

'Lady Slatterly, ma'am. She was none too pleased
to find that his lordship's not here, you see. Didn't
believe Mr Treddle when he told her. Kicked up a bit
of a fuss, she did.'

'He's gone over to Foss Beck,' I said.

'Yes, ma'am, though we didn't tell her ladyship that.
She drove out of here like the devil himself was after
her. She'll ruin her horses if she drives 'em like that.'

I would like to have asked if she'd gone to Abbots
Mere where my Jamie was, but that would not have
been discreet. 'Yes,' I said, looking away down the
covered passage to the street beyond, imagining Veronique clattering through, desperate to see Winterson.
Well, there was nothing I could do about it, but my first
thoughts were for Jamie's safety rather than for
Veronique's peace of mind.

I cannot say I enjoyed the drive to Osbaldwick, being
forced to concentrate fully on the frozen mud ruts that
knocked the phaeton about in a most uncomfortable
fashion. I was obliged to walk the horses for most of
the way, to save their hooves. The countryside was
white, the dried grasses laced with cobwebs that shim-
mered in the sun, and soon we caught up with other carriages travelling towards the sound of tolling bells, then
groups of black-clad people walking from cottage to
church. It was obvious that Prue's parents had been
well loved, for there were several phaetons and car-

riages already lining the narrow street, and crowds passing through the lych-gate into St Thomas's Church.

Inside, I sat with our staff from the shop, and because I was placed to one side of a thick stone pillar, I doubt that Medworth Monkton knew I was there. But it gave me the chance to watch him closely, to see how he fluffed his lines and almost dropped his prayer book as he turned the pages with shaking hands. Something, I thought, was wrong with the man, usually so amiable and at ease. The traipse out to the burial site was, as always, a sombre affair that reminded me too closely of my late lover and his winter resting place, and had it not been for my promise to support Prue, I would have chosen to stand some distance away so as not to see. As it was, I stood with my arm around her shoulders as she had done for me, which appeared to do nothing to ease Medworth's trembling, and he hurried through the service of commital as if he too would rather have been elsewhere. Perhaps, I thought, this was too near his brother's burial for him to distance himself.

I looked for him after that, while Prue greeted her friends, but he had disappeared. This was very odd behaviour, for a curate ought to stay with the bereaved as a matter of courtesy, if not duty. So I slipped quietly back to the church ostensibly to congratulate him on his forthcoming advancement, though in fact to remind him where he was needed most. He had offered me the benefit of his advice; I would offer him some of mine.

The sound of voices from the vestry ought to have made me turn about and return to Prue, having only recently eavesdropped on a private conversation. I was not at all comfortable with the underhandedness of it, but while it was not in my nature to enjoy such a thing, my curiosity was at once alerted by Medworth's unusually sharp tone and by the answering one, in some distress, of Lady Veronique Slatterly. Yes, I was quite sure it was her because it was her name that Medworth snapped out, impatiently.

'You should not have come here, Veronique, on such a day. You *must* know I cannot see you. Go back home.'

There was a sound like a cough or a sob, and I froze, hating myself for staying, half-turning to go, but held back by my heart that told me I was in some way involved, willing or not. This was undoubtedly not a good time for her to seek counselling from her adviser, and his tone must have convinced her of his lack of sympathy, in case she had other ideas.

'You're avoiding me,' she whimpered from the vestry side of the curtain, a heavy purple thing with a fringe along the bottom meant to conceal the changing of vestments rather than conversations. 'Everybody is avoiding me. And you lied to me about Mrs Monkton.'

'Shh!'

She ignored his command. 'You told me you and Mrs Monkton were not intimate any more, but you were, weren't you? And you let me find out about her condition at the ball, of all places, when I couldn't…couldn't…' The sobbing voice faded and choked. 'So…so unkind of you. I don't suppose *she* knows about *my* condition, does she?'

'Hush, for pity's sake, Veronique. Of course she doesn't. Why would I tell her *that*? It has nothing to do with Cynthia. And I did *not* lie about not being… well…affectionate. It was true at the time.'

I heard again the sanctimonious tone he'd used to me, excusing, validating, squirming with righteousness. I wanted to burst through the curtain to take her side and demand a proper hearing, but perhaps I had no need, for he had made her angry too, and she was unwilling to be brushed aside simply because he had a funeral party to attend.

'Stop! Don't go!' she insisted. I saw the curtain billow. 'You'll *have* to tell her, Medworth. *This* is your doing too, you know.'

If I had not been told of her condition beforehand, I would not have guessed that she must be pointing to herself, the connection never having occurred to me after what he'd told me on Wednesday. Her accusation hit me like a thunderbolt. Not Winterson, but Medworth himself, taking advantage of those advisory sessions with his patron's unhappy daughter.

'Of *course* it isn't,' he rasped, half-whisper, half-yelp. 'And I have not been avoiding you. I have duties to perform that I've already neglected for your sake. And I told you before that it *must* be Winterson's. You know the reason, Veronique. He's free and I'm not, and with enough pressure from you and your father, and from me, and eventually from Miss Follet, he'll be obliged to accept it. Think of that. You'll be Lady Winterson. That's what you've always wanted, isn't it?'

'No!' she snapped. 'Not at *that* price, Medworth. He would not give in to that kind of pressure when he knows as well as I do that it cannot possibly be his.'

'Cannot? What nonsense is this? Of course it can.'

'No. I lied to you too.'

'What d'ye mean, lied? About what?'

'I've never been to bed with your brother. It's *your* child, not his.'

There was a pause, then the shocked, disbelieving reaction that I was fortunate not to have received from Linas when I'd told him about Jamie. That was something that had lain heavily on my conscience ever since, that I had been obliged to lie to everyone about the child's father for *his* sake, not for my own. It had been unforgivable, even while sparing me the gossip.

'I don't believe you,' Medworth said, coldly. 'You told me—'

'Of course I did. It was what you wanted me to say, wasn't it? That your brother and I had been lovers too. Well, now I'm telling you the truth—I have *never* been to bed with him, not ever. He would never be alone with me, and, yes, I *did* want him, have always wanted him more than anyone, but you didn't want to hear that, did you? You said you could offer me your comfort for his offhandedness, and now you don't want to know about it. But you can't foist it off on to your brother, Medworth. It won't work, and he knows it. It's his twin's woman *he's* always wanted, not me.' Her voice wavered and, at that point, I almost turned and left, for my guilty heart was not so well seasoned that I was immune to her anguish. She had felt his indifference too.

'You're lying again. I thought you and my brother would surely have…'

'I'm not lying. It's the truth. Why d'ye think I needed your comfort? Because you're irresistible? I've resisted better men than you, Medworth.'

'The father must be one of those you didn't resist, then. There have been plenty of them, I'm sure.'

'Not recently there haven't. You'll have to accept it because you're the only one responsible and there's no reason why I should pretend otherwise. *You* told me Mrs Monkton was ill and that you'd always wanted me. You said you loved me more than anyone. You didn't say she was ill with morning sickness, as I have been, did you?'

'Oh, God, this is terrible. It will be the end of me.'

'Have you told anyone about…about *my* condition?'

'No, of course not. I have to go, Veronique. I have people to see. I've done all I can for you. Really…no… let me go…*please*!'

The curtain billowed again as I watched, horrified, imagining the tussle that was being enacted in that confined space, her desperation, his determined cowardice, the terrible spinelessness that convinces men that black is white, that up is down, that no means yes if that is what will serve their purpose best. Guiltily, I shrunk back into the shadows, expecting one of them to emerge like a bullet within the next moment.

But it spoke volumes for Veronique's mettle when her shape appeared with arms outstretched, bulging across the curtain, preventing his escape. 'Oh, no,' she whispered, growling with menace, 'oh, no, Medworth Monkton. Don't you walk away this time and pretend innocence just because you think your word will be believed above mine. This time, there's your brother's word too, isn't there? Tell him about it, if you wish, and see what *he* tells you when he's stopped laughing. And tell my father too. *He* knows that Winterson isn't stupid enough to get *me* pregnant while he's hoping to catch Linas's woman, even if *you* are.'

'*You* tell your father,' he replied, cuttingly. 'You tell

him and see if he can't come up with half a dozen names who could easily have fathered your brat, Lady Slatterly. Why, you could have had a stableful by now with the kind of generosity *you* practise. How else could it have happened but by your own stupid carelessness?'

The bulge in the curtain disappeared, and a loud crack swayed it in the draught. Then, after a hiss of pain from within, the curtain was thrown aside with a rattle and Medworth stumbled through the gap with one hand pressed to the side of his head, bent very low.

Pressing myself back against the wall, I saw him pause and cling to one of the pews, take a look at his hand, then continue on round the corner to the small north door, the way he had apparently entered. Inside the vestry, the low sound of sobbing tore at my heart and filled my lungs with the painful beginnings of a wail. I could have gone in to her; I could have offered her whatever comfort a rival has to offer, but I had to choose between her and Prue. And I chose Prue because that was why I had gone there.

If I had been in the same dreadful position, I told myself, I would have preferred privacy after what had just happened, and that poor Veronique would probably want the same. And for all my odious guilt at having overheard what I had absolutely no right to know about, my regard for her privacy and my silence on the matter gave me some comfort all through the wake that followed the burial, the usual noisy gathering for refreshments, condolences and reminiscences.

Prue's appreciation was demonstrated in a motherly hug that, had she but known it, I was in need of almost as much as she, while the shock of what I'd discovered resounded in my head like the clamour of church bells. When Prue asked me where the curate had disappeared to, I murmured something in his defence that he had looked very unwell and had probably had to hurry home, which was better than saying that he would not wish to appear with a distinctly red hand-print on his cheek.

Prue understood when I asked to leave the wake before it had run its course, for now she was amongst friends who would talk far into the evening. Naturally, my mind dwelt on what I'd heard, on Medworth's betrayal of his position, on Veronique's misery and on my own decision to withhold offers of help for fear of being thought intrusive. It was none of my business, my conscience told me, without conviction. It was a lie, of course. If it had not concerned me, I would not have stayed to listen. Yet my guilt gave me little respite, and my punishment was a pounding headache.

Back at Blake Street I sat beside a roaring fire with my child and his nurse, a tray of tea, lemonade, and a dish of buttery muffins hot from the kitchen, listening to his back-to-front accounts of how he'd ridden without a saddle, 'To strengthen my thighs,' he said, glowing with three-year-old pride. 'And now they ache, Mama, but Uncaburl's man says it's good for me.'

I hugged him to me, smelling the straw and stables on him. 'Well done, little one,' I said. 'You shall have a warm bath to soak the aches away. Did they show you how to groom Penny and make her shine?'

'Yes, I stood on a box to reach her back an' she stood still an' liked it, an I fed her carrots, and I ate all my...' a mighty yawn interrupted the flow before the final '...greens for Nana Frances and Grandpa, Mama.'

To keep him awake until bedtime, I took him with me to the shop's deserted workrooms while I assessed all the available spaces in the property that Prue would have been able to use as living quarters if she'd not been obliged to live with her parents. There was no reason now why she could not live above the shop, rent free, if only we could clear some of the rooms and provide the basic amenities for her. It was an arrangement that might help to soften the blow of not having Pierre's bounty to sell.

After dinner that evening, as we sat by the fire in the drawing room, the sound of the door-knocker made us look up in the hope that it might be Lord Winterson, although I did not expect him. The footman tapped and entered. 'Lady Slatterly, ma'am,' he said.

My astonishment must have lingered on my face as she came forwards, for although she had indeed been at the forefront of my mind, I never expected her to show up here. 'What a pleasant surprise,' I said, responding to her curtsy. 'Please forgive the informality. Will you sit with us a while?'

I had seen her in all sorts of conditions over the years, ever since her first acid comments meant to wound me and, more recently, when she had been thankful to accept my goodwill. So my reading of her manner on this occasion was well informed, and clearly she was not a picture of happiness. There were red rims to her eyes, and she wore an air of uncertainty that was very different from the usual and, although she concealed her anguish with courage, it showed through in so many small ways. Forcing a smile, her eyes darted to Mrs Goode and Jamie.

'Mrs Goode,' I said, 'will you take Jamie up for his bath now, please?'

Once we were alone, Veronique's shoulders sagged with relief. As if unsure whether she was doing the right thing in approaching me this way, she took sleep-walking steps to the nearest chair and sat sideways on the edge of it. This was most unlike the Veronique I knew. And no wonder.

Fidgeting with her reticule, she blinked at me as if deciding how best to explain her visit. 'Helene,' she said at last, 'you were once kind enough to speak out for me.'

'At the ball. Yes, I remember. Men can be so insensitive, sometimes.'

'Yes. So I've come to ask…er…to ask you a favour. To ask your advice, actually…er…not for me, but for a friend of mine. She has a problem, you see, and I told her you might know how to…er…advise her what's best to do. She has no one else but me to turn to. Her other friends would not wish to be involved. It's all so…so difficult.'

My heart softened and ached for her. No one else to turn to but the one who had last said something kindly in her defence. Such unhappiness. What rejection she must be feeling. 'Of course I'll help your friend if I can,' I said. 'Is she about our age, or older?'

'Yes, she's our age. My age, actually. We've been close for years. She's done something foolish. Very… very…foolish.'

I saw that she struggled to hold back her tears, so

while she took a few moments to compose herself, I went to pour a glass of wine and place it beside her. 'Take a sip,' I said, 'then tell me how I can help your friend. I take it there may be a man involved?'

She sniffed, then nodded, but this time the fair ringlet did not bounce. The white fur collar reflected its pallor upon her mottled skin, and despite the brightly patterned pelisse-robe, she was far from the winter cheer it was meant to represent. At last, her wide-brimmed bonnet lifted. 'Yes, there is a man involved, but he doesn't want to know.'

'Know what, Veronique?'

'That she's going to be a mother. You're not shocked?'

'No, I'm not shocked. I am an unmarried mother too.'

'That's another reason why I thought you might know what to do.'

'If the man involved doesn't want to accept his responsibility, it makes life very difficult. Do her parents know about her problem?'

'No. She has only one parent.'

'I see. I had only one parent too.'

'Did you? That makes it even harder then, doesn't it?'

'Not really. Not if the parent is on her side, and loves her.'

Her eyebrows lifted at that. 'Doesn't it?' she said.

'No. There's only one opinion, one reaction, one shock. It often makes things simpler. Is there some reason why your friend may not wish to tell her parent? The point is, you see, that if she lives at home, her parent is going to discover it sooner or later, so perhaps it would be best if she said something herself before someone else does.'

'But it would hurt him so, wouldn't it?' she whispered.

'My dear, it would hurt him even more if he found out by accident. If it's from her father your friend is hoping for most help, then surely it's only fair to confide in him at the beginning so that they can discuss what to do about it. Is he the kind of man to fall into a rage, your friend's father?'

'No, he wouldn't do that. I'm sure of it.'

'He loves her very much, does he?'

'Indeed he does, but he'd want to know who's responsible, and she cannot tell him that.'

'She cannot…because…?'

'Because he's married, Helene. That's why he doesn't wish to accept the responsibility. I believe,' she added, as if she wasn't sure.

'Then I would not wish to persuade her otherwise,' I said, thinking quite the opposite. 'She's obviously a loyal young lady whose affection for the father runs very deep. Most of us would prefer him to be honest and admit that he has a part to play in the affair, and most parents would wish to know who'd sired their grandchild. But that decision must remain with your friend, after all.'

'I suppose it must,' she said, looking into the fire, 'and I'm sure she ought to take her father into her confidence. He'll be very upset, though.'

'Veronique, I think you'll find that fathers often understand how such things can happen. He may well be upset, and angry, and concerned for your friend, but if he loves her as you say he does, he won't wish to hurt her more than she is already. My advice would be for her to go and talk to him about it without delay, apologise for the pain she's caused and ask for his help. No hysterics. No blaming anyone. No threats or unkind words that she'll regret later. And no packing of bags, tell her.'

'Yes. I will. Thank you.'

'If you would like to talk about it some more, I shall be happy to listen, and to help, if I can. But go to your friend now and see what she thinks. Let me know, will you?'

'You've been very kind,' she whispered, pulling on her soft kid gloves. 'Men can be so unpredictable, can't they?' Placing a light hand on my arm, she brushed a kiss upon both my cheeks, which surprised me.

'Men are governed by different forces from us, but there are some exceptions out there. Does your friend have any exceptional men friends?'

Stretching out the fingers of one hand, she stroked the back of her glove as if imagining a wedding ring there. 'There is one… yes…who's been in love with me… *her*…for years. It's possible that he may help her out of her troubles. But it wouldn't be quite fair, would it?'

'Only if he's given the full story and is allowed to choose, not otherwise. He would have to know the facts and, even then, only if your friend truly believed she could be a loyal and faithful wife to him. Such things are not uncommon and often turn out to be very happy. I feel hardly in a position to act as adviser here, but it may be worth thinking about, especially since the child's father is not in a position to offer any help.'

'It would serve him right if I made his name known

to *everyone*,' she whispered, fiercely. 'He's getting away without a blemish.'

'Yes, probably. But he's not the only one who'd suffer, is he?'

She turned her hand over to stare at the palm, then closed her fist. 'He didn't let that thought bother him. I shall go and tell her what you've said, Helene. Thank you. It's at times like this when she misses her mama most.'

'When did your friend lose her mama, Veronique?'

'When I was fourteen, she left Papa for another man, but then she died only six months later in Scotland and we never saw her again. Papa was broken-hearted. He loved her too.' The distress still showed in her voice.

'Which is perhaps why,' I said, hearing the shift in her account from third to first person, 'you ought to confide in him, to let him know that he's needed. It sounds as if you may need each other's comfort.'

'Yes,' she said. 'I don't know why I didn't see it before.'

I surprised myself then by taking her into my embrace and holding the motherless miserable creature as if she were my sister while my secret knowledge burned holes in my conscience.

When she had gone, I found that my legs were shaking, whether from the effort of the last half-hour or from relief that Veronique had unwittingly verified all that Winterson had said about their relationship. I could not condone his apparent heartlessness any more than I could condone his earlier coldness to me, and I was sorry, in a way, that my own peace of mind had been bought at the price of her deep unhappiness. Yet it *had* been bought, and I was both glad and flattered that she had come to me, of all people, for honest objective advice. That was the least I could offer her, though I would like to have done more. On reflection, the only other thing I could do was to keep silent and respect her confidence, as her faithless lover had failed to do.

As for my enquiries about the possibility of a beau who might help her out, I had no qualms on that score, impersonal though it may seem. Wealthy fathers were often able to find bidders in the marriage stakes willing to take on an erring daughter, with enough inducement. The added benefit of knowing a man who had loved her for years cast a very positive light on the proceedings, and clearly Veronique was not against the idea in principle. In fact, I had never known her speak with such a lack of waspishness or self-pity.

With my head in my hands I stared into the fire, watching the flames lick around the logs and thinking how fortunate I had been compared to Veronique, whose life of wealth and luxury had not compensated one bit for the tragic loss of her mother at the age of fourteen. I was exactly that age when my father had gone from us in such frightening circumstances, yet although I'd had to venture out into the world owning next to nothing and expecting little, Fate had treated me with kindness, though until now I had failed to appreciate its methods. Is that what it had taken, I asked myself, to make me see how carefully Fate had taken me under her wing, providing me with a protector, then a child, and finally a promise of marriage to the man I loved? So, there had been deceptions, but not of the kind that Medworth used on Veronique and his loyal wife. There had been a loss of pride when I discovered how I had been used, as mistresses *are* used. But of what good was it to perpetuate my grumbles when I had my adored Jamie to bring me such joy? The rejection Veronique had suffered from both Winterson and his devious brother was of a more heartbreaking kind than I had suffered, including the thoughtlessness from his twin.

As my thoughts turned to Linas, I saw another day passing without having found the notebooks that might tell me, if nothing else, what his accounting was like and how much he had paid out for my upkeep. So when I had tucked Jamie up in bed, told him a story and said prayers, I left him in Goody's safekeeping and went down to begin the search again, eventually finding the books in a cupboard where the spare napkins and table covers had been put away.

Placing Veronique's untouched glass of wine at my elbow and the three leather-bound notebooks on my knees, I turned up the wick of the lamp and opened the first and smallest of them. As I suspected, it consisted of payments to the grocer, the chandler, the butcher and fishmonger, the carriage-maker and farrier, money paid to his tailor, bootmaker and hatter, the snuff-maker and, before my time with him, a record of payments to the jeweller for trinkets, a fob-watch, chain, and quizzing-glass. Running my finger down the more recent pages, I saw expenses for Jamie—bed linen, a cot, a small chair and a walking-frame from the carpenter—though all his clothes had been made by myself and Mrs Goode from fabrics obtained from the shop, costing Linas nothing. Even my own clothes, except for shoes, has cost Linas nothing. There were no surprises here.

The second notebook was no more than a catalogue of the volumes in his study on ethnography, geology and geography, on Greek and Roman sculptures and artifacts from Japan and India, on seashells and fossils, and rare plants from South America. Linas was never happier than when he was studying amongst his books.

The third one appeared to be a collection of his own essays on various topics, like one on Charles Townley's collection of antiques in his Park Lane house. That, I remembered, had been on our last visit together to London. Flipping through the pages, I saw another one headed 'Greek Vases in the Sir John Soane Collection', and another, 'On Earthquakes and Volcanoes'. I was just about to close it when I saw the familiar name of Helene, which I assumed would be Helen of Troy in that kind of company. It was his last entry, and I would have closed the book but for the word 'Burl' that sprang out of the pages as if it had been written in red ink instead of grey-black.

I was intrigued, feeling once more like the eavesdropper choosing to listen in to someone's private musings. This was getting to be a habit. I closed the book and sat with my hand on the cover, hearing the voices of conscience yet again, then Linas's voice telling me to go on.

Open it. Read it. It's meant for you.

I caressed the pages where his hand had rested, absorbing the touch of him from the faintly lined creamy paper. The voice faded and left me to my own devices and to the burning need to know why my name was there with Burl's. There was no heading to this last essay, only the date, October 10th, 1805, which was only days before he was taken to Abbots Mere to live out the last of his time. It was addressed to me, *Beloved Helene*.

Beloved? He had never called me that. 'Love' was his only tag for me, the usual Yorkshire form of address to anyone remotely friendly. 'C'mon, love,' he would call to me. Adjusting the book to catch the best light, I sat back in my chair and, to the sonorous ticking of the clock, began to read.

Chapter Fourteen

Beloved Helene. Dubiously, my gaze hung over the words.

The house is quiet now and I am unable to sleep until this story is told, for I shall leave here in the next day or two with little prospect of a return. You came to me this evening with our Jamie, as always, to perform those countless little services for me, too intimate to delegate to anyone except family. I never thought a three-year-old child could be so helpful or bring us such happiness, nor did I ever think I would have the love and devotion of a woman like you to take me to the end of my life. Beloved, I am truly blessed, and I wish I could say that I have no regrets, but, alas, that would be untrue. I have. And it is those regrets that must be explained while I still have time and strength, and although I would prefer to have explained them to you face to face, I fear that I would express myself so clumsily, thus undoing any advantage of spontaneity. No, I see you smile, spontaneity was never Linas's forte, was it? A planner, a deliberator, a scholar, perhaps, but hardly a creature of impulse.

You will know by now the regrets to which I refer, for although you never allowed that knowledge to colour your devotion to me, it placed upon you an unfair burden that was sometimes too hard for you to carry.

Oh, Linas, it *did* colour my devotion. If only you knew.

To tell you how and why may not earn your forgiveness, after all, but perhaps Burl will put in a good word for me now that he is claiming what was rightly his to begin with. How do I know that? Because I know my brother well; he would not delay for a day on something as important as this, and by now he will have begun his re-conquest of you.

You were seventeen when we met, beloved Helene— no, Linas, I was not seventeen until April—*a flower of a woman, a dazzling beauty who outshone every other female at the Assembly Rooms on that St Valentine's Day, and if I am not so articulate now, I was even less so then. Tongue-tied. Mute. I did not stand a chance with you. Together, Burl and I saw you enter, and I felt his reaction immediately. Yes, felt it. Don't ask me to define it. I cannot, except to say that his quietness took on a different quality that only a close relative would recognise. It was never his way, was it, to crowd in with the others?*

Nevertheless, it was not long before you stood up with him, nor was it long before everyone who saw you together knew that something momentous was happening before their eyes, and when Burl introduced us, I doubt if you heard a word he said. I remember it better than you think, dear Linas. Still, you politely danced with me without realising that I was as smitten as he. How could you have known that my desire was like a pain, all the more intense because whenever Burl looked at a woman, she was as good as his?

You could not have known how it was between us, Burl and me, close-coupled in mind and spirit, though not in body. The very best of friends, yet rivals in love. Whatever woman came my way, Burl's magnetism drew her irrevocably towards him instead. Any woman I managed to attract, one-tenth of Burl's tally, would also see him, and whether he responded to her or not, I might as well have been invisible for all the attention I won. I grew used to it, yet I resented it even though I knew it was never his intention, and, although I did have flirtations, I was glad to move to Stonegate where the chances of keeping a woman to myself for longer were marginally better.

But that St Valentine's Ball, dearest Helene, was a milestone for me, having just received from my doctor a period of three years at the most in which to cram every happy circumstance before it was too late. So live life to the full, he advised me. I had never been strong, as you know, but I think his prognosis surprised even me. And now I had seen the woman of my dreams, the one I wanted above all others, already beyond my reach. What galled me most, I think, is that Burl's relationships with women had always been fleeting affairs before the inevitable diversion of another more alluring creature. Yes, it was the hunt that Burl enjoyed most—the chase, the capture, the capitulation. And that night, I saw the possibility of you being caught, flaunted and then left while I watched again from the side, seeing my chances and my life slip quietly away together. He was in love with you, there is no doubt of that, but then so was I. Impotently, disastrously, angrily in love.

But I knew something that, at the time, Burl did not know, that you had no means, that your family were unable to help you, that you had been supported by two lovers for a short period, and that you worked for the milliner and mantua-maker on Blake Street. How did I know that? By overhearing the gossip that spread like a forest fire through the ballroom while you and he were dancing. You were vulnerable, chère *Helene, and while Burl would offer you the moon to hold for a few fabulous weeks, or even months, I wanted to offer you the security of my home and all the amenities that a mistress needs who has nothing of her own. I had only three years left; no long drawn-out sentence for you to endure and better, I thought, than being yet one more of Burl's cast-offs. I was what you needed, dearest love, and you were what I needed. You were all ready to fall into my brother's arms. I decided to take matters into my own hands, truly the closest I have ever been to being spontaneous.*

The next day I went to Abbots Mere, ostensibly to tell Burl of my doctor's prediction for my short future. We wept, trying to think of ways round the sentence, but there were none. Our parents and Medworth should be prepared, he said. It was only fair. He would see that I had everything I wanted in my last years. Everything. Nothing would be denied. What was it I wanted most? Funds? To travel to Italy? Or Switzerland?

Wanting only you, I saw my chance. 'Miss Helene Follet,' I said. 'She is my only desire.'

Oh, Linas. Dear Linas. Is this how it happened, then?

I recall how Burl went to stand by the mantelpiece, resting his head on his arm across the shelf as if it was too heavy for him, and his silence almost made me change my mind. 'Why?' he said at last. 'Why her?'

'I need her,' I replied. 'Three more years are of no use to me unless I have her beside me, and I doubt I could even live them at all, seeing her with you, Burl. That's asking too much of me.'

It was asking too much of him too, I knew that, but I was convinced that although he too was in love with you then, it would not last and you would soon be broken-hearted, bewildered, and no better off materially than you were before. As love triangles go, this was the worst it could get, I thought. I was wrong, as you know.

For a while, the light seemed to go out of him, Helene. 'What do you want me to do?' he said.

'Leave her alone,' I told him. 'Leave her to me. She'll accept me, if only because I'm your brother and what I can offer her will be too good to refuse. She needs a patron, Burl. And anyway, I have only three years. If you feel the same way about her then as you do now, you'll be able to carry on from where you left off. She'll only be twenty. But I want an heir, Burl. Sounds daft, I know, but the thought of leaving without even a son to carry on my line is the saddest thing that could happen. I've never got a woman with child yet, but with her I could. I know it.'

'How can you be sure she'll accept you?' he said.

'I've told you. She needs a place of her own and long-term stability. If she becomes a mother to my child, she'll be glad of my protection.'

'At Stonegate? Let her have Blake Street, then. It's not far to walk.'

That much of the conversation I can remember clearly, but I was winning him over, Helene. Blake Street is his property, and he was already planning to give you the use of it as if it was mine. Looking back, I see that it must have given him some small pleasure to know that you would be living in his house, even if you didn't know it. He offered me the use of his servants, too. And to pay all the running costs. He was always generous.

He did, however, have some provisos of his own. About the offspring. If it happened, he said, that you were to produce a Monkton heir, then the child would need a guardian, the obvious person being himself. I must appoint him as such in my will. I agreed. It will bind you two together for many more years after I have gone, for one thing. Forgive me, Helene. I did it for the best. If I had known then what I know now, I would not have made such a fateful request of my brother, but how could I have foreseen that Burl's passion for you would burn so fiercely for so long? At the time of our agreement he tried to put me off, saying you were sure to be unreliable, a vision too good to be true. But my heart was already yours, my dear, and my three years already beginning to shine with contentment.

Ah, the unreliable part. I see now. But Burl's passion? Is that true?

He agreed to leave you alone, not to do anything to attract you or to win his regard, not to allow you one speck of hope or to add fuel to your desire for him. Oh, yes, I could see it, dear Helene. You tried to hide it, but *yours are not the kind of emotions that can easily be hidden. And though you did your best to hide your anguish too, and your hurt, you kindly accepted my offer for reasons I shall never quite understand except that the arrangement would allow you to see the one who had misled you about his interest.*

No, Linas, that was the hardest part of all, seeing him. I accepted your offer because, as you said, I needed you and you needed me, and the fact that the house on Blake Street was so convenient for my work with Prue Sanders.

Naturally, I had to tell you of my lifespan and to give you a choice; to do otherwise would have been barbaric. But you bore the news well, and maybe it was that which gave you a reason to put on a brave face and to give me all I could have wished for in devotion, nursing and loving. I always found it impossible to tell you, dearest beloved Helene, that your loving companionship was the heaven for which I had bargained with my brother. I should have written to you sooner about my adoration.

You may be wondering, beloved, when my regrets began. Not during those nights of tender lovemaking, to be sure, but on those days when we visited Abbots Mere and I could see how well Burl stuck to the letter of our agreement and, worse, its effect on you. There were times when I wanted to revoke it, to beg him to be a little kinder to you, but it was a risk I dared not take, being selfish, wanting you all for myself. I know now how very unhappy I made you even while you had my protection, yet my regrets on that score were to multiply.

Two years passed without a sign of my much-wanted

heir, and my doctor and I were forced to the conclusion that the infertility was linked to my illness, not to you. You may also have wondered why I never asked you to marry me in those early years, but to be honest I saw no reason to. You will be well provided for when I am no longer with you, dearest Helene, for I have always known that Burl will claim you and our son, especially as he was so far-sighted as to lay claim to my heir's guardianship, even before he knew the exact circumstances. Moreover, widowhood brings its own complications of inheritance and relationship and, in short, I felt that for you to remain as a spinster would make things simpler for Burl and for you to come together without blame or scandal. For both your sakes, I pray that it has already happened.

But when I realised I was not likely to produce an heir, I decided to share my concerns with Burl and, once again, beg him to help me. I need not tell you how much he fought against my suggestion, knowing how it would immediately wreck the relationships we had put in place, how distraught you would be by the second inexplicable withdrawal of his affection, how bitter you would have every right to be when you began to realise the purpose of it, and how worried you would be about the initial deception to myself, the one who had provided for you. So I brought to bear all the ammunition to the argument, how I'd already used up two-thirds of my predicted time and how, if you became pregnant by him in the near future, I would have only a few months in which to see my son. Could he deny me that? I asked. Could he also deny himself, and you, one night of bliss as a foretaste of what was to come? Would the damage outweigh the benefits, did he think? Were you likely to allow him access to your bed?

No, he said, you most certainly would not. You had pride, and who did I think I was talking about...a whore who shares her body with anyone she fancies? He could have one of those any day of the week, he said. He was astonished I could even ask. Yes, he was very angry.

I begged him, Helene. Yes, it was my doing, not his. I promised him I would not lay an ounce of blame on you or him, but take any offspring as my own, male or female, even though it would look like a miracle. I would love it as my own too. I told him I would not want the details, the how, or when, or where. I would leave it to him, and then to you to break the good news, having not the slightest doubt about the success. It was not, however, the kind of request I could expect to be answered there and then, and indeed he never did answer it in words, only in the deed. And even as I write, I am not in a position to guess how, or even if, he explained himself to you. Needless to say, the very thought of sharing you even briefly with my brother was like a knife wound in my soul.

Oh, dear Linas, I begin to wonder if you had a soul and, if so, where you hid it. How could anyone use a woman so, without a word to her?

But although my joy at Jamie's birth was boundless, dearest Helene, I saw how shame, humiliation and sadness showed through your lovely dark eyes, and how Burl's coolness towards you was unchanged, and there has not been a day since then when I have not tried hard to justify the impositions I placed on you both for my sake. Yes, to save my face, you lied to everyone

*for me about our Jamie's parentage. You swallowed
your pride and hid your pain from everyone but Burl
and me, yet I suffered not one word of reproach from
either of you. I could give you no comfort, my Helene,
because that would have been to admit my treachery,
and ruin with distrust what were to have been my last
few months. As it turned out, the wonders of fatherhood
gave me an extended lease of life that I have always
accepted as a precious gift from you, Burl and little
Jamie. It has been more than I deserve. And now we
have worked out the complicated plot and my story is
at an end, at last.*

*Forgive me, dearest beloved. I have thought too much
of my own desires and not enough of yours. When I am
gone, you may find it in your heart to understand the kind
of love I have for you that asks far more than love is
allowed to ask. Or give. Burl has burned for you through
all these years in a way I never believed was possible
and, if I had not already done enough damage to last one
lifetime, I would beg you to listen to him, and believe, if
ever he tells you so. His suffering was for my sake, too.*

*God Bless you, dearest Helene, and our beloved son.
Linas Monkton.*

Yelping, gasping with grief, I put the book down, for
it was trembling too much for me to read and my sobs
shook my arms uncontrollably. Blinding hot tears
crumpled my body into a heap, slamming the book shut
between my knees and dropping it to the floor. His
writing was so eloquent, yet he had never once hinted at
his feelings in spoken words, never remembered special
days, never voiced what his heart felt or what he knew
death was about to take from him. But worse than that

was the way he had abused his brother's love. I had
accused Burl of using me; now I saw how he too had
been manipulated, his emotions bribed into submission
by Linas's demands. Knowing his brother's generosity,
Linas had wrung him like a sponge to get what he wanted
for his last three years and, although this had caused the
birth of our darling Jamie, to do so in such a self-serving
fashion at the expense of our happiness was unforgivable. He had asked for understanding, but my wretch-
edness could not find even the smallest crumb of it.

The clock struck nine and, as if obeying some kind
of signal, I tried to slow my roaring into my handkerchief and clear my mind.

The tears began again. Stopped again.

The servants must not hear. They already had.

There was a tap on the door and Mrs Goode slipped
into the room through a haze of my tears. Saying nothing,
she came to hold me in her arms, bringing me back to
earth with the smoothing and patting of her hands. 'It's
the funeral isn't it?' she said. 'It's brought it all back to
you. Shall I make you a cup of hot chocolate? I'll tell
Debbie to go and warm your bed. You've had a busy day.'
She bent to pick up the book and restore it to the pile,
perhaps suspecting something in the handwritten pages.

'No, Goody. Bring me the woollen cloak. I'm going
to Stonegate.'

She took me by the elbows. 'Can it not wait?' she
whispered.

I shook my head, hoping she would not ask why.

'Shall I come with you?'

'No, you stay with Jamie. I just want…to…' Tears
flowed again.

'Shh, it's all right, I know. But you ought not to go out alone.'

'It's not far. I won't be long.'

She brought my cloak and changed my shoes for me, frowning the perplexed footman into silence as I left the house. I clung to the railing beside the ice-covered steps, staggering like a drunk along the slippery pavement that twinkled with new frost under the lamps, passing the dark frontages of Blake Street, most of them shuttered for the night. Linas's house on Stonegate, now his brother's, was in darkness except for the brazier stuck into the metal holder beside the door.

Mr Treddle answered my knock, admirably concealing his surprise at my tear-stained face, extending a kindly hand to help me up the last step, drawing me like a father into the darkened hall as if he needed no explanation for my presence there. 'My dear lady,' he said. 'Come inside.' It was familiar, I know, but familiarity was what I had come for.

But if he had asked me why I had come, what I needed, what I would see, I could only have told him that I needed to be where Linas and I had been together, to try to make some sense out of those years, to chronicle the events and try to justify the pain he had inflicted on his over-generous brother. I pointed to the beautiful winding wrought-iron staircase. 'Up,' I whispered.

'Allow me to light your way, ma'am.' Picking up the hall lamp, he went very slowly ahead of me, waiting on the top landing for me to indicate the room I had once called my own. Passing through the doorway, now painted a fresh pale grey with gold beading, I saw that nothing inside had been changed, not even by a detail, same bed-curtains, same rather threadbare carpet, same towels and soap on the wash-stand, so dowdy compared to the rest of the house, newly decorated. 'Would you like me to draw the curtains, ma'am?' Mr Treddle said. 'And I can have a fire lit in no time, if you wish?'

'I only want to sit a while, Mr Treddle, thank you.'

'Very good, ma'am. I'm downstairs if you need anything.'

'I'll ring,' I said. The room smelled musty, damp and unloved.

Like a wraith he disappeared, and I sank down upon the velvet-cushioned window-seat that overlooked Stonegate's frosty cobbles, just as I had done countless times before to gather my thoughts together from the jumble of parts that intertwined like the figures in a dance. I had believed myself to be the one most wronged, the one most hurt by hopeless love, the one who had sacrificed most for Linas. Now I saw that it was not so. Burl had loved and wanted me and I had never known it, thinking that I was no more or less than a woman to be caught, and bedded, and then discarded once she had fulfilled her purpose. Now, all his coldness could be explained by Linas's dying wish that he should leave me well alone.

Mine. You belong to me, Helene Follet. Me alone. I have you at last.

Those words, fiercely spoken against my cheek, had haunted me for days, for they were words of possession, not love, though I had been right in my hunch that comfort was what he most needed then. It was what he'd needed for years, though he'd hidden it much better than me. How he must have suffered.

Sighing, I went to lie on my bed still, with my cloak wrapped round me, my mind unwinding the ravelled story that was too full of alternatives, assumptions and speculations to offer me any reason at all for forgiveness. The only mitigating factor I could dredge up from my charity was that Linas had been very ill, and desperate, and probably very afraid, and that in such an atmosphere, his resentment of Burl's success with women finally drove him to play God, before it was too late.

Downstairs, the muffled slam of a heavy door broke into my tangled reverie, hurting my head, but I thought no more of it until my bedroom door opened to let in another light and another figure, and then the cold icy scent of the night. Horses, leather, larches after rain.

'Burl!' I croaked. 'Oh Burl...dearest man...dearest beloved.'

Shadows lurched and skidded across the bed-curtains, and then I was being pulled up into his arms and held close with my wet face warmly nudged by his. Our lips met and breathed soft words into each other's mouths, words of wanting and the pain of loving too much.

'I didn't know, Burl. I didn't know until now,' I sobbed. 'I had no idea that's how it was for you. And I love you...love you...have always loved you...and you should not have allowed him to do this to us. It was so very cruel, my darling. Your pain, Burl, when...'

'Hush, my love. Sweetheart,' he whispered deep, low, velvety words that warmed me like fur, 'my only love, my darling Helene. You must not weep for me, lass. Come now, no more tears. It's done. Past. How long have you been here weeping?'

'Since I read it…oh, Burl. I'm so sorry.'

'For what, dear heart?'

'For my accusations. I've been so unfair and selfish. You did it for love of Linas, as you told me, but I thought it was some cold-hearted scheme you'd both devised to get Linas a son.'

'It was not cold-hearted on my part, my love. Anything but that. I had strong objections, but he made it too difficult for me to refuse him. I ought to have done, I know, but that day at Abbots Mere the chance arose and I took it. You were so unhappy, and I thought that just for one night I could show you how it could be. It was wrong, I admit it, but I had wanted you for so long and I felt that you wanted me too. Darling, it was never my desire to hurt you so much. Can you forgive me?'

'I didn't know you loved me, Burl. You kept it hidden.'

'I dared not let a word pass between us. That was part of the bargain. He pleaded with me to let him have first chance, thinking it would be for only three years, but then he took three more. How could any of us have known that would happen? It was almost unbearable. I didn't *want* his death, sweetheart, but I wanted you so desperately.'

'I think I might have left him, Burl, but for you. It was you who kept me here, that and the thought that I might lose Jamie. He was my comfort, my part of you that I never expected to have. If I'd known you loved me, I could have borne it all with patience, but he told you to leave me alone.'

'I couldn't let you suspect it. You would not have

been able to conceal your feelings. You've never been good at that, have you, sweetheart? But how did you discover all this? Has he left you a letter?'

'Yes, I found it this evening. Perhaps I ought to let you read it.'

'Poor Linas. So he explained his reasons?'

'Yes, and now that he's gone, Burl, I ought not to criticise him to you. He was your twin and my lover, and I suppose he *gave* us more than he demanded from us. At least he kept us together, didn't he? Like it or not.'

'I would have found a way, sweetheart, never fear. There's never been a woman, not one, that I would have waited six years for. Until you.' His arms tightened around me and, in his kiss, I felt all the longing and desolation of those six years, the ache of desire and the release of love that had been so long denied by us both. 'I knew I'd have to work hard to get you back,' he murmured, stroking the hair off my damp temples, 'but I didn't realise how useful your family would be, and the snow and ice, then the floods. And all that nonsense talk of rewards and prices, my darling, was only a device to trap you into accepting me. I had to do something to make your mind up. Think no more of it. For you, I would do whatever it takes, family or no family. So don't think too harshly of Linas if that's what he did too. They were his last years and his only chance to be the proud lover of Miss Helene Follet and, who knows, if I'd been in the same boat, I might have done the same.'

'You wouldn't, Burl. You're too big-hearted. You would never forget your sense of fairness. Linas seemed to forget everything.'

'We have six years of lost ground to make up. Shall I take you back home now, so we can make a start? And will you marry me now, Miss Follet, without any ifs and buts? No bargains? No delays?'

'I *will* marry you, Burl Winterson,' I said, feeling a strange sense of elation rush into my chest like the first stirrings of a young woman's heart. Breathless with happiness, I took hold of his head as I had done on that April night four years ago, letting my fingers roam in the semi-darkness to remind myself that this was not a dream. His skin had warmed, his lips kissed my finger-tips as they passed and I knew I was not dreaming. 'Yes, take me home. I have things to show you,' I said.

Under my fingers the lips smiled and whispered. 'You would not prefer to stay here, in your own room?'

'Not until it's been decorated,' I said. 'A pretty spring yellow, I think.'

Dear Mr Treddle ushered us out with a smile at my blotchy face. 'Goodnight, Miss Follet. Goodnight, my lord. The step is icy…take care…hold the railing, ma'am.'

That night, the short walk to my home was punctuated by several stops to remind ourselves and each other that, however many questions still awaited answers, the main one had at long last been resolved. Yes, it was true. Burl had loved me from the very beginning, and although I might have argued that for him to accept Linas's suggestion without consulting me was less than gentlemanly, I found it easier to forgive Burl than Linas. Though we had both suffered for it, we had also lived off that brief memory for four years, gaining an adorable child as a consolation that bound us together irrevocably. I could not blame him for that any longer. It was time to let the past take care of itself.

For me, the day had been packed with incident, most of which I was not at liberty to talk about. For Burl, who had been to Foss Beck again, the day had been a tiring one and he had plenty to tell me. Yet in the dim warm intimacy of my room at Blake Street, there were more important matters to keep us occupied than our respective families, for now our loving could take on a new dimension that would stretch ahead into years of trust and understanding. I had never thought that particular freedom would be mine so soon.

Setting all modesty aside in his honour, I first acted as his valet to make him comfortably naked in the chair beside the fire with a glass of wine, and myself standing some distance away where the lamplight could catch at only the palest surfaces. Although I was tired and emotionally drained, my slow and erotic removal of each item of clothing was suitably lethargic, like that of a sleepy woman who has other things on her mind. Each garter, each stocking was peeled off and discarded with a tantalising display of my body, just enough to delight him and, although he was relaxed and silent, I knew how focused was his attention and how delicious this was for him after a long day attending to my family's welfare.

Pretending to be alone, I took my time with each button, hook and tie, letting one side slip a little, then another, loosening my hair to reveal and conceal, swinging it aside, lifting it and letting it drop for me to make all those minute examinations of this limb, that hand, that foot, which we women make at such times as a matter of routine. Sliding my chemise down over one hip, inch by slow inch, I held it before me to conceal that part of me which I have never found particularly attractive, finally stepping out of the soft cotton fabric with the deep broderie-anglais hem while looking at him through the screen of my hair. I could go no further in my pretence.

Like a large cat, he stood up, dark against the firelight. 'Siren,' he whispered, 'you have captured my dream. How did you know, wicked black witch? Eh? Can you read my dreams now?' He came to me, taking the cotton shift out of my hand and tossing it on to the chair.

'Now I can,' I replied, softly. 'Now I can call you mine at last, after all these years. I can have you all, body and mind. And I am yours, my love.'

After bearing our child, and suckling him for nine months, my figure was no longer that of a seventeen-year-old. My hips and belly were rounded, my breasts full, still firm, but with all those years of virginal innocence gone for ever. Burl's heavy-lidded examination and the path of his hands over my body, however, was as leisured as my undressing had been, and I stood trembling like a girl with my knees turning to water at each touch, the tenderly teasing brush of his thumbs melting me, then his warm lips over my shoulders and neck.

No longer able to wait upon him, I linked my arms about his neck, knowing that he would lift me and take me those few short steps to the turned-down bed and lay me there with the blanket of his beautiful body to warm

me, each of his kisses fusing into the next, emptying my
mind. And because we were both physically weary, yet
aware of the change in our relationship, our loving was
sweetly languorous and indulgent, teasing time itself into
eons of pleasure that washed over us like waves, taking
us further and further into the deep waters of our passion.
Our cries were softly calling, tuned to each other,
wordless and evocative, arousing, yearning. With years
of discovery ahead of us and no more misunderstandings,
our loving was made all the sweeter and more poignant
by words of love in all its forms, words we had saved in
the secrecy of our hearts and never thought to use.

'Never leave me,' he whispered. 'Never...never leave
me, Helene.'

'Beloved, I am yours. I have always been yours,
even when you—'

'Don't say it. Darling woman, what can I do to make
you forget?'

'That's easy, my lord. Brothers and sisters for
Jamie, please.'

'I can arrange that, Lady Winterson. Leave it to me.'

'Now?'

'Of course now. Immediately. A little co-operation
is all I ask.'

Needless to say, I co-operated fully. So well, in fact,
that the deep sleep that followed our exhaustion took
us through until dawn when Jamie and Debbie appeared
to draw the curtains and place our tea-tray on the table.
With no sign of surprise at seeing his Uncaburl in my
bed, Jamie crawled across the prone and tousled body
to burrow between us like a mole, grinning as if he was
personally responsible.

Chapter Fifteen

~~~❦~~~

With our love for each other firmly established and our future as a family assured, everything else seemed to matter less than before, even though there were some serious issues still to be discussed. Linas's letter to me had certainly cleared my mind of misconceptions and left it wide open to receive his brother's love, but Burl himself had some doubts about the manner of Linas's explanation.

Some days later we sat by the fire in our house on Blake Street. Shaking his head, he closed the book and turned it over once or twice to study its leather binding. 'Tch!' he muttered. 'How like him to write it as an essay and then leave it to chance that you'd find it one day. It might have been *years* before you found it, Helene. What if I'd thrown the notebooks out, or put them into a bookshelf? Then you'd never have heard his side of the story, would you? Why couldn't he have told you, while there was still time?'

Snuggling deeper into his arms, I took the notebook

from him and returned it to its companions. 'Because he was unsure how I would take it,' I said. 'Because he could never have said it the way he could write it. Because he was not even sure he wanted me to know, after all. Let's not give it any more thought. It's of no consequence now. Tell me what you discovered about Pierre. You said you had something to tell me.'

'It was your brothers who solved the mystery, sweetheart. They were doing some clearing up ready for the renovations and they found some lists that Monsieur Follet had left behind in his hurry.'

'Lists of what?'

'Names. French prisoners of war kept in prison ships off the Essex coast, some of them crossed off or underlined. They showed it to me, and I recognised some of the names that have been circulated to all the Justices of the Peace in the county. They're men who've gone missing, presumed escaped. We've known for some time that there are French connections over here helping prisoners to get back home across the English Channel or the North Sea, but personally I never thought they'd come all this way up north. But it seems that some of them made their way up as far as York where your cousin has been meeting them.'

'In the coffee houses? Once a month, when he went to collect my mother's medication and bring the goods to the shop?'

'Very likely. The coffee houses are perfect meeting places.'

'Then the man who was with him when we saw him might have been one he was helping. He looked very rough and tired, didn't he?'

'Yes. He would have taken him to Bridlington to wait there for one of the smugglers' boats to ship him back to France. The men who come to collect these prisoners pay handsomely for human contraband, and Pierre has probably been doing it for several years, growing nicely wealthy from it.'

'Which is where the extra money comes from.'

'No more, dear heart. He pulled up the ladder and made a run for it. Things were getting too complicated for him. He'd waited for you, and then realised it was futile, and maybe he suspected I might know a thing or two about what was happening. Who knows? But Greg and Finch are not a bit sorry. They had no wish to call him brother.'

'So my mother has not been receiving her potions lately.'

'If I were you, I would not be too concerned about that,' he said, twisting a strand of my hair round his fingers. 'Your mother appears to be improving daily. Due, perhaps, to the absence of pain-killing drugs.'

'Burl…you cannot believe…*surely* not!'

'I'm keeping an open mind, sweetheart. I think we should allow the matter to drop, since it really serves no purpose to find out, does it? I don't think your mother suspects anything sinister.'

'So do you still think it was Pierre who told the Customs and Excise Men to look in our shop for French goods?'

'No. It was not him.' He answered with such finality that I knew his enquiries had revealed something.

'Do you want to tell me?' I said.

'Difficult. Maybe I should not.'

'Then it's someone I know. It would upset me. Is that it, my lord?'

He took a deep breath, and I thought how unlike him it was to hesitate. 'It upsets *me*,' he said, 'to think that I've had not one, but *two* brothers who see me so much as a rival that they are driven to prevent my happiness. On the other hand, Miss Follet, looking at you here in the crook of my arm with your hair all over the place and the neck of your bodice indecently open…'

'Which *you* opened, my lord!'

'…which I opened, I dare say I could forgive them both for wanting to knock me off my high horse, once in a while. However, I find it rather uncomfortable, to say the least…'

'Oh, *do* say the least, darling Burl. What *are* you saying, exactly? That Medworth…oh, no, you can't think that he…did he?'

'Yes, I'm afraid that's what I am saying. He dropped a rather indirect hint to two of the men who work for the Customs Controller, so I'm told, just as the floods began, a hint that they're trained to pick up with ears like bats. The truth is, my love, that although Medworth was quite content to see you as Linas's mistress, he's less than content to see you as my wife and mother of my son. Jealousy of my good fortune? Envy of my inheritance compared to his? Yes, love, he's not immune from the vices any more than the rest of us, though I'd not have believed he'd allow it to get as out of hand as he appears to have done.'

'He wanted to see me arrested? Oh, Burl, surely not.' My arms prickled, and the hair at the nape of my neck sent shivers down my spine.

'I really don't believe he'd thought too hard about what the exact consequences might be. I think he was more set on pulling us apart than what might happen to you. In a way, what he tried to do is potentially more serious than what Linas tried to do. Envy is a terrible thing.'

If ever the time was right for me to say what I knew about Medworth's other attempt to pull us apart, it was now. But I said nothing, for it was not my way to worsen a sibling relationship that had begun to falter. So I kept my peace, and I was glad that I did, for Burl himself told me the rest.

'He's moving house, by the way,' he said, 'so we shall be seeing less of him in the future. We had a meeting at Abbots Mere the other day, and my father has offered him a small living just on the other side of Harrogate, so he'll be near them. Mama is very pleased, of course.'

'Oh! That's rather sudden, isn't it? What of the rector's position at Osbaldwick? Has it…?'

'Fallen through. Lord Slatterly has found someone he believes will be more suitable. An older man. They'll be moving out next week.'

'I see. Is Medworth very disappointed?'

'He's philosophical about it. Cynthia won't want to leave, but curate's wives must move on. She'll take it in her stride. But I have some other news that will please you, Miss Follet. About Lord Slatterly's daughter.'

For one moment, I was not sure what I was meant to know and what to conceal. 'Veronique? Is she well?'

'Well and happy, according to her father. She's soon to be married.'

'Heavens above! That *is* good news. Anyone I know?'

'One of Viscount Wetherclough's sons. Been keen on her for years. He can't believe his luck, at last. I think I know how he feels.'

I hugged him. This was good news indeed. 'I must go and see her. We're on good terms now, you know.'

He looked down at me and smiled. 'Thanks to your kindness to her. You are, Miss Follet, the most wonderful woman, and I am the most fortunate of men. And if you hug me any closer, wench, your bodice will drop off altogether and I shall be shamelessly compromised. Is that the idea?'

'Mmm,' I said, as his hand moved the matter forwards.

'Wait, hussy,' he said, diverting the hand into his inside breast pocket. 'I have a halter to put round your neck while I have you half-naked here. Hold still.' Opening a flat red leather-covered box, he revealed a lining of white satin upon which lay a fine gold chain with a pendant hanging from it, the largest smokey-grey pearl I had ever seen. It was tear-drop shaped, with a diamond dripping from the base. 'Burl sounds like pearl,' he whispered. 'Keep saying it, sweetheart.'

'Burl,' I said. 'Thank you, dear heart. Thank you for waiting.'

'I would have waited for ever, my love, but I'm glad I didn't have to. Six years is more than enough to wait for a woman like you.'

It was on my birthday, April 18th, 1806, when the fifth red rose appeared on the hall table before breakfast, and it was then that I had to accept that the anonymous donor could not have been Linas, after all. Smiling, I placed it on my table between the toast and the milk-jug and waited for comments.

'Another rose, Mama?' said Jamie.

Burl looked across at me. 'Get them regularly, do you?'

'Mmm.' I nodded.

'Mama gets one every year on her birthday, Uncaburl. I think she should marry the handsome prince who gives 'em out. Shall you, Mama?'

'Yes, love. I think it's time I did. Will some time soon be good?'

Burl was staring, but then his expression changed, his eyes softening and desirous. 'Very soon, you mean?' he said, slowly.

'Yes, my lord. As soon as possible,' I said, nibbling at my lip.

His hand reached across the table to cover mine, caressing, protective and thoughtful. The tender expression deepened into a smile and I knew he understood that I was saying more than that, and I thought he looked like a young lad with his first girl. 'This time,' he whispered, 'I shall be able to do all those things I couldn't do before, shan't I? Shall we go over to Foss Beck and tell them? We can stay overnight at Fridaythorpe so as not to tire you.'

'To see Nana Damzell,' Jamie said. 'And when you marry Uncaburl, Mama, will he be my new papa then?'

We looked at each other without answering him, until he insisted. 'Will you, Uncaburl? If Mama gives the red rose to Papa, he won't mind then, will he? We'll tell him about it. Shall we?'

Tears prickled my eyes. 'That's what we'll do, little one. We'll call and see him on the way there, and you can give him the rose. He'll like that.'

So we did, making it the start of a tradition we kept up each year on my birthday, even when our retinue extended to our two nurses, the two younger boys and one girl, and a handsome young man of twelve who looked exactly like his papa.

MILLS & BOON
Historical

On sale 6th March 2009

Regency

THE RAKE'S DEFIANT MISTRESS
by Mary Brendan

Snowbound with notorious rake Sir Clayton Powell, defiant Ruth Hayden manages to resist falling into his arms. But Clayton hides the pain of betrayal behind his charm, and even Ruth, no stranger to scandal, is shocked by the vicious gossip about him. Recklessly, she seeks to silence his critics – by announcing their engagement!

Regency

THE VISCOUNT CLAIMS HIS BRIDE
by Bronwyn Scott

For years Valerian Inglemoore, Viscount St Just, was a secret agent on the war-torn Continent. Returning home, he knows exactly what he wants – Philippa Stratten, the woman he left for the sake of her family… But Philippa won't risk her heart again. Valerian realises he must fight a fiercer battle to win her as his bride…

To unmask her secrets, he will have to unlock her heart!

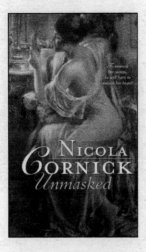

Wickedly handsome Nick Falconer has been
sent to stop a gang of highwaywomen.
But the woman he suspects of leading them
is intoxicatingly beautiful and Nick sets
out to seduce her.

Mari Osbourne's secrets are deeper and
darker than Nick could ever imagine.
Will trusting the one man she wants lead
Mari to the hangman's noose?

Available 20th February 2009

www.millsandboon.co.uk

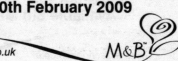

Passion. Power. Suspense.
It's time to fall under the spell of Nora Roberts.

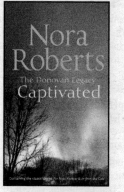

Nora Roberts
The Donovan Legacy
Captivated

2nd January 2009

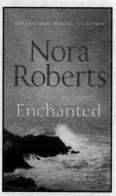

INTERNATIONAL BESTSELLING AUTHOR
Nora Roberts
The Donovan Legacy
Enchanted

6th February 2009

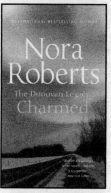

INTERNATIONAL BESTSELLING AUTHOR
Nora Roberts
The Donovan Legacy
Charmed

6th March 2009

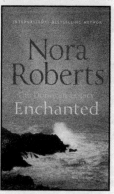

INTERNATIONAL BESTSELLING AUTHOR
Nora Roberts
The Donovan Legacy
Enchanted

3rd April 2009

The Donovan Legacy
Four cousins. Four stories. One terrifying secret.

FREE

2 BOOKS AND A SURPRISE GIFT

We would like to take this opportunity to thank you for reading th
Mills & Boon® book by offering you the chance to take TWO mo
specially selected titles from the Historical series absolutely FRE
We're also making this offer to introduce you to the benefits of th
Mills & Boon® Book Club™—

- ★ **FREE home delivery**
- ★ **FREE gifts and competitions**
- ★ **FREE monthly Newsletter**
- ★ **Books available before they're in the shops**
- ★ **Exclusive Mills & Boon Book Club offers**

Accepting these FREE books and gift places you under no obligatio
to buy; you may cancel at any time, even after receiving your fre
shipment. Simply complete your details below and return the enti
page to the address below. You don't even need a stamp!

YES! Please send me 2 free Historical books and a surprise gift.
understand that unless you hear from me, I will receive
superb new titles every month for just £3.69 each, postage and packir
free. I am under no obligation to purchase any books and may canc
my subscription at any time. The free books and gift will be mine
keep in any case.

H9ZE

Ms/Mrs/Miss/Mr.............................Initials ....
                                                    BLOCK CAPITALS PLEA

Surname ....

Address ....

....

....Postcode ....

Send this whole page to:
The Mills & Boon Book Club, FREEPOST CN81, Croydon, CR9 3WZ